EAST OF THE MOUNTAINS

DAVID
GUTERSON

EAST
OF THE
MOUNTAINS

Harcourt Brace & Company

NEW YORK   SAN DIEGO   LONDON

Requests for permission to make copies of any part of the work should
be mailed to: Permissions Department, Harcourt Brace & Company,
6277 Sea Harbor Drive, Orlando, Florida 32887-6777.

ISBN 0-15-100229-0

Text set in Centaur MT
Designed by Lori McThomas Buley
Printed in the United States of America

To Robin, always,
and for Henry Shain——he loved the mountains

There were ten thousand thousand fruit to touch,
Cherish in hand, lift down, and not let fall.

—ROBERT FROST, *After Apple Picking*

ONE

On the night he had appointed his last among the living, Dr. Ben Givens did not dream, for his sleep was restless and visited by phantoms who guarded the portal to the world of dreams by speaking relentlessly of this world. They spoke of his wife—now dead—and of his daughter, of silent canyons where he had hunted birds, of august peaks he had once ascended, of apples newly plucked from trees, and of vineyards in the foothills of the Apennines. They spoke of rows of campanino apples near Monte Della Torraccia; they spoke of cherry trees on river slopes and of pear blossoms in May sunlight. Now on the roof tiles and against his window a vast Seattle rain fell ceaselessly, as if to remind him that memories are illusions; the din of its beating against the world was in perfect harmony with his insomnia. Dr. Givens shrugged off his past to devote himself to the rain's steady cadence, but no dreams, no deliverance, came to him. Instead he only adjusted his legs—his bladder felt distressingly full—and lay tormented by the unassailable fact that he was dying—dying of colon cancer.

Three hours before first light in the east, wide awake and in defeat, he turned on his lamp, put his feet on the floor, and felt the pain bearing down in his side that plagued him through all his waking hours. He felt it where his colon, on the left, made a turn before dropping toward his pelvic cavity; if he pressed his hand into the flesh there, it produced a sensation of irritability seeping through his abdomen. Ben Givens put his fingers against it and began the insistent, delicate caress that had of late become his habit. He plucked his glasses from the side table, fitted their stems behind his ears, and once again probed his side.

To the west the city where he had passed his adult years lay incidental to the force of the rain, and mostly obscured by it. Eastward the rain fell hard against the hills, but higher up on the flanks of mountains it turned to snow dropping silent against glaciers, on slopes of broken talus rock, and on wind-worn buttresses and outcrops. East of the snow-covered crests of the mountains the sky lay almost clear of clouds; save for a few last spectral wisps of vapor floating beneath the chill points of stars, one's view of the heavens was unimpeded. October moonlight illuminated hay fields, vineyards, sagelands, and apple orchards, and the land lay dry and silent. On the sloping, dark verges of the Columbia River, where Ben Givens had entered the world, the apples hung heavily from fragrant trees, and the windfall fruit lay rotting in the night, gathering a pale sheen of frost.

Ben thought of lonely canyons, of how today he would travel eastward to wander in pale, autumnal light with his dogs quartering the ground in front of him and the quail holding when the dogs went on point—and then he rose with the unsteadiness of morning, shuffled to the bathroom still rubbing his side, propped one hand against the wall above his toilet, and waited with bitter, desolate impatience for the muscles of his pelvic region to recollect how to pass night water. He reminded himself that by dusk of that day—if everything went according to his plan—he would no longer be in this world.

Dr. Givens was a heart surgeon, retired, who had specialized in bypass operations. He had been admired by other doctors for his steadiness of hand, his precision, his endurance, his powers of concentration, and his grace. His assistants knew that when the heart was isolated—when everything human was erased from existence except that narrow antiseptic window through which another's heart could be manipulated—few were as adroit as Dr. Givens.

Now he lived in a much-contained fashion: a restrained, particular man. At seventy-three he had a thick chest and broad shoulders, though the muscles in his limbs had gone soft. Since youth he'd climbed mountains and more mountains, and hiked many miles in all seasons. He'd walked in the high country every winter and snowshoed into lonely canyons. These past nineteen months, since his wife died, he'd returned to a haunting, autumn pastime: he'd hunted birds to shoot on the wing for the first time since he was a teenager. This was a pursuit that stole his soul shortly after Rachel's death, after he'd turned from his work as a surgeon and found himself with too much idle time.

His face was weathered and furrowed, his eyes two dark shields. His coarse gray hair looked permanently wind-tousled, and he walked a bit gingerly, with a bowlegged gait, to keep the weight from his instep. He was so tall that, without thinking about it, he ducked his head to pass through doorways. His patients, in past years, had admired his hands: precise, large, and powerful. When he palpated their chests or listened to their hearts, they were infused with his professional confidence. Dr. Givens had believed fervently in medicine and deferred only grudgingly to its limitations. He had not readily accepted defeat and had struggled with the weaknesses of his patients' hearts as if those weaknesses were an affront to him personally. In this way he had removed himself so that when patients died on the operating table he did not have to feel unduly burdened. He did not have to feel haunted. The main questions for him had been tactical; the rest, he'd felt, was all mystery, and so beyond his governance.

None of this meant that Dr. Givens was devoid of tenderness. His heart wavered when the truth of another's lay exposed and irreparable before him. Always at work he had been aware of his divine power of intervention, and of his helplessness, too. He understood the mortality of human beings and the fallibility of their beating hearts, though these things had kept their distance from him, until his own diagnosis. Now he'd been told—it was the dark logic of the world—that he had months to live, no more. Like all physicians, he knew the truth of such a verdict; he knew full well the force of cancer and how inexorably it operated. He grasped that nothing could stop his death, no matter how hopeful he allowed himself to feel, no matter how deluded. Ben saw how his last months would be, the suffering that was inevitable, the meaningless trajectory his life would take into a meaningless grave. Better to end it now, he'd decided; better to avoid pain than engage it. Better to end his life swiftly, cleanly, and to accept that there would be no thwarting the onslaught of this disease.

As had been his practice since the death of his wife, Ben went out to let his dogs in the house immediately after rising. There were roses growing beside their kennel—summer damasks his wife had planted—and their stalks shone in the rain. The dogs were awake when he came their way to lift the latch to their fenced-in run, the wizened Tristan staring at him where he stood at four o'clock in the morning with an umbrella tightly over his head, the two-year-old Rex leaping high against the wire mesh as if to scrabble over with his forepaws. When Ben swung the gate wide, the young dog leaped and clutched him at the waist, then ran unbounded out into the rain, leaped at nothing, and returned.

They were brown-and-white Brittanies—Rex ran more toward a bronze hue—with fawn-colored noses, tapering muzzles, and eyes well set back in their heads. They were both broad and strong in the hindquarters, and had little feathering at the legs. Tristan, in another time, had been boundlessly energetic; he'd had the habit of pursuing birds with earnest, exuberant good intentions. Now, in his later years, he was increasingly deliberate, more reluctant to plunge into thorns, and generally stayed closer to hand. His tendency to range had been quieted.

When the dogs were coaxed in out of the rain, Ben fed them in the kitchen. He poured a tumbler half full with prune juice—constipation was one of his symptoms—then swallowed two capsules of Docusate sodium and set his tea water to boil. He was accustomed to reading a newspaper over breakfast, but at this hour the boy who brought it around was no doubt blithely sleeping. Ben laid out melba toast, orange marmalade, two small bags of lemon tea, and a jar of applesauce. He arranged a small plate, a knife and spoon, a bowl, and a cup and saucer. When the water boiled, he filled his thermos, then draped a tea bag over its lip to steep while he attended to breakfast. Despite his contest with sleeplessness, he felt keen of mind on this morning, as well as a calm, compelling urge to establish domestic order. There was a protocol to the day that would be pleasurable to follow, in spite of everything.

The dogs lay easily at his feet while he ate and were still there when he pushed his bowl away, gently rubbed his tender side, and sipped his lemon tea. Both of them rose at the same moment he did and followed him soberly into the bedroom, where he took his gun case from the corner of the closet and slid his shotgun free. At this the dogs froze and looked at him with uncertain curiosity.

Ben sighted down the barrels once, flicked the safety on and off, and broke the gun so as to hold it to the light and inspect the condition of the bores. It had once been his father's shotgun, a Winchester 21 side-by-side, choked for quail and chukars. It dropped an inch and a half at the comb, which was, as it turned out, right for Ben, but the length of pull that had worked for his father had not been entirely comfortable and Ben had added two inches to the stock butt. His father took him when he was eight years old to shoot mourning doves at the edge of the apple orchards. The doves flew up from the Columbia to feed, very swift and flocking wildly in the pale light of morning. Ben's father did not broach the subject of hunting's moral perplexity. He only showed Ben how to establish his lead, how to swing through smoothly and easily. Ben's mother, on the other hand, did not approve of bird hunting, and had made her sentiments known to them. Food for the table was necessary, she maintained, but pleasure in killing small birds on the wing was reprehensible in the eyes of God. Ben killed three mourning doves that day and watched them fall at the report of the .410 his father had placed in his hands. He buried their viscera, wings, and heads in a small hole in the ground. Their breast meat was dark and small in the frying pan, dusted with salted flour. He ate the meat with vague regret while his mother watched in silence from the sink, until after awhile she came near to touch his cheek. Then she went to the sink again and scrubbed the pan for him.

Now, in the bedroom, the Winchester in hand, Ben snapped the action closed. He shouldered the gun and swung it along the picture molding, and with his forefinger lightly against the front trigger he squeezed off a silent shot at the seam where the wall met another wall. Rex pranced, high-stepping.

Then Ben set the gun butt against his bed and wrapped his lips around both barrels, as though to fellate them. In this posture he ascertained that in fact the front trigger was just in reach; he had only to extend the full length of one arm, which pushed the sight bead against his palate. If he seized the shotgun in this way, wholly willing, embracing it, allowing the metal to prod his mouth, he could blow the top of his skull off without logistical difficulties. The knowledge that this was indeed possible, that such an act was not out of reach, suffused Dr. Givens with a glandular fear that washed through him like a wave.

Ben put the gun down and packed for his journey with the same judicious deliberation that had been his foremost professional trait: he weighed everything at immoderate length, but made few errors in judgment. He packed his duffel with his upland vest, a box of twenty-five number 8 shells, his shooting gloves, his shotgun sling, a canvas cap with a canted brim, and a whistle hung from a lanyard. He loaded his rucksack with a headlamp and battery pack, maps of Chelan and Douglas Counties, an altimeter, a compass, an aluminum cup, three paraffin fire starters, a roll of waterproof adhesive tape, a medical kit, a needle and thread, an entrenching tool, a folding camp saw, a rain poncho, a length of Manila cord, a pair of field glasses, a vial of lip balm, a tube of sunscreen, prescription sunglasses in their case, a cigarette lighter, insect repellent, a snap box of water-purifying tablets, and a sandwich bag full of toilet paper.

In the kitchen he filled his two water bottles, closed the thermos of tea securely, and turned all three on their heads briefly to check for leaks around the cap seals. He wiped them dry, wiped the table, and washed the breakfast dishes. He had hoped to move his bowels before leaving—the first hour in the car would stop them up firmly, sealing them closed for the length of the day—but he knew there would be no success to the enterprise should he endeavor to sit and wait on the toilet. That would swell his incipient hemorrhoids and encourage the frustration incited in his stomach when he could not void his bowels. Ben was sorry that at the heart of things this day he would carry the sensation of a poisoning fullness and a heavy reminder that he himself was now a blight on the world.

He had taken much of the previous night to page through photograph albums, to read his files of correspondence, and to hold in his hand the earrings and lockets his wife, Rachel, had worn. He had found, in a box, a jar of her sewing buttons, a bulbous-head lavender wand laced with ribbon, a pair of her shoes, a pack of foxglove seeds, and a sketch pad less than a quarter filled with her pencil drawings of trees. He had unzipped the garment bag in the storage room closet and, yielding to sentimentality, burrowed his face into the dresses there in order to retrieve the faint smell of her. He had done like things all evening long and so had found in the endpages of books his mother's neatly fountain-penned signature, and in a hinged cedar box his father's pocket watch, its face glass missing for fifty years. After midnight he came across photos long forgotten, at the bottom of a box, most of Renee, his daughter.

There were photos of him, too. He hadn't been handsome, but he'd been strong and tall, blue-eyed like his mother, lean-jawed like his father. There were photos taken in apple orchards, on the summits of peaks, in uniform, on leave in the mountains of northern Italy.

Now it was morning of the next day. And Ben could not bring himself to extinguish the kitchen light and turn away quite yet. He listened to the hum of the refrigerator and remembered how Rachel had habitually commented on the taste of things they ate together—Jerusalem artichokes dug from the ground, or apples at their sugared prime. He remembered her, too, slicing carrots with a paring knife, the ball of her thumb a stop. Ben shook off his memories, turned out the light, and called the dogs from the living room. It was time to go away from there. It was time to begin his journey.

Dr. Givens kept in his garage a 1969 International Scout, which he used as an adjunct to his sporting life. He had purchased it new twenty-eight years before, and although since then he'd bought and sold other cars, he had not been able to part with the Scout for reasons he could not readily give voice to. He was not a man who fell in love with cars or spoke of them in endearing terms; nevertheless, he felt for this one a certain enduring fondness. The Scout was modestly well-preserved, but idiosyncratic in keeping with its age, with the tics and uncertainties of passing time. It included a four-wheel transfer case and locking hubs one turned by hand after coming to a halt on the road verge. Its heater fan made a hollow din, and through the moldings where the doors met the windshield—the car's top could be removed in good weather—the wind whistled tonelessly. More disconcerting was that the driver's side window regulator had developed with time a modicum of play: the pane chattered at high speeds and irritated Ben deeply. Twice in three years he had taken the door apart and peeled back the plastic vapor shield in an effort to address the problem. To no avail, however. The play in the regulator was fundamentally ambiguous, or perhaps organic to the entire apparatus, which was deteriorating in all its particulars.

He slid his shotgun across the backseat and set his rucksack and duffel next to it. Then he slung down the rear door and entreated his dogs to load up, urging them to leap against their will. As it turned out, he had to lift Tristan in, because there was no room for a running start.

He opened his garage door to the beating rain, but then it occurred to him he had not made certain that the house was left in
proper order—the home of a man who intended to return at the
end of an ordinary bird-hunting trip—and he went inside once
more. He moved methodically from room to room, until he felt
secure in his impression that nothing could prompt a postmortem inquiry, going so far as to leave on the kitchen table the
12-volt bird plucker he'd sent away for last Christmas but never
used. He also pulled from a wall cabinet a small file-card recipe
box and turned the recipe for quail on toast loosely on the diag-
onal. He left the box standing on the counter beside the sink
with its hinged lid open.

This strategy had possibilities, he realized, so he programmed
his VCR to record a show called *Great Railway Journeys* playing on
public television, and turned back a copy of *Scientific American*—a
Christmas gift from Renee, his daughter—which he placed on
his bedside table. He wished he had reserved some bills unpaid
to leave behind on top of his dresser: he might have arranged
them artfully to appear artlessly strewn.

He had visited his family the evening before, eaten dinner with
Renee and Chris, his grandson, in the pretense that everything
was ordinary, but in fact to service his end-game ruse. He was
going over the mountains, he'd said, to hunt for quail in willow
canyons, he had no particular canyons in mind, he intended to
return on Thursday evening, though possibly, if the hunting was
good, he would return on Friday or Saturday. The lie was open-
ended so that his family wouldn't start worrying until he'd been
dead for as long as a week—so none would miss or seek him
where he rotted silently in the sage. Ben imagined how it might
be otherwise, his cancer a pestilent force in their lives, or a pall
descending over them like ice, just as they'd begun to emerge
from the pall of Rachel's death. The last thing they needed was
for Ben to tell them of his terminal colon cancer.

He sat at Renee's table with a fork in his hand, admiring her durable, quiet beauty—at fifty she was slender, thoroughly gray, aging in a poignant, tender way—and taking note of Chris's forearms, which were vein-cabled, thickly corded. He asked after his granddaughter, Emma, who had married a man from Wellington, New Zealand, and was rarely seen in Seattle anymore; he asked after Renee's husband, John, who was on a business trip. Ben urged Renee to talk about her work—she wrote screenplays for children's movies and had penned two highly respected scripts—but she was, as usual, reticent about it out of a native modesty and preferred to deflect the conversation toward Chris, who had embarked on his third year of medical school. He'd begun his clinics, he told Ben. He was seeing patients for the first time, but only for the purpose of asking questions and to practice diagnosis: he found it more interesting than labs. "What about a climb?" he asked out of nowhere. "We haven't gone since August."

"Well, I don't know," answered Ben.

"What about Silver Peak?" insisted his grandson. "Up in the pass. A shakedown cruise. A tune-up run. A day hike."

"I don't know if I can do it anymore. My legs are beginning to wobble."

Chris held a piece of bread in his hand. "What are you talking about?" he demanded. "You're still the toughest old goat in the mountains. Don't start talking like that."

"I'm not the toughest goat in the mountains. That's you, Chris."

"Silver Peak," said his grandson.

They'd climbed together for fifteen years. Chris had been with him on fifty summits. They'd taken lunch on mountaintops, sprawled back easily on their elbows, peaks spread out before them. The boy was strong and confronted his climbs with an admirable good cheer. Ben enjoyed his company. Early he'd taken the boy to the mountains, but of late the boy took him.

"All right, Silver Peak," Ben said, and it was this lie he found most disturbing now, as he stood in his bedroom arranging more lies. "We'll go up there when I get home."

Ben decided he hadn't packed to produce the illusion he wanted. If this was at least a six-day hunting trip, beginning on a Saturday and ending on a Thursday, his outfit would certainly include more clothing, and so he gathered more together— socks, shirts, long underwear, and a worn pair of canvas-faced brush pants. In the bathroom he made up a full toilet kit, including a tube of hemorrhoid cream, a bottle of aspirin, his second pair of glasses, and his bottle of calcium gluconate pills for easing leg cramps at night.

The truth was that at the end of this day of hunting, he intended to set his dogs free on the sagelands, hang himself up between strands of barbed wire—as if he'd been making a low fence crossing—and shoot himself in the carotid artery: shoot himself in the neck. Only his doctor, Bill Ward, would suspect the truth, but even Bill wouldn't feel certain about it, given all the evidence to the contrary, and anyway he wouldn't want to hurt anyone by suggesting that Ben had committed suicide. For Bill, Ben knew, there was a protocol about such matters, a principle governing them. Unless obliged by a coroner's inquest or an insurance agent's inquiry, Bill Ward would keep Ben's cancer to himself.

Pausing in his bathroom, staring in the mirror, Ben recollected his pact with Rachel on the train from Mantua to Bressanone: that the ashes that were the remains of them both would someday make a bed for roses—his for a red rose, hers for a white: the two to grow and intertwine with the passing of many years. It had been the foolish desire of romantics, the sentimental vow of young lovers. It had been the sort of thing young people wish for in their recklessness and passion. He and Rachel, on growing older, had been amused by the idea of these roses, but had not let go of them, either. And he prayed now, thinking of her, that their pact might yet be consummated. He'd preserved her ashes in such a hope.

But perhaps the price of his suicide was that such a thing couldn't happen, and he imagined his bones bleached to dust in the sagelands, scattered about by coyotes. He imagined, too, that his dogs might wander into hunger, hardship, death. He hoped they would somehow fend for themselves and find their way to another hunter, yet he still felt he owed them more than to abandon them in that expanse of empty canyons. His last meal, too, he understood—the breast of a quail, spit-cooked on a fire— would go to nurture nothing but the worms and maggots feeding on a dead man.

When he returned, Rex had jumped across the car seat and had his forepaws over the rucksack. Ben had to prod against his haunches in an effort to force him rearward, Rex resisting stubbornly until Ben caught him at the throat. He spoke frankly to the dog about his behavior, then turned the Scout's engine over. As always it expired momentarily and required a half dozen strokes of the accelerator before the choke sustained itself.

Briefly, he sat idling in front of his house—a half-timbered Tudor, modest in scale—where the telephone answering machine was on, the heat set at fifty-five degrees, and the timers on the lamps in the living room and bedroom set at five and ten P.M., respectively. The rain beat hard so that the house seemed shrouded, beleaguered, and somehow reduced. A neighbor had been solicited to collect the daily newspapers and mail and to move the garbage out to the curb by eight A.M. Tuesday morning. Ben noted, to his satisfaction, that all had been left in proper order. He'd made his arrangements carefully, seeing that every detail was covered. To the last he'd attended to particulars.

Working himself into a seizure of purpose, Ben drove away

without looking back at his home of forty-three years. The rain rattled off the car roof, fell in long streaks through the arcs of streetlamps, and ran torrentially in the gutters. He could not see more than a few yards in front of him, even with the wipers barreling at full speed. Through the glass the streets he passed along seemed only half real, half formed. He leaned forward, squinting a little, switched on the defroster and made an adjustment to the heat lever. It was shy of six o'clock on a Saturday morning; no one else was on the road just yet. No other travelers, just Ben.

On the interstate he poured a cup of lemon tea, steadying it before him on the dashboard so that it shed a crescent of steam against the windshield, and settled back in his seat. There was the high smell of dogs in the car, the sharp odor of their animal digestive tracts, the rain evaporating from their rank fur. There were whitecaps southward on Lake Washington as he crossed the wind-wracked floating bridge. To the north the water was a black expanse, and on the east side, beyond Mercer Island, loomed half-built exit ramps dressed in skins of intricate concrete pouring forms. The wind tore tired leaves from the alders and blew them onto the freeway. The long shore of Lake Sammamish, once a place of marsh and cattails, now lay throttled by condominiums, their yard lamps bathing the valley. At Issaquah, there were more lights: a Triple X Root Beer, a Texaco gas station, a Dairy Queen, Boehm's Candies. Then the last of the suburbs dropped away, and he was climbing the grade above Issaquah Creek beneath the rain-embattled trees.

A tractor-trailer roared past on the right, and a sudden slap of road water, lashed from its tires, washed across his windshield. He could not make out the borders of the lanes or much beyond the rain in his headlights, as white as sleet and flashing rapidly like small electric sparks. Another truck passed, and then there was no one, and Ben took a sip from his lemon tea and fell into fretful meditation.

His cancer had metastasized, traveling from the mucosa of his colon to the lymph nodes close to his tumor, and from there to sites in his liver. Each day he fortified himself once again to accept this intractable state of affairs; each day he started over. He was, he knew, incurable; he had seen too much in his years as a doctor to delude himself that things were otherwise. He knew exactly what to expect and could not turn away from meeting. After the bed-sores and bone fractures, the bacterial infection from the catheter, the fluid accumulating between his viscera that would have to be expunged through a drainage tube; after the copious vomiting, the dehydration and lassitude, the cracked lips, dry mouth, tube feed-ings, and short breath, the dysphagia, pneumonia, and feverishness, the baldness and endgame sensation of strangling; after he had shrunk to eighty-five pounds and was gasping his last in a nursing-home bed—only at that point would Bill Ward put him down under a drip of death-inducing morphine. That was how his life would end if he did not end it first.

He was well aware of countervailing arguments, but these, he saw now, had been forwarded by people not yet confronted by death. He, too, had articulated at times the consolations of a gradual dying: how the trivial paled in the face of death, yet the veins in the tree leaves and the evening slant of light were brought to the forefront of existence. How all was intensified, heightened, compressed, vivified, transformed, appreciated. How love deepened and ordinary tribulations sank into insignificance. How one had time for a summing up, days on which to meditate in search of a divine composure. Yet what had he really known of these matters even as soothing words about them flowed easily from his mouth? What had he fathomed of dying? Ben knew there were regions of pain so bleak they could not be traveled without surgery to sever nerves in the spinal cord. There were re-gions of pain so terrible, they obliterated all argument. The cancer-ridden, often, preferred to die as the only antidote to their suffering. Such was predominantly the case at the end; such might be the case for him, too.

It did not seem to him cowardly to want to avoid pain. He had seen enough of it in his seventy-three years to understand its indifference to character, temperament, or virtue. There was no real bravery in enduring it, but only fear of pain's alternative, the cessation of everything.

The biology of the body, which he'd confronted every day, had not in the least taught Dr. Givens to disbelieve in God. On the contrary, he had seen that the body was divine, and he had witnessed the ceasing of its processes often enough to know that something holy left the body at the very moment of death.

It was sometimes possible—the perception came and went—to view the imminence of his own end with a calm, fearless detachment. In his grave he would experience nothing, the condition of death would not be painful, it was nothing, a kind of sleep. The problem, then, wasn't death but dying, and if the trial of dying could be got through—like any horrifying or painful ordeal—death, the other side, would be endurable. And so the best one could do, it seemed, was to remove the pain and horror from the process by choosing an intelligent suicide. A course well thought out, rational, the least of many possible evils. The worst of it was his present melancholy, and the illusion that after his end came, he would experience an eternal regret. In this nether-life he now endured, he experienced regret already. He felt no longer a part of the world. Everything reeked of the grave.

The rain fell even harder over Tiger Mountain, and by the time he had crossed the Raging River, he had slowed to fifty miles an hour. He passed Echo Lake and Rattlesnake Peak, and in the darkness of morning the hills all around—or what he could see of them through the veil of rain—were a bare shade darker than the sky. The faint first light from out of the east made the crests of the hills just distinguishable from the heavens, and as he traveled down the long grade to North Bend, the profile of Mount Si became visible. Ben had scaled it three dozen times, mostly to test his strength and endurance before more difficult ascents. Its abrupt black fault-scarp seemed to rise up directly from the lights of North Bend's main street, and the promontory of its summit—the Haystack, it was called—appeared forbidding against the sky.

The highway began to climb in earnest, following the south fork of the Snoqualmie River, past Harmon Heights, Cedar Butte, Grouse Ridge, and the low summit of Mount Washington. Here the trucks worked around one another and the wind whistled through the window moldings. Ben passed the cutoff to McClellan Butte—another promontory he had climbed often—and the Tinkham Road cutoff where in the growing light he could see the river steaming. The rain was pummeling the flats along its bank and melding into its currents. Power lines traveled over the hills. As the light of morning grew more expansive, the mist tucked low in the valleys was revealed, and the first snow dusting the high couloirs. It occurred to Ben to follow his present heart and on the spur of the moment change everything, hike in the rain to the summit of Silver Peak, and there simply lie on the crest of the Cascades and wait for the end to come. The plan had a soothing elegance, and the prospect of succumbing to a hypothermic torpor was not really so dreadful. It was less like taking one's life than allowing it to be taken. One just stopped living, that was all.

The mountains beckoned in this way, the green wet flanks of mountains breaking out into windswept scree and snow. Ben shrugged them off and continued on his way. He was bent on crossing into the country beyond. He had been born in the cradle of apple orchards, and it was this world he wanted to return to.

Past Humpback Mountain the road turned north and began to climb more steeply. A trio of haul trucks, convoy-fashion, took the grade at thirty miles an hour in the far right-hand lane. The darkness had mostly given way to the low gray light of early morning, and Ben could see red huckleberry brush and vine maples on the hillsides. Everything glistened and swam with rain, and the creeks plashing down their deep-cut ravines were white and fast with it. The Scout seemed to float for sudden interludes, as if riding weightlessly on shallow surf—there was the spatter of water beneath the wheels and the sense of being unmoored from the earth—and then it would seize the road again. And there were the headlights of a car behind him now, and the tail-lights of two cars in front of him, shimmering beyond his windshield. Ben slowed to forty miles an hour and leaned tautly forward. The rain, the wet pavement, the trucks to his right, the windows around him fogged with the breath of dogs—the moment was so fraught with dangers that when Rex hurled suddenly over the seat to settle his forepaws again on the rucksack, Ben felt a surge of anger. The dog had to learn his place in things, as Tristan before him had. He had to understand how it was.

Ben spoke beseechingly at first, then with urgent command in his voice, then with the low melody of gentle threat. When nothing happened—Rex did not move—Ben took him firmly by the collar. "Get back there," he said between clenched teeth, exerting himself to pull the dog off the rucksack, but Rex only whimpered and held his ground.

Ben anchored himself against the Scout's steering wheel and tried to dislodge his dog. Half-turned in his seat, his hand behind him and locked at the dog's throat, he did not have time to correct or control matters when the Scout began to slide toward the median. He let go of the dog and swiveled forward, the car skating silently and as if in slow motion, and clutched the steering wheel. The Scout struck the concrete road barrier and rebounded across all four eastbound lanes, sliding miraculously between two haul trucks and down the summit exit ramp, where it slammed into a small fir tree.

TWO

The rain beat hard on the Scout's roof. A boy pulled open the driver's door and placed a hand on Ben's shoulder. "Are you okay?" he asked.

"I don't know," Ben answered. He was holding his head in his palms.

"You need some help? You need a doctor? You're bleeding pretty bad, it looks like."

"I am a doctor," said Ben.

The boy took his hand from Ben's shoulder and shut off the ignition. There was a squall of whimpering from the rear of the car—Tristan and Rex both sounding unnerved—and the boy urged them to settle down. Swinging his wet hair from his eyes, he squatted in the door of the Scout.

"You're going to need some help," he said. "It looks like you need stitches."

"My dogs," said Ben. "How are they?"

Suddenly there was a girl behind the boy, a tall girl in a yellow slicker. "Are you okay?" she asked.

"He's all right," the boy answered gently. "Everything's all right."

"I'm fine," said Ben, "but what about my dogs? How do they look back there?"

"They look good," the boy assured him. "It's you we're worried about."

Ben held the heel of a palm to his forehead, just above his left eyebrow. With his other hand, he slid free his glasses: one lens was broken, the other had popped out, the frames were twisted and mangled. Blood trickled into his left eye and along the left side of his nose with warm constancy. "Your head must've hit the wheel," the boy said. "Here you go. Use this."

From his hip pocket he slid a blue bandanna folded into a square. He leaned into the car and with no hesitation cleaned the blood from Ben's face; then, turning the bandanna inside out, he pressed it against Ben's forehead. "Drop your head back," he advised gently, "and hold this here for a minute."

Ben did. His neck hurt.

"Why don't we get him in the van?" asked the girl. "It's pouring out here and everything."

Ben couldn't see her or anything else with any power of distinction. A dense black shroud lay over his consciousness, and he felt that his brain had been jarred loose. At the same time, he felt startled awake, infused with adrenaline, raw. There was the giddy exhilaration experienced by those who survive accidents intact; there was a sense of freedom and good fortune, of his place among the blessed.

Without his glasses, on any given day, his sight was compromised. Now, with the blood running into his eye, he was vertiginously half blind. He could discern, in the foreground, a few stray details: the boy's long hair pasted against his scalp; the girl tall and slim in her rain gear, its hood pulled over her forehead. He guessed them to be in their early twenties. The boy wore a spindly goatee.

"How's the car?" Ben asked.

"Mangled," said the boy. "Wrapped around a tree. You want me to take a better look?"

"Is it drivable?"

"Your radiator's gone, at the very least. You don't have a cooling system." The boy shrugged and shook his head. "We were right behind you coming through the pass. It's like a miracle you're even alive."

"It's a total miracle," the girl added. "You slid between these two huge trucks. And they didn't even stop or anything. They just kept right on going."

"My dog," Ben said. "I turned because the dog jumped across the seat and . . . the road was wet. I lost control."

He leaned forward, took the bandanna from his forehead, and squinted at himself in the rearview mirror, tilting it in his direction. "That's right," the boy said. "Take a look."

There was a laceration just above his left eyebrow that would require three or four stitches. His glasses had pinched against his face, leaving several minor abrasions. The left eye's lower orbit suggested a tenderness that would darken rapidly into a bruise. He was going to look like a defeated boxer before this episode was over. His eye would swell shut, too.

"You had a little scuffle with your steering wheel," the boy said, squatting beside the car. "Looks like the wheel got the best of it."

"It could have been considerably worse. I actually feel very lucky."

"It's incredible," the girl agreed. "You could have been dead, you know."

"Yes, I could have," Ben said. "It's a kind of miracle."

He swiveled toward the door of the Scout and exerted himself to stand up. The boy assisted him, smoothly. Ben spun dizzily toward the rear of the car and slung down the tailgate. Rex bounded out—Ben cursed the dog as he leaped past—but Tristan stood still and sniffed the rain.

"You still alive, Tris?" Ben asked. And he ran his hands along the dog's flanks and held his muzzle gently. Searching with one eye shut, he found the tire iron. "I'd better pry open my hood," he told the boy, and set the tire iron on the tailgate.

Leaning gingerly through the driver's door, his neck and shoulders stiffening, Ben plucked his coat from the seat back. He rummaged through the rucksack for his spare pair of glasses and slid on his hunting cap. The glasses were antique, steel-rimmed ovals, very small and delicate, bought in 1954. He hadn't worn them in thirty-three years.

When Ben came out into the rain again, the boy had the Scout's hood levered open. He and the girl stood looking underneath it, the girl with her hands in the pockets of her raincoat, the boy holding the tire iron in one hand and rubbing his head with the other. "It doesn't look good," he warned.

The radiator had rammed into the fan shroud; the shroud had split and twisted sideways. The fan had been pushed against the water pump, which was fractured and leaking steadily. The front seal and pulley had bent, and the alternator had been torn from its mounting bracket. The battery had tipped over and lay against the steering box. It was cracked and slowly seeping acid.

The boy bent to peer beneath the car. "Bet your frame's been torqued," he said. "And I can see where you cracked your left front mount. Block could be cracked, too."

The girl had caught Rex by the slack in his collar and was caressing his throat and withers. "Let's go," she said. "We'll leave it here. Let's check out the Traveler's Rest."

"He doesn't deserve that," Ben told her. "Damn you, Rex," he added.

"There's a phone there," the boy said. "You can call a tow truck and everything. Deal with your forehead."

"Let me lock it up," said Ben. He shook his head as he looked things over. "I've had this car for twenty-eight years, and this is the first time it's been scratched."

"I know how you feel," the boy answered, easing the hood down against the rain. "I totalled my Travelall last year. It was the best car I ever had."

Ben looked at him for the first time with something approaching a proper interest. Through the old glasses he could see the world with only moderate, swimming clarity. The boy looked back at Ben earnestly, smiling with a charming ease. He was smooth-faced, brown-eyed, and handsome—as handsome as a movie star. The girl, too, was beautiful, kneeling beside the dog in her rain gear, graceful as a ballerina. Her hair was blond, her eyes blue, and she smiled directly at Ben, holding his gaze with a poise that stirred him. "I like your glasses," she said.

The girl's beauty was a torment. Her wet hand moving against the dog's throat and slowly down the length of the dog's chest filled Ben with a hollow yearning. He turned away from it.

They took him in their van toward the Traveler's Rest, a place he knew in Snoqualmie Pass, a haven for skiers and climbers. The rain beat hard off the windshield and roof, and the dogs were wet against his legs and boots. To the right Ben could see bare ski runs, their distant chair lifts idle; to the left rose slopes of huckleberry brush, subalpine fir, and vine maple. The van, he thought, smelled of lavender, but when he asked about it, the boy explained that the summer previous he and the girl had gone trekking in the Nepalese Himalaya and had come across this distinctive incense of sandalwood, musk, and saffron made by Tibetan monks. While the boy told of finding this fragrance in a village little visited by westerners, very close to the Sikkimese border, Ben sat patting the cut on his forehead and peering through his steel-rimmed glasses. The van had a sleeping berth cleverly up top, a built-in sink, a drop-leaf table, a refrigerator, and a chemical toilet. A length of purple climber's webbing hung in a loop from the rearview mirror, a well-worn carabiner clipped to it, dangling a ring-angle piton. On the dashboard sat an incense holder, an open bag of pumpkin seeds, and a few sprigs of ancient sage.

The girl eased off her yellow slicker—she wore a pile pullover underneath, her ponytail thick against it—and the boy sat drying his hair with one hand, driving easily down the summit road and talking over one shoulder. On the floor to Ben's left, in a cardboard box, were a white gas stove, two stainless steel cooking pots, a handheld water filter, and a candle lantern. Beside that was a grocery bag with the end of a long baguette poking out of it, and wedged in the corner were two sleeping bags inside nylon stuff sacks.

"How's your head?" the girl asked.

"I think it's okay," said Ben.

"You need anything? A drink of water? There's a water bottle in the cooler."

"I'm fine for now. Really."

"There's a first-aid kit," the boy remembered, then leaned across and popped open the glove compartment. "There's some Mercurochrome in there, I think. If you want to use it, go ahead."

The girl put the first-aid kit in her lap and found the Mercurochrome. She closed the glove compartment and smoothed her hair. Smiling, she turned to look at Ben, and at the same time flipped her ponytail deftly over one shoulder.

"We're just about to the Traveler's Rest," she said, as if he were in need of optimism. "We'll be there in just a few seconds."

"I know the place," said Ben.

"We ski up here," the boy explained. "If there's powder up here, we go."

"Otherwise we go over to Mission Ridge," the girl added with enthusiasm. "There's way more powder there, usually. It's way better snow."

"We hit the Rest for coffee," said the boy. "We've been there a million times."

He pulled up in front of it and shut down his engine. There were two other cars in the parking lot, the rain pounding off their roofs and hoods. The Traveler's Rest looked like an old-fashioned ski chalet—Ben remembered it from another time—but in fact it was mostly a convenience store. In the aftermath of hiking and climbing trips he had often stopped here to fill his thermos with tea for the dark westward drive home.

In the foyer, he stood beside a pay phone, where the business cards of towing companies were pinned to a bulletin board. On a placard a man named Steve advertised roof shoveling at "reasonable rates"; a '49 Studebaker was for sale. Plenty of mud had been brought into the foyer on the boots of mountain travelers. Ben held his head—his temples were throbbing—and waited with resigned patience while the phone rang seven times. Then a man answered in a curt, sleepy tone, as if in his life he'd fielded hundreds of such calls, and Ben told him what had happened.

"So what do you want me to do?" asked the man.

"I want you to tow the car," said Ben. "Get it out of there."

"You call the state patrol guys yet?"

"Not yet. But I'll get to it."

"You got insurance or anything?"

"Yes. But not for towing."

"Well, it's a hundred bucks for me to tow you, guy, so I need a credit card number."

"All right," said Ben. "A hundred." And he gave the man a credit card number, reading it from a sleeve in his wallet.

"You want us to make repairs?" said the man.

"I don't know yet. Maybe."

"Well, when will you know? For my information."

"I have to call the insurance agent. It's a Saturday morning and it may take awhile. Besides, it's a '69 International Scout. You'll have a hard time locating parts."

"We can find 'em," the man said. "We can get International, depending on what you need."

"I need a lot," Ben said. "The whole front end is totaled."

"Two days, probably, be my guess. Depends. We have to order from Chicago."

"I'll think about it some, okay?"

"It's five dollars a day to leave it in the yard. You're willing to pay five bucks a day, you can think about it a hundred years."

"That's perfect," Ben said. "You hold the car for me."

"Now what about you?" the man asked. "We've got twenty-four-hour taxi service I can have there in thirty minutes."

"That's okay," Ben heard himself say. "I won't be needing a ride."

"You won't be needing a ride," said the man. "You're up in the pass with a busted-down car. What are you going to do?"

"I have a ride. That's taken care of."

"All right," said the man. "I'm on my way. You say it's in the first summit exit?"

"Yes. Eastbound. Against a small tree."

"I'll see you there, then. About an hour."

"Maybe not. I need a couple stitches. So the key will be sitting on the driver's side leaf spring in case you need to get in."

"That's a good place for it," the man said.

In the rest room Ben leaned toward the mirror to inspect the wound in his forehead. He was surprised at himself for refusing the taxi service—but what did he have to go home to? And why shouldn't he continue with his journey? The young people would certainly give him a ride, and after that he could rent a car—in Ellensburg perhaps, there had to be a place—and continue to his destination.

Prying the wound open with his index fingers, he turned it toward the light. The boy entered with the first-aid kit and stood patiently beside Ben at first, then leaned against the wall with loose-jointed ease, one foot propped up behind him. "What do you think?" he asked.

"It needs to be sutured," Ben answered, though he knew sutures would be a waste of time, given his intentions. He removed his glasses delicately, slipping their stems from each ear with care, bent slowly, stiffly at the waist, cupped his hands beneath the tap, and doused his face, twice. He worked soap into the laceration. When he finished, the boy was at his side, handing him a paper towel.

"There's a couple of choices here," said the boy, rummaging through the first-aid kit. "There's the Mercurochrome. There's hydrogen peroxide. A tube of ointment. This dermal wound cleanser we got in Colorado, it's made from aloe vera."

"I could use some sterile gauze," Ben said. "What kind of ointment is it?"

The boy handed the tube to him. "It's bacitracin," he said.

Ben worked the bacitracin into his wound. After severing the gauze lengthwise with a small pair of scissors, he sliced it into narrow strips and laid them against the adhesive side of a length of waterproof tape. He pressed the dressing to his head and pressed it again, forcefully, with the tips of his index fingers. He put on his glasses, washed his hands, and ran his fingers through his hair, trying to arrange it neatly.

"What about stitches?" the boy asked.

"I know a doctor in Quincy," Ben lied. "It's another two hours east of here. I'd like to get him to do it."

"We're turning south at Vantage," said the boy, "but for sure we can get you that far."

"I could rent a car in Ellensburg. That way I'd be out of your hair."

"Little known fact," the boy said. "There's a rental place in Vantage at the RV campground. I had to use it once."

"You're sure?"

"For sure I'm sure."

"I never noticed it there before."

"It's a small place, but they'll rent you a car."

"All right," Ben said. "Let's do it."

The boy and girl in the Volkswagen van ferried Ben to his car again. He placed the key on the driver's side leaf spring and carefully sorted through his belongings, meditating on every item and casting off whatever seemed useless. He broke down the shotgun and put it in his duffel. He left all the extra clothing in the car—with the exception of two pairs of cotton socks and his thermal underwear—and he jettisoned the dog food and dog bowls. He considered the thermos but left it where it lay on the seat beside his broken glasses. The prescription sunglasses had dropped off the dashboard and fallen onto the floor mat. He slipped them inside his rucksack.

It would look, he hoped, as if he had decided to press on with a modified hunting trip. No one would read the truth, he felt, from the way he had left things here. He imagined his daughter trying to make sense of it: his car abandoned in Snoqualmie Pass, the credit card record of his car rental in Vantage, his corpse rotting in a sage canyon across the Columbia. She would trace his steps, or most of them, he hoped. She would see how naturally it had all unfolded. Her suspicions would be erased.

Ben hauled his duffel bag and rucksack to the van. He opened the side door and set his things on the floor. The two young people stared at him. He glanced at each and then stepped in. "I'm ready," he said. "Let's go."

He rode with them through Snoqualmie Pass to the east side of the mountains. He settled back with the dogs against his legs and let the terrain seep into him. To the northwest, he knew, was Denny Mountain. Twice before he'd walked the ridge to it from Chair Peak and The Tooth. He'd climbed Mount Wright and Preacher Mountain, the winter of 1959, in a pelting downpour of sleet. He remembered climbing Alta Mountain, and the brief, truncated glissades he'd made to work his way back down. He remembered a journey with his grandson to climb Mount Thompson and Kendall Peak, and the high camp they'd established in the lee of a ridge, where the cold caused Chris much misery. Ben had showed him how to warm his fingers by burying them in his armpits.

The girl in the front seat took a water bottle from between her thighs and extended it in Ben's direction. He thanked her for it and drank a little. He fingered the tape against his forehead and worked the vertebrae in his neck. Holding his side, he stared in silence out the window. The girl offered him some pumpkin seeds, and he let her pour them into his hand and ate them at the same rate she did. She'd roasted them, she said, in olive oil, and sprinkled them with sea salt. They were excellent, he told her, and she smiled at this and poured still more into his cupped palms.

"You must be bummed about your car," she said.

"Oh, well," said Ben.

"That's a pretty good attitude. That's what I try to do."

"Yeah," said the boy. "It's great."

"Now where were you going?" the girl asked. "Before you crashed and everything."

"Up near Rock Island," Ben said. "I was born up there. I'm going home."

"It's so beautiful," the girl answered. "All those apple orchards."

"Yes, it is," said Ben.

The boy reached out and touched the girl's cheek with the back of his index finger. She reached across and touched the boy's arm, and then she moved her hand to his shoulder, and from his shoulder to the muscle of his thigh, where she let it linger comfortably.

They were passing Keechelus Lake now. Its waters sat low at this time of year; the basin lay full of weathered stumps. On the far side, off to the south, the big hills were furrowed and deeply eroded, smooth, contoured, treeless. The land, already, was more arid than it had been. The rain had slowed considerably and had spent itself, as it always did, against the green mountains to the west.

"You're a doctor, you say," the boy asked.

"That's right," answered Ben.

"I kind of thought," the boy said, "that you had to hurry with stitches. Like if you waited too long, it didn't work."

"Not true," Ben lied again. "That's a misconception."

"I cut myself bad in the Dolomites," said the boy. "I took a header and laid my shoulder open. The doctor wouldn't even sew me up. He said it had been too long or something. He said it just had to heal."

"In the Dolomites," Ben repeated.

"Yeah."

"They don't know about stitches in the Dolomites," Ben lied. "They're living in the Middle Ages."

"It was incredible there," the girl said. "We totally loved the Dolomites."

"I've been there, too," said Ben.

"Did you go to Cortina?"

"Yes. Some. Mostly further north."

"What did you do?"

"I went hiking and climbing. Years ago. I had my honeymoon there."

"That's great," the girl said. "You don't meet a lot of climbers or anything that are, like, your age."

"This was years ago, " Ben said. "This was fifty-two years ago."

"We climbed the Marmolada," the boy replied. "We stayed at San Martino di Castrozza and went climbing every day. I totally loved the place."

"It's beautiful there," Ben agreed.

"We went up Sella Pass," said the boy. "We climbed all up around Cima Pardoi. We went over to Tre Cime di Laveredo and climbed up in there, too. We would have stayed forever," he added, "except that we ran out of bucks."

"That happens," Ben said. "Reality intrudes."

"Only if you let it," the boy said.

Ben made no answer. He sat with his right hand cupping his waist and his left fingering his bandaged temple. He remembered that long ago in the Dolomites, he and Rachel had taken the high trail from Vigo di Fassa to Ciampedie to see the glow of the setting sun against the Torre di Vaiolet spires. At their hotel on the Lago di Carezza, the electricity was unreliable. At Falzarego they'd bought wine and crostini and traversed uphill to Lagazuoi. At dusk a roseate glow had suffused the world. The mountain walls appeared buffed and polished. In the twilight they came to the Refugio Scotoni, a small inn in a narrow valley. They'd been

married only ten days. The mountains were in the scent of
Rachel's shoulder blades. The odor at her throat was salt and
pine, the smell of her hair, wood smoke.

The Hotel Monte Sella in San Vigilio de Marebbe had been
done up in the Jugendstil fashion: rough pine doors with
wrought-iron grilles, grisaille tile in the corridors. The plaster
had been painted to look like marble. In the vestibule, a lake pastoral, painted delicately against the walls: pleasure boats on
turquoise waters, birds aloft over cypress trees, tranquil skies,
pines. At midday, the headwaiter used his handbell with a delicate, calm persistence. Bruschetta and saltimbocca, consommé,
tortellini filled with mashed potato, scallope di vitello with egg-
plant. In the lounge, late, card games. An atmosphere of pastoral
extravagance. Bottles of grappa set out; carafes of the hotel's
house wine—slightly bitter, tannic.

They'd bathed together in a claw-foot tub. The moon risen
high over the mountaintops. On the chill, clean air, the chiming
of the village bells. In the hall, late revelers moved toward sleep.
The smell of the sheets, of bath soap; then no smell but hers.
His mouth against her hairline, slow. A long descent toward
those incidental places he found he did not want to neglect: the
shallow channel in her lower back, the bones in her wrists, her
heels. The rest of the world obliterated. Time arrested now.
Everything possible, all manner of entanglement pleasurable.
When they understood there was no choice anymore, they
watched each other without shame.

He'd felt himself at the height of life. He told her so. He said
that he loved her. He said that he wanted to hold her forever. He
kissed her deeply, sweetly.

Sitting in the back of the Volkswagen van, Ben mistrusted his
memories. Everything in memory achieved a truth that was only
a brand of falsehood. He remembered what was beautiful—a
torture unto itself, really—while all else receded and blurred,

dwindled into insignificance. It pained him to think that with his death the narrative of his time with Rachel would disappear, the story of their love expire. He could not explain it to anyone. It would leave the earth when he did.

At the far end of Keechelus Lake, the sky eastward opened wide over distant coulees, buttes, and canyons, all swathed in morning light. Ahead lay a low film of red on the horizon where the sun was new; the road wound down through a stand of grand firs with long, broad, flat needles. Ben sat back and watched the country grow larger and more sparsely treed and gentle. They drove down out of Snoqualmie Pass and left the mountains behind. The girl gave Ben more pumpkin seeds; the boy flipped down his sun visor. They asked him his name, and he gave it to them, and the boy introduced himself as Kevin Lamont and the girl as Christine Reilly. The road ran straight and true into the southeast, the hills spread out beneath the sky, and there was no sign of rain now. Along the Yakima River, the cottonwoods had gone russet yellow. The light was huge and unadulterated. West of the mountains the light ran to gray, hushed and annealed by ocean clouds, but here on the east side the world yielded and lay unguarded beneath the sun.

They came down into the pine flats past the town of Easton, where half a dozen horses grazed on the north side of the highway. They passed the cutoff to Roslyn, the road grading down toward Cle Elum, the river twisting past gravel bars and islands, leaving sloughs and eddies behind, the tincture of autumn woodstove smoke hanging heavily on the air. As they climbed eastward into Elk Heights, the land was all pastures, hills, and range, the big hay sheds loaded to the rafters, the hay wintered under tin roofs. Off to the north was the Stuart Range, distant and ethereal as a mirage.

The country was given over to cattle graze, and the cotton-woods lay in folds and vales that rose toward the east horizon and north to the foothills of snowy peaks. Christine pointed out for Ben the autumnal beauty of all those trees, smoothing her hair just over one ear, and Ben quietly agreed. They climbed over Indian John Hill, where power wires marched west across the land as though cobbled together by the children of giants passing their time playfully. In Elk Heights Pass they saw to the east the hills of bitterbrush and ponderosa pine, and the rangelands of sage and bunchgrass. There were treeless, fruitless, sad buttes, their soil barren as the moon.

"You must be feeling better," said Christine. "You seem nice and mellow."

"I'm fine," said Ben. "I'm comfortable."

"We got the van for that," said Kevin. "It's nice to kind of stretch out."

"We travel a lot," Christine added.

"We're going climbing," Kevin explained. "We're going out to the Sawtooths for a while and then down into Sun Valley."

"If things work out, we'll ski all winter," Christine said hopefully. "That's what we did last season. There's this friend we know in Ketchum who can hook us into the ski patrol."

"Free lift tickets and a crash pad," said Kevin. "Only thing is, it's too crowded."

"We thought we'd get into heli-skiing," said Christine. "You guide people up in the backcountry, get away from the crowd."

"That's a few years off," said Kevin. "We don't have that focused yet."

"We're sort of poor right now," explained Christine. "We just have the cash to get there."

"Not even that," Kevin countered.

He opened the glove compartment, found his sunglasses, and slid them onto his face. They were mirrored glasses of the sort skiers wore, and he looked less handsome in them suddenly, with the mirrors concealing his brown eyes. "The sun," he said. "I'm driving straight into it."

"Better than rain," Christine said.

They passed the Thorp Fruit and Antique Mall. The hills in the distance were barren; eastward the land lay lifeless. They passed a grain silo, fenced pastureland, a row of willows planted as a windbreak beside a forlorn farmhouse. There were long wheeled irrigators lined up by ditches and canals full of runoff water. The river spilled broadly past cutbanks.

"Listen," said Ben. "It's apple season. If you're out of money, you could go up and pick. They'll be looking for people now."

"That's a good idea," Christine said.

"Yeah," said Kevin. "Maybe."

"You know what? It sounds really great."

"It does sounds great, you're right."

Christine put a hand on his thigh again. "I've always wanted to pick," she said.

"We ought to do it," agreed Kevin.

At Ellensburg they passed into the stench of a slaughter-house—the reek of blood spilled into the earth and of the exposed viscera of cows. The yards and gates stood empty now, the corrals deeply pocked by hooves and pools of muddy water. Plumes of steam rose off the ground; hundreds of cows fed until the last on a dirt hillside nearby.

"There's a good reason right there," said Christine, "to totally go vegetarian."

"We tried it once," Kevin said. "Then we sort of slipped."

"We made exceptions. It all fell apart."

"Thanksgiving," said Kevin. "We went to her mom's. What were we supposed to do?"

"We could have stuck to potatoes, you know. We just didn't, was all. We were weak."

They rolled on into the eastward country. The hills were more windswept and vast as they graded up out of the valley. A pig farm stood on the north side of the road, and the pigs wallowed in thick black mud beneath the shade of cottonwoods fast shedding their leaves. Ragged cover followed the fence lines, and the fields in the distance were muddy and furrowed, with the ditch water reflecting sunlight. They were leaving the cultivated, well-kept country and entering hills that had been there before the farms, hills dotted with islands of wheatgrass sprouting up between the sage.

"This stretch of road is spooky," said Christine. "Everything looks so old."

The country appeared bleaker, more desolate. WARNING! a sign read. NEXT EXIT 23 MILES. LAST CHANCE FOR FOOD OR GASOLINE. They drove on past the Kittitas exit, where cottonwoods stood on both sides of a ditch swollen with running water. Big irrigators loomed in the hayfields. Everything was still, silent, and sad; everything looked dilapidated. Against a fence grew Russian thistle, most of which had turned to tumbleweed. At the edge of the highway sat a run-down farmhouse, the ruins of a shed beside it. A swaybacked dog paced its front porch, halting to sniff at a sofa. The sage desert began in the farmhouse's sideyard and ran infinitely eastward.

Ben sat kneading the right side of his belly and staring out the window. The hills rose tan, olive, and brown, and the ribbon of asphalt cutting through them was the darkest thing on the landscape. They passed beneath a railroad trestle; they passed a concrete spillway. The power wires appeared feeble against the hills, like old telegraph lines. Now the road before them steepened, and as they ascended into Ryegrass Summit, Kevin downshifted into third gear. "Everything up here is crumbling," he said. "Erosion city or something."

"Basalt lava," Christine said.

"Old volcanoes."

"Very old volcanoes."

"Like fifty million years."

"Even older."

They made their way over Ryegrass. The country broke open into long barren slopes falling to the Columbia. Off in the distance, off to the east, Ben saw the breaks on the far side of the river shimmer in the October sunlight.

"We're coming into Vantage," said Kevin, moving into the right-hand lane, slowing to take the exit ramp. They emerged from the shadows of the talus buttes, where the river lay throttled behind Wanapum Dam, still and flat, a green lake. A flock of mallards, tightly packed, bobbed together in the lee of the bridge. A magpie perched on a stop sign.

Ben pointed north, upriver. "I was born out there about thirty miles," he said. "Up past the canyon and around a few bends. Back before there were any dams."

"Those were the good times," said Kevin.

Vantage sat sheltered behind windbreak trees—venerable Lombardy poplars. There was a Shell, a Texaco, an RV campground, a restaurant called the Golden Harvest. Kevin turned at the general store and stopped beside a phone booth. He came around and slid open the van's door, his sunglasses in his hand. "Stay," he said, pointing at Rex. "Just hold it right there, dog."

He gestured toward the campground office, through the break of poplars. "If you need to rent yourself a car, you can do it over there."

"Good," Ben said. "Thanks."

"We'd take you on," Kevin added, "but we're turning off toward Othello."

"It's all right," Ben said. "I'm glad to have gotten this far."

"Your eye's swelling up," Kevin observed. "Looks like you're going to have a black eye. It's going to be kind of gnarly."

"That's okay. I can live with that."

"Your neck looks pretty stiff, too. You better just take it easy."

Christine got out and stood in the sun with her hands in the front pockets of her jeans. "What about your dogs?" she asked. "Can we let them run loose out here? Or do you want to tie them up?"

"They can run," Ben said. "They won't go anywhere."

The boy and girl stood to one side and watched the dogs sidle out. Ben followed and slipped on his hunting cap. His side burned. His back hurt. He still couldn't see clearly.

"It's a great day," Kevin declared. "Everything smells like sage."

"It's warm out," added Christine.

The young couple stood by their van holding hands while Ben called his insurance company. He called the state patrol, too. The girl slipped her fingers into the boy's rear pocket, then around his slim waist. The boy pulled her to him, and they kissed briefly. They were seriously in love, Ben could see that. They were easy and familiar with each other. He turned from the sight of them, hung up the phone, and made his way to their van. He hauled his rucksack and duffel bag out, propped them beside the phone booth, and rummaged for the Manila cord he would need to leash Tristan and Rex.

"What's the deal?" asked Kevin.

"My friend's on his way," Ben said. "He'll pick me up right here."

"Okay," said Kevin. "Perfect."

"You forget anything in the van?" asked Christine. "You got everything out here?"

"I think so," Ben said. "I left your bandanna on the seat back there. It probably goes in the trash." He slid his wallet free of his pocket, plucked out four twenty-dollar bills, and thrust them into the girl's hand. "Don't argue," he said. "Just take it."

"We don't want your money," Christine said. "We didn't help you out for this."

"You can skip picking apples this way. That money will get you to the Sawtooths."

"Not a good reason," said Christine.

"Take it. You need it more than I do. So just take it and let's not talk about it."

"No way. Come on."

"Yeah," added Kevin. "Come on."

Ben backed away and put his wallet in his pocket. "You keep that money," he told them.

They stood for a moment looking at him. Then Kevin pulled open the van door. He came out with the bag of pumpkin seeds, a small carton of the Himalayan incense manufactured by Tibetan monks, and the length of purple climber's webbing, threaded with the carabiner and ring-angle piton, that had hung from the rearview mirror. "Here," he said. "Our gift."

"That 'biner is really good luck," explained Christine. "We found it up in the Dolomites."

"You're an old climber," Kevin added. "You ought to take this 'biner."

"I don't know," Ben said.

"Take it. We want you to have it." Christine took the webbing from the boy's hand and looped it over Ben's neck. "There," she said. "It's yours."

"It looks right," Kevin said. "It looks perfect on you."

"Take this other stuff, too," said Christine. And she gave him the incense and the pumpkin seeds. "It's not worth eighty bucks," she said. "But maybe it'll come in handy."

"Thank you," said Ben. "I appreciate it."

They stood looking at him awkwardly, uncertain about taking their leave. "You don't have to wait around," said Ben. "My friend's on his way. It's all taken care of. I can't thank you two enough."

"Okay," said Christine. "Good luck and all."

"Yeah," said Kevin. "Hope it goes well."

The girl reached back for her ponytail and laid it over her left shoulder. Her features, Ben saw, were much like Rachel's: her beauty was in her fine bones. Her beauty was not an ephemeral thing or a condition of her age alone. It would still be there in fifty years, underneath her aging skin. "If you haven't done it already," said Ben, "you two ought to get married."

Christine smiled and nudged Kevin, who put an arm around her neck. "I'm never going to leave her," he said. "I don't need a piece of paper."

"We're soulmates," Christine said. "We're forever."

When they had pulled away in their Volkswagen van, Ben sat down by his rucksack and perched his head against his hands. The van crossed the bridge in the distance, small against the rising hills.

Ben remembered that in Italy, he and Rachel had slipped down between rows of apple trees on the plain of the Po, deep into the cool and dark of orchards, and there they had kissed with the sadness of newlyweds who know that their kisses are too poignantly tender and that their good fortune is subject, like all things, to the crush of time, which remorselessly obliterates what is most desired and pervades all that is beautiful.

THREE

The wound in his forehead throbbed now. There was not a soul to be seen in Vantage; the town appeared lifeless, barren. Below was the silent highway and the river, and to the east spread a sky unfathomably vast, becalmed, devoid of clouds. Everything close, the stones and the grass, seemed hard-edged and vivid to Ben's eyes, but in the distance the clear substance of things gave way to mirages and shadows.

Tristan sidled over to lie at his feet and to rest his throat on Ben's boot. Ben put one hand on the dog's muzzle and with the other prodded his own wounded forehead and massaged his aching temples. He stayed that way for a long while, taking in the dark hills to the south; then he stood and leashed up the dogs with the length of Manila cord. He spoke to them gently, explaining the state of things, but the sound of his voice was strange to his ears and he retreated into silence. Stretching his neck, back, and shoulders, he tried to fend off the lassitude growing in him even at this hour of the morning. It seemed to him he had to move or risk falling into a pause that might become a stupor. At last, drumming up his energy, he maneuvered into the rucksack straps and, bearing his duffel over one shoulder, hiked up toward the campground with his dogs trailing, leashed.

The campground's office smelled of cigarettes, and on a shelf in the front window lay a dusty collection of quartz and petrified wood. On the counter sat a five-gallon aquarium of desultory neon tetras milling behind algae-tinted glass. There was a black velvet scroll, perhaps made in Hong Kong, of a sequined and benign-looking tiger. There were ceramic finger vases, ceramic snakes, and ceramic miniature flamingos. Behind the counter, on a couch in the corner, two small children, a boy and a girl, sat curled under a sleeping bag, watching a cartoon.

"Good morning," Ben said to them. "How are you?"

Neither child answered at first; instead they gawked at his swollen eye, the boy with the sleeping bag pulled up to his chin, the girl with a corner of it in her mouth. "Did somebody punch you?" she finally asked.

"Yes. But I don't want to talk about it."

The girl sat up to see his eye more closely. "What happened? You got busted good."

"I had a fight with a coyote."

"You didn't fight with any coyote."

Ben shook his head, as if disappointed. "Don't believe me," he said.

"I don't. Cuz you're just teasing."

"That's what they all say," said Ben.

She rose haughtily to leave the room, her torso thrust forward and misshapen. She had a severe case of scoliosis and was as bandy-legged as a cowboy. Yet she exited with the hauteur of a duchess who has been toyed with too often. The boy, younger, stared at Ben as if he were an apparition. "Really?" he asked. "For real?"

"Really."

"You should have climbed up a tree," said the boy, "or throwed rocks at him."

"There are a lot of things I should have done. But I didn't think straight."

"What happened?"

"He punched me, I punched him. You know." Ben shrugged.

The boy blinked and put his thumb in his mouth. "The coyote looks worse," Ben said.

The boy's mother came through the door then, trailing the girl behind. She was a heavy woman, not yet thirty, stout in the neck and shoulders. She wore a string of puka shells at her throat and a yellow hooded sweatshirt. "What do you need?" she asked Ben.

"I'd like to rent a car," Ben told her. "I've heard this is the place."

"Not really, not anymore. There was a guy in the campground used to rent a couple cars, but he's gone awhile."

She slid one hand into the pocket of her sweatshirt and inspected his damaged face. "What happened?" she asked. "That looks nasty."

Ben explained that he had crashed his car and banged his head on the steering wheel. "You were just teasing," said the boy. The girl put one hand against her hip, cocked her head, and sighed. "I knew you didn't fight any coyote. Can't nobody fight with a coyote."

Ben sighed in mimicry. "You win," he confessed. "I lied."

"You didn't even lie good. I never believed you for a second."

"You hush now," her mother said. She looked at Ben and shook her head. "She's just like a little grown-up sometimes. I can't figure out what to do with her."

"I have a daughter too," Ben said.

The woman nodded, leaned her weight on the counter, and yawned without embarrassment. There was probably a room at the motel, she said, if he wanted it. The Greyhound bus was coming through later that afternoon. He mentioned the two dogs waiting outside. She shook her head and explained that unless they were Seeing Eye dogs, the bus driver wouldn't let them board.

The motel, she suggested again. He could rest there, get his eye healed up, figure things out tomorrow. It wasn't any trouble for her to call over, let them know he was coming. Their rates were reasonable, she added.

Ben thanked her and picked up his duffel. "I think I'll just call a friend for a ride. But thanks for everything."

"Good-bye, liar," the girl said.

"You hush," said her mother.

Outside, his dogs sat impassively on the ground, watching him as if they expected something. Ben sat beside them, contemplative. The sun stippled the surface of the river, autumn-warm and pleasant. He reconsidered the attractions of a motel. But what would be the point of passing time in Vantage, sprawled out on some melancholy bed, watching television and dozing? It wasn't this he had come for. He patted Tristan's flank for a while, caressed Rex's belly and withers, until gradually he came to accept that his expedition had been thwarted by his accident, that it was time to get home any way he could—time to retreat, regroup, recuperate, then to reconsider this matter of how to meet his end.

He stood, and hauling his rucksack and duffel—his dogs straining on tightly held leashes—headed back to the highway. Ben hadn't hitchhiked in fifty-five years, but now it seemed unavoidable.

He climbed up onto the highway shoulder and stood there brazenly breaking the law with his bags sprawled on the ground next to him and his dogs restless at his side. Ben held his thumb out for a long time, but no one stopped for him. Who would stop for an old man with two dogs and a black eye? The drivers speeding past were from another universe—the universe he'd inhabited as a Seattle physician—and hurled past his extended thumb without concern or apology. One woman shrugged, but Ben couldn't translate the substance of her message. Perhaps she only meant to suggest that while half her heart wanted to serve, the other half was wary of strangers. Or perhaps she meant something more specific, that she was only going as far as the next exit and couldn't be of help to a traveler. Whichever it was, she didn't stop, and neither did other drivers. He was stuck outside of Vantage.

He hadn't reckoned with this possibility; he'd assumed his right to get home. After all, in times past, when he'd been a boy in orchard country, there was nothing illegitimate about hitchhiking or improvising a journey. He'd lived in a world of orchard tramps; a wanderer fell in with other wanderers. Though unwelcomed in settled places, they were not long scorned on paths or byways but generally treated to a ride. Now the cars flew by so fast, a driver could start in Seattle one morning and make North Dakota the next. No one waved or gestured. No one risked stopping at roadside. The world was full of madmen and strangers. Ben understood that he was one of them and that he had no chance of a ride.

Walking north on Wanapum Road, heading toward the Vantage Motel, he met another traveler. A long-haired drifter with thick tresses across his face, lean, tall, sun-burnished, he wore an oversized black leather jacket, its belt hanging limply from worn loops. He hadn't shaved recently, the hair sprouted mostly on his chin and upper lip, and he smoked a hand-rolled cigarette. "Hey, partner," he called to Ben. "I like those hunting dogs."

"Why don't you take them?" Ben answered.

"Can't," said the drifter. "I'm on the road." And he showed Ben his thumb, pointing east.

"I just spent an hour and a half doing that."

"It's the dogs, probably. Hide them in the bushes."

"Why didn't I think of that myself?"

The drifter shrugged. "Who knows?" he said. "Where are you trying to get to?"

"West," said Ben. "Across the mountains."

"The other side," the drifter said. "I haven't been over in a long time."

"Well, I was there a few hours ago. I came over earlier this morning."

The drifter shuffled his shoes in the dust, city shoes incongruous with the sagelands, his black leather jacket incongruous too, cut as if to be worn to a coffeehouse by a traveling blues musician. "Quick trip," he said to Ben. "You came over the pass this morning?"

"Three hours ago, about."

"Well, what are you going back for then?"

"It's a long story," said Ben.

The drifter tossed his cigarette in the road and perched his hands on his hips. "I hate to ask, but could you maybe spare a little change? I'm in need right now."

"I guess so," said Ben.

He set his bags on the road shoulder, experimentally fingered his forehead, then produced a twenty-dollar bill. The drifter took it in easy fashion. "Good man," he said.

"It's all right," Ben answered.

"Good man," the drifter said again. He folded the bill and slid it in his pocket. "So you're headed back, you say."

"I'm not headed anywhere," Ben replied. "I just had my thumb out for an hour and a half. Nobody even slowed down."

"Well, why don't you cross the river there? Go over and pick up Highway 26. People slow down at the intersection."

"It's the wrong way," Ben pointed out. "That's east, and I'm headed west."

"Well, maybe, but it's only a mile east. Put the thing in perspective."

"It's still the wrong way," Ben argued.

"There's no wrong way," the drifter said. "Whatever gets you there."

He propped Ben's duffel on his shoulder like a longshoreman, one arm looped over the top. "I've got this," he said. "Come on."

They set out toward the river. The drifter asked Ben about his damaged eye, and Ben told the story of his accident, the young people in the Volkswagen van, the attempt to rent a car. He said he'd come over the mountains to hunt quail, but with his eye swollen the way it was, he couldn't see well enough to shoot, so he may as well go home.

"Hey," said the drifter. "You can still hunt quail. A lot of people shoot one-eyed."

"It's not the best. No depth perception."

"Adjust," said the drifter. "You can do it."

They were at the west bank of the river now. They set out to cross the highway bridge, the drifter with Ben's duffel over his shoulder, Ben with his rucksack against his back, his dogs checked on tight leashes. The way was narrow, so they went single file, the drifter leading in silence. Ben followed him across the bridge. The Columbia here lay broad and flat. He was glad to see it, after all, glad to make this river crossing. To the east the breaks rose toward the plateau, and it occurred to Ben to hunt chukars. He had never hunted this stretch of country. It was all new terrain, unknown. But what difference could that make to him? Hunting birds in the open air was exactly what he'd come for.

They crossed on the north side with the traffic coming at

them, and as they did, the mallards in the lee of the bridge got up in a great slow easy flush and winged downriver, low, a hundred yards, where they settled again in long skating skids that raised pockets of white water. "Too bad you're not a duck hunter," said the drifter, calling back over one shoulder. "You'd be knocking 'em dead right now."

"Nothing against duck hunting. They're just not what I've come for."

"You're hunting other birds," observed the drifter.

On the far side the drifter stopped at the intersection with Highway 26. He eased Ben's duffel onto the ground. "You made it," he said. "All right."

"I'm here," said Ben. "I don't know exactly why. But anyway, I'm here."

The drifter lit another hand-rolled cigarette with a kitchen match struck off his pants zipper. "Park your dogs down there in the bushes," he said, "and try sticking your thumb out."

"I don't think I will. These breaks here might have chukar in them. I came to hunt. I'll hunt them."

"You changed your mind," said the drifter.

"I did," said Ben. "That happens."

"I change my mind all the time," said the drifter. "That's what's normal for me."

Ben tied his dogs to a fence post, spread his tin-cloth coat on the ground, opened the upland vest beside it, and laid out the items in the two bags neatly, where he could contemplate them one after the other. The drifter smoked, watching, and flipped the hair from his eyes. Ben turned the twin barrels of his shotgun to the sunlight, aligned the lug with the hinge pin, and snapped the gun together. "Winchester 21," said the drifter. "Top choice of heroes."

"I've had it forever," said Ben.

Deliberately, he pressed twenty-three number 8 shells into the loops in his upland vest and slipped the remaining two into a bellows pocket where he could bring them easily to hand. The tin-cloth coat he rolled up tightly and lashed it with the blanket and folded duffel against the bottom of his rucksack. Finally he put on the vest and the shooting gloves and pulled down his canvas cap tightly. He slid the whistle lanyard over his neck, then nestled the Winchester in the crook of his arm. "Hey," said the drifter. "Metamorphosis. You look like one ace hunter."

"Cyclops," said Ben. "Cyclops the hunter."

"Orion's the hunter," said the drifter.

Ben stood, looking up at the breaks. "You're out of here," the drifter told him. "Put your pack on, and you're free of it all. You're off into the hills."

"I'm dying of cancer," Ben told him. "So I guess I can do what I want."

The drifter drew on his cigarette, as if he'd heard nothing special. He spoke with the smoke streaming out of his mouth. "What kind of cancer?" he asked.

"The dying kind," Ben answered.

"We're all dying. You're just closer to it."

"You've been reading too many books. Or watching too many movies."

"Whatever," said the drifter. "But it's true."

"It's true, but it's like talking about the weather. I'm really dying. It's different."

The drifter picked up a stone and threw it into the Columbia. "No, it isn't," he insisted. "Except, maybe, that you're dealing with pain. Hey, wait—I've got something you can use, a little bit, along those lines."

He took from his jacket a breath-mint tin. He opened it and drew out three hand-rolled cigarettes. "You've heard about this," he said to Ben. "Medicinal marijuana. Joints."

"I don't want them."

"Yes, you do."

"I wouldn't use them."

"They've got magic powers."

"Put it away."

"It's a pain reliever."

"Put it away," repeated Ben.

The drifter slid the three marijuana cigarettes into his own jacket pocket. "This half is mine," he said. Then he knelt beside Ben's rucksack and stuffed the tin with its three other cigarettes into the cargo compartment. He stood again and smiled, snaggle-toothed. "You can toss them out in the desert," he said. "But I wouldn't, if I were you."

"I'm going to," said Ben.

"Well, either way, best of luck out there."

"I'll need more than luck, shooting with one eye. The hunting gods better be with me."

"They are," said the drifter. "I can feel it, partner. The hunting gods are with you."

"I hope so," said Ben.

A car approached from out of the east, and the drifter bounded up to the road shoulder. "We look like a tag team," he called to him. "You'd better get out of here."

"Okay," said Ben. "I'm sorry."

"Smoke that dope," the drifter advised. "And take care of those dogs. And happy hunting."

"I'll see what I can do," said Ben.

He set free his dogs and they quartered ahead, into the desert country. Ben went after them, traversing uphill, climbing the breaks above the river. Putting discomfort out of his mind, he passed between rough bands of basalt stained in pale streaks with bird droppings. Twice he stopped to ease his breath and rest half-bent with his palms against his knees. Far below lay the bridge he'd crossed and the silver-tinted river. He could see the dam at Wanapum, the sun pale in the southern sky, the canyon walls scalloped and scoured, the petrified drift of the basalt flows. He could see the drifter, still hitchhiking. To the north the river narrowed again and squeezed between bland rock walls before disappearing around a bend. The prairie smelled of sage and of the dampness held in the earth. Overhead the vast expanse of sky ran so deeply and unbroken to blue that he felt a momentary vertigo.

Ben knew he was leaving the world behind. He took courage from the pungent smell of the desert, and gradually—as he knew they would—his life and death became less disturbing, inconsequential somehow.

He hunted northward in open country, following the broken line of the ridge top, the river running below him in the west, the dogs working at a cross angle to the soft October breeze. Rabbit brush and purple sage festooned the bunchgrass prairie. A dozen times the dogs flushed flitting sparrows, who at the last minute bolted forward into far-off patches of cover. Rex would roust them out once more and send them in spurts of three or four, banging like popcorn out of the sage, then away across the hills. The shadow of a hawk passed over the land, and then the hawk bore down in lazy circles, caught the swelling river breezes, and rode broadside across the breaks, working south with ease. Ben stopped, slipped free of his rucksack, and drank from his water bottle. He felt broken in, less raw and fragile, though a ligament behind his left knee seemed bound up from the steepness of the climb, and in his left hip joint there was bone-against-bone clicking and sliding beneath the fascia. Yet vaguely he felt improved by the high air. The desert fragrance had cleaned his sinuses. He rested, fingered his side, and soon rose to hunt again over the breaks behind his pointing dogs.

He found a fire ring full of charred fence posts, a rusted coffee can holding dry, leached stones, and a plastic bucket turned upside down, tattered and torn along its flanks where shotgun pellets had passed through it. Two beer bottles were set against a strand of rusting, low barbed wire, and then no further sign of people. Ben felt right inside his loneliness. It was just as he had wanted.

He came across deer droppings against porous rock and beside them a patch of orange lichen. The sun came more laterally from west of southwest to burnish the left side of his face, and in the breeze his hands felt dry and worn. As he walked, he poked up under his sunglasses at the tender lower orbit of his eye and pulled and prodded gently against it to keep his depth of field intact, since the swelling had greatly reduced the world and unhinged his sense of distance. He knew that when it came to it, he would shoot the way beginners did, aiming deliberately with one eye shut. His view of the fleeing bird would be foreshortened, deluded, lacking in perspective.

Late in the day, he sat for a long time, drinking water in great swallows. He ate a handful of the pumpkin seeds the girl in the van had given him, worked the hinge on the Italian carabiner, and touched the ring-angle piton. He remembered using ring-angle pitons on the North Peak of Mount Index in 1957. He thought of Christine Reilly, then of Rachel in Italy: the train from Mantua. He and Rachel had boarded late, in sunlight that bathed the window of their sleeper car with a warm copper hue. It had inundated Rachel's face as they moved past the ocher and sienna walls of the flats on the edge of town.

He remembered it all so vividly: how the two of them sat in silence while the train gathered speed. The trembling of the train subsided gradually into a steady, pleasant vibration. The land outside seemed to travel with them, as did the sun and the violet sky, against which a church spire rose high, slim, pale as the moon.

Only the birds, swooping south from tree to tree, seemed free of the force that propelled the fabric of the world northward.

That night they lay in their mingled scent, in the heat of each other's breathing. At midnight they swallowed the last of their wine. He remembered taking her face in his hands. "Roses," she'd said. "Red and white. They'll make a single bush of pink roses."

"All right," Ben had said. "Roses."

She mentioned it a final time the day before she died. "Remember," she told him, two hours before her surgery. "You're red and I'm white."

"The mortality rate in a mitral-valve replacement for someone in your state of health is approximately one in a billion," Ben said. "You're going to be just fine."

"I'm not planning on dying, Ben. But if I do, remember about the roses. And remember how much I loved you."

It was early evening, the light fallen low, when he came across his first chukars. The air had cooled with the dying of the sun, and the birds were on the move to forage on the succulent blades and seeds of bunchgrass growing along the ridge crest. As they fed, they separated and called to one another reassuringly; Ben heard their gregarious, staccato clucking before his dogs could catch their scent riding on the wind. He stopped to listen and to fix their location. He cradled the shotgun in the crook of his arm and called the dogs in close. He listened with his palm cupped around his ear, turning his head down the long route of the horizon. The chukars, he thought, were feeding to the north, though with them there was no real certainty, for their low fast call always seemed to Ben to come from everywhere at once.

He had not pushed ahead more than thirty paces when Tristan became hotly agitated. The dog raised his snout to the breeze and trotted forward twenty yards, and with this the chukars stopped calling. Rex cut hard and fast behind Tristan, down into the breaks to follow scent where no doubt the birds had laid up through the heat before abandoning their cover for the ridge crest. It was silent now. Ben moved up between the dogs and dug in his thumb against the safety tang. Tristan had gone all stalkingly tight and was edging right and left again. Ben understood that when the birds broke at last, they would hurl themselves cleverly over the break and he would have the low sun in his eyes. He held his shotgun lightly. Rex bounded up into view from below with his withers flattened and his ears back. The dogs worked aprowl before him with their noses trailing fresh ground scent and Ben stopped to collect himself, should the birds suddenly flush. He relocated forward, set his feet, and adjusted the tilt of his sunglasses. He had just swung his rucksack onto the ground when Tristan halted twenty yards out and locked up high at both ends beautifully, classically gone on point.

Ben edged tensely forward. "Stay where you are," he said to Rex, who had not stopped pounding insatiably through the cover as if to put up all the birds. The dog, against his will, held up.

Then everything was still and silent. Ben had time to think. In his teenage years it had been his habit to pass on the initial shot at chukars, since they always posted a sentry, like the cow guard in a band of feeding elk. The first bird often flushed wild at a distance from where the feeding covey would flush outside of shooting range. More than that practicality, there was something poignant in passing on a first shot and standing in silence while the bird fled. There was something haunting in it.

When the lone bird got up at last, it held low to the purple sage, and in the late October light Ben saw plainly its dark barred markings, its vermilion feet, and its chestnut tail feathers. There was the quiet stirring of a single bird's wings while swiftly the chukar dropped over the breaks and sailed out freely above the river, where suddenly it grew incidental and disappeared down the hill.

Immediately the dogs moved forward, as though the flushed bird had been a shadow. Ben worked wide to his right and ahead so that the shots he might take would be more direct and less like passing shots. In the next moment, the dogs went on point together, a few yards apart in a patch of high bunchgrass, Rex pitched leftward with one paw raised, Tristan low and stretched solidly. Ben flicked off his safety and calmed his reeling heart.

It was always at this moment that he hesitated to take the life of a bird. It had been this way since he was eight years old, shooting mourning doves alongside his father. It had been easier for him in his teenage years, though still he had felt a flicker of doubt, been haunted by the feeling that something was amiss—and, of course, after the war, after killing was a part of him, he'd stopped hunting altogether. He had stopped fishing, too. He'd been done altogether with killing. Yet he'd embraced it again after Rachel died, the killing had become a substitute life, and in the past two autumns he'd taken up again the pastimes of his childhood— shooting small birds in canyons and sagelands, deceiving geese from cold pit-blinds, killing mallards in the bends of sloughs.

Ben stood waiting for the birds to flush. A chukar got up under Rex's nose, winging low toward the river breaks, and he shot it with the open barrel bored as if for shooting skeet, and suddenly chukars were everywhere, leaving cover in a bold flush, a dozen or more leaping from the bunchgrass while Ben was frozen by the weight of his astonishment and swung through on one bird and then another, and at last gave out with the second barrel, which was choked down tightly for a distant shot, and the chukar rose higher on the wing, as if assailed by a fast-rising breeze, and sailed wounded toward the sagebrush.

Ben broke open his Winchester and laid it over his forearm.

He was befuddled to have shot so well with the use of one eye only. There was a terrible injustice in it for him, as though shooting well were only luck. Or bad luck for the birds who fell at the hollow report of his father's gun.

Down the breaks below his feet, the remaining chukars settled. Ben knew they would sit for a lonesome interlude and finally in frantic desperation call with a yearning to meet again, until the covey reassembled. He wanted to hunt them while they were likely to hold, waiting for him to pass by.

He worked Tristan after the cripple. When the dog maneuvered close enough, the wounded chukar abandoned cover and dragged its left wing through the sage. Ben felt sullied by what had happened and watched helplessly while Tristan gave chase, pounced to seize the running bird, and clutched it softly between his teeth in a puff of gently floating feathers.

At the crest of the breaks Ben stood, bird in hand, and watched while Rex brought the other slain bird in and laid it neatly on the table rock. He praised his dogs, though not too profusely, as they stood panting at his side. Ben slid the first bird into his coat pocket and picked up the second to examine it, a young male with small, rounded spurs. He tucked it in beside the first.

The sun lay low against the mountains, but there was still good shooting light. He slid off his sunglasses, fingered the dressing over his eye, and worked on his steel-rimmed glasses. He drank some water—he emptied one bottle—and then he went after the singles slowly, leaving his rucksack behind on the ground, urging the dogs to stay close.

Last hunt, he told himself.

He hunted three hundred feet downhill. He missed on the first, but then there were others, and he felt satisfied. One bird he took straightaway on a second shot, staying beneath it as it barreled downhill; the next flushed from behind a stone tower and, unlike most chukars he'd seen as a boy, flew toward him along a steady contour twenty yards below his gun, so that he had to swing patiently for the longest time and kill it on the late going away.

He held this last bird in his hand. A dark band passed rakishly over its eyes, and the black bars along its flanks lay symmetrically, sleekly ruffled. The tail feathers were chestnut brown and the feathers elsewhere an olive color, in places darker or a blue-tinted gray; they lay well-ordered in delicate waves and were soft and thick against its breast. The warmth of life was still in it.

It was unfathomable to Ben that he had decided to die under circumstances so cruel. Odd not to have thought of this before—a death in the arid sageland, alone, in the aftermath of killing small birds. He could not understand the end he'd chosen except as an act of stoic machismo, and that was not enough. The shooting and the land were not enough. Hunting small birds as his final earthly act—it was inadequate, somehow, and misdirected, at odds with the life he had lived as a doctor, a husband, and a father. But so was the act of taking his own life instead of seeing it through. So was killing himself. Suicide was at odds with the life he knew, at odds with all he understood, of himself and of the world.

Ben put the bird in his coat pocket. He climbed the breaks in the last light of day with a steady pain in his side. The day was closing around him now. Things could not hold light any longer. Weary of climbing, short of breath, he paid no attention to his hunting dogs. The darkness seeped into and over the land, and inevitably into Ben too, as he saw the world swallowed by night.

He was too tired and in too much pain for the long hike back into Vantage. He sat and waited for things to improve, but there was only the sweep of the night wind blowing and the discord of his breathing. Reluctantly, he climbed fifty feet, and fifty more, until he came to his rucksack.

Somewhere in the night a coyote called, tremblingly high like a melancholy flautist, and with such ornate, long-winded insistence, it was impossible to know if it was one animal or many out toward the Frenchman Hills. A night music native to this country of Ben's birth; a grievous howling, as if the land mourned itself. Ben remembered a Wanapum man, with whom he'd boxed apples sixty years before, saying that the cry of a single coyote often sounded like the cry of many.

Now Ben breasted one of the chukars and fed the boned meat to his dogs. He tossed the remains of the bird down the hill; he watered his dogs from his aluminum cup, pouring a ration for each. He ate more of the pumpkin seeds Christine Reilly had given him and drank his own water ration. Then, digging in the rucksack for his headlamp, he came across the breath-mint tin of three marijuana cigarettes. Ben took one out and sniffed it. He pondered what he knew of *Cannabis sativa*. That it eased the pain of cancer was a well-established medical fact. And yet he remained adverse to it. Its associations were foreign to him. On the other hand, why not?

He got out his lighter and lit the cigarette against the grain of his principles, astonished at himself. The smell, inhaled, was pungent, raw. He felt the searing of the smoke in his lungs, and his windpipe rejected it. Exhaling, he gasped roughly. A veil soon dropped over the world. He brought the cigarette to his lips again and sucked on it until its tip glowed orange, then blew thick smoke through his nostrils in long double plumes.

Ben noted the strangeness of things. Nothing particularly troublesome, but certainly an odd difference—the desert poised, crystallized.

He drew again on the cigarette. Its acrid, green odor sweetened the chill air. He drew again deeply into his chest and held the smoke until his face turned a strangled red.

After that, he felt inured to pain but hungrier and thirstier than before. He ate more of the pumpkin seeds. He indulged in them and drank half of his water. He spread the duffel bag and the rain poncho on the ground, stuffed the remaining chukars in his rucksack, and lay down wrapped up tightly in his blanket like a nomad in the desert.

Ben's dogs excavated and maneuvered in the sand, settling in at his side. He urged them closer for the warmth they could provide. It was good to have them near, companions. They were sentinels, too, beside him there in the frigid, inhospitable night.

Resting his head on the folded hunting vest, he watched the stars with his one good eye, their light blurred through his glasses. His mind raced, his thoughts were rich, his memories vivid, graphic. He felt he could touch the past.

FOUR

Ben's parents had planted rows of apple trees on the east bank of the Columbia River. Their orchards were sheltered by Lombardy poplars and fell toward the river in an immaculate sweep, the rows full of irrigation ditches, sharp-bladed quack grass growing dense, and branch props leaning against forked limbs. There were thirteen acres of Golden Delicious, two of Winesaps, two of Rome Beauties, and eight of cherries and apricots. There were shanties for the pickers who came in June, a weathered shed for making boxes and for packing apples in oiled tissue, a barn loaded with hay to the rafters, a stable for the horses, a chicken house, an outhouse, an icehouse, and a small-well pump house. The Givenses' farmhouse sat on a knoll surrounded by shade elms and willows. Even inside, the world smelled of sage, and from the front window the setting sun bronzed the hills stretching westward. When the wind came up, the tops of trees swirled, so that with the windows flung open on summer evenings the crash of branches came startlingly loud. Year around was the wind in the trees, the drifting fragrance of sage.

Ben made apple boxes out of pine shook, pulled weeds in the kitchen garden, split cordwood for the fireplace, and milked cows twice a day. In the spring he helped his father and brother put out the pollinating hives. When the rains came, the sluice gates clogged with weeds, and Ben and Aidan stood in the ditches to clean them out by hand. There were also windbreak trees to plant and Jonathan pollinating trees. In April and May there were young trees to plant and finished trees to pull out. In early summer they disced between the rows to keep the mice from the orchards. In July they put spreader sticks in the yearling trees and strapped the branches back. Midsummer there was always fruit to thin and branches to prop and strap back carefully to keep them from cracking beneath the apples. In August came the picking season; in fall and winter there was pruning to do, and piles of water sprouts to burn.

Where the orchards ended, the desert began—buttes, coulees, unnamed canyons, arid expanses of infinite reach, sun-beaten, silent, and lonesome. Ben and Aidan took the dogs into this country in search of quail, chukars, and sage grouse, and occasionally got a shot at a jackrabbit. They rode on horseback when they had the chance, their shotguns slung across their backs, their canteens slapping against their saddles. Sometimes they camped in the sage at night, where they drew and spitted their birds carefully, stuffed sage sprigs inside the empty bellies, and cooked the meat on a twig fire. Then they lay back with their hands behind their heads and talked and watched the heavens.

Aidan was older than Ben by twenty months, stocky, sturdy, even-tempered. He worked with a pine sliver set between his teeth, a sheen of sweat on his collarbones, and the front of his shirt soaked in a line from breastbone to navel. Generally he wore his hat low on his forehead, so that his eyes were heavily shaded by its brim, but when somebody spoke to him he canted the brim up and listened with much animation around the eyes before answering.

Aidan was agreeable, amiable. His skin was brown, his eyes blue. He liked to swim in the river at dusk, just upstream from the ranch house, in the backwash of a small eddy. Ben and Aidan would strip on the bank, tossing their shirts and pants up high against the warm, polished shore rocks. They stretched their limbs and ran their hands along their bellies and through hair flecked with pollen dust, apple litterfall, or blossom petals. Then they splashed into the river. It rippled gently across their backs, and in the eddy they rode the current and swam against it while up the hill the orchards glowed in the last light.

In late fall the Givenses went mountain climbing. They took the train into Stevens Pass with a picnic lunch inside their knapsacks and walked open ridges in all weathers, ascending to unnamed summits. Their mother and father sat on a blanket while Ben and Aidan leaned against stones to look down on forests foreign to them in their density and reach. Ben claimed he could smell the salt of the sea, though it was off two hundred miles, carried on the mountain breeze. To the east the mountains gave way to sage, but westward loomed impenetrable forests, and they spoke of hiking into them to places no one had ever seen. They spoke of traveling for weeks in the mountains to see the uncharted high country, as though they were explorers or pioneers and not the sons of orchardists.

In Leavenworth, one year, they bought wooden skis with bent-metal toepieces and leather straps, to ski down Big Chief Mountain. Ben's mother taught them first to snowplow, then the trick of a telemark turn and stopping in a christy. They took their skis on winter trips, slaloming from summits on still afternoons, and tried the amateur ski-jump trestle near Leavenworth on Ski Hill Road, strapped to eight-foot hickory skis and falling badly and often. They skied along Peshastin Creek or up along the Chumstick River, then hiked uphill with their skis on their shoulders until they had earned a downhill run, or they took the railroad into Stevens Pass and telemarked back down.

Once they stood on the summit of Mission Peak with the December wind in their faces but the sky cloudless and lit by the pale sun low among the peaks. Ben was working his boots into the toe irons when Aidan pointed at a mountain goat risen out of drifts not twenty yards off, poised to flee with its head turned toward them, already certain of flight. It swiveled on its hind hooves and was gone in a puff of snow behind an outcropping, and Ben, closing his binding clamp, felt poised on the cusp of the world, as close to God as he might ever get, with no place higher but heaven itself, and nothing to obscure the truths of the wind, the sky, the snow, the winter sun.

At ten he rode horseback with his father and Aidan, deer hunting for the first time. They rode into the hills just after lunch, when new snow covered the ground. They crossed the river at Coleman's Landing and followed the Colockum Stagecoach Road, his father with his 270 Weatherby Magnum in a leather saddle scabbard at his right hand and a .22 pistol at his belt. It was dry-cold, winter-still; the land lay white and paralyzed. They saw no one and no deer sign in the clean snow of the road. When the stars were thick and brilliant in the sky, they stopped at a bench overlooking the river. Wright Givens buttoned his canvas coat and cupped his hands to light a cigarette, his jaw and mouth and the end of his nose glowing in the flaring match light. "This'll do," he said to them, and they stamped the snow down, staked out the tent, and hobbled the horses for the night. They started a fire of lodgepole pine slabs, on which their father boiled water for coffee, and they ate elk jerky from a leather bag and chewed dried apples and apricots.

Wright Givens smoked, his collar turned up, the brim of his hat turned down. He said that in the morning chances would be good, since deer were always nocturnal in their habits, moving at dusk and dawn. Deer watched their back trail as they moved to bed down, and traveled with their noses into the wind, but there was no wind now to assist them in their caution and they might well be approached from above. Then Wright settled in before the fire, tapped a pine ember with his boot, and said that in the early days it was hard along this stagecoach road where they were camped tonight. Wagons were lowered toward Wenatchee by rope; trees were dragged behind wagon axles to supplement the wheel brakes. A schoolhouse was pulled on skids from farm to farm each summer to spread justly the burden of heating it and of boarding the accompanying teacher.

Had they heard of the Rock Island wheat chute? At first the wheat smoldered and burned in the pipe because of its speed and friction. Before the railroad came through Rock Island, there'd been a tram between Waterville and Orondo for carrying gunnysacks of wheat to the steamboat and for hauling coal back up. The Indians back then grew squashes and pumpkins in the bottom of Moses Coulee. They moved east when the sheep came in and farther east when the tractors came, the tractors fueled by sagebrush, bolts of pine, anything that burned, even greasewood. Ben's father had seen Hutterites up on the plateau who lived in hovels in the ground and boiled their soup on dung fires. He'd been to Soap Lake, where a sanatorium had been built by the muddy shore for sufferers from rheumatism, eczema, and gout. He'd been to the Yakima powwow at White Swan and to the Yakima horse races in the huckleberry country up in Indian

Heaven. He'd floated logs through the Yakima Canyon on the spring floodwaters past Ellensburg and down to the mill near Selah. He said that where his grandfather had lived, just outside of Walla Walla, freight was carried toward Hell Gate on the backs of African camels. There were channeled scablands down that way, where rich, kilted Scotsmen ran ten thousand sheep herded by indomitable miniature dogs and by men who spoke the Basque tongue. Ben's father had traveled by steamboat once all the way to the mouth of the Columbia and had seen the Pacific Ocean. He'd also been on the railroad to Minneapolis and had prospected the Black Hills in South Dakota. He'd passed a summer at a placer mine north of Ketchikan, Alaska. He'd been to Chinatown in San Francisco, where he ate raw sliced octopus and squid and baby eels.

Wright Givens told of how his grandfather led west a train of covered wagons in 1879. John Hale Givens was a fruit grower and nurseryman in the vicinity of Marion, Indiana, who built two wagons as soil beds in which he planted newly grafted fruit trees and bushes to bring across the plains. Apple starts, pears, cherries, plums, currants, gooseberries, peaches: they were canvased over for protection from weather, but on balmy days the canvases were removed and the traveling gardens bounced sun-drenched across the plains, hauled by teams of oxen. The Indians, Wright's grandfather claimed, had vouchsafed the westering party's passage in the belief that the traveling gardens were protected by the hand of the Great Spirit.

Wright Givens said that the boys' maternal grandfather had patented the Rainier Delicious apple. James Chandler purchased two dozen seedling trees from an itinerant peddler passing through Wenatchee—they turned out to be Golden Reinettes from Virginia—and when the offspring of one of these, sprung from a windfall, eventually produced an extraordinary fruit, huge apples growing mild yellow on each branch, he bought up the propagating rights. He built an iron cage around his tree to prevent the theft of bud sticks and took to promotion vigorously. In 1921, the American Pomological Society presented James Chandler with its Wilder Medal; in 1926, a carload of his apples was shipped to the men of the St. Louis Cardinals to honor their World Series triumph. The boys' grandfather had once been wealthy, but had invested with too much confidence in the stock market before it crashed in 1929.

The embers of the fire went quietly red while Ben sat listening. His father nodded across the coals, where Aidan was curled asleep on a log, his mouth hanging open. "Not interested," his father said, and shrugged.

"I am," said Ben. "Keep going."

"It's time for sleep," said his father.

In the morning they broke camp in the dark and rode up Stray Horse Canyon. Ben watched his breath boil off into the dawn, until his father motioned him alongside and pointed out the deep track of a buck, heart-shaped and split down the middle. The buck had passed the dark hours at the creek because there was no other running water, and now at first light was working west toward higher elevations. The track made an easy meander in the snow with the dewclaws readily visible, and finally they came across droppings in a pile, as if the buck had stopped unalerted. "This is good," said Ben's father. A quarter mile farther was an opening in the trees, but they held up below it in case the buck was watching his back track from a vantage point. They turned their horses directly up slope to keep the track below them.

They made the ridge top in gathering light and rode north, studying the hills on either side for signs that the buck had crossed ahead of them. They came to a saddle where no tracks showed, the world as still as if it had been painted, the snow loading up the boughs of pines in cumbersome white thick mantles. Wright Givens instructed his sons to tether the horses fifty yards downslope, then return to the ridge saddle. He took his Weatherby from its scabbard, turned up his coat collar, and pushed his hat down firmly. "This is good," he said again.

They sat with their backs to one another so that all points of the compass were covered. After forty minutes of waiting, Ben heard his father's rifle click as the hammer was brought back into full cock. Turning, he saw a buck of modest size, in high alert with its gaze full on them, seventy yards down the hill, its sleek left flank exposed. There was no time for Ben to ponder things or to wish they might be different. His father's Weatherby roared, and the buck buckled forward on tenuous forelegs, flailed weakly for a few seconds, and did not move anymore.

Ben's heart beat wildly. He leaned against his father, who put a hand on his shoulder. "Looks like we got one," his father said.

They approached the deer cautiously. Wright Givens touched a stick against its eye. Then he knelt, looked closely, and showed them the place where the bullet had passed through the buck's hide. He explained how his bullet had splintered the left shoulder joint, next the spine just below the neck, and finally the right shoulder. There was blood on the snow underneath the buck, and he said it was good for the blood to drain and for the meat to cool quickly. Pointing with the tip of his dressing knife, he showed them the sticking place on the buck's soft chest, and then with no warning he thrust in the knife, lifting its hilt until the artery was severed. The buck's eye remained open. More blood colored the snow.

Ben's father stepped back to look at his sons, pulled off his hat, and rubbed his chin. He was lean in the face, unshaven, wind-worn, with a head of neat black hair. He propped his Weatherby against a tree, knelt with one hand on the buck's warm flank, and motioned the boys to kneel. "I promised your mother," he sighed.

They took their hats off, as he had. They all three laid a hand on the buck, and their father began to pray. "Dear Lord," he said, "our thanks to you for this meat you have granted. Our thanks for your goodness and your bounty, Lord. In Jesus' name, amen."

He stood and worked his hat on. He cut the scent glands from the deer's hind legs, severed the testicles, and tied a knot in the penis so no urine would taint the meat. He explained what he was doing and why he was doing it, and Ben and Aidan watched. Then they brought the horses around, lashed the deer quarters over the saddles, and left the hide, the head, and the guts on the stained, snowy ground.

Five minutes later, riding down the ridge, their father halted his horse. There was blood across the front of his coat and on his jaw, nose, and hands.

"That's how it's done," he said to his sons. "That's the way you'll want to do it when I'm not around anymore."

At the Grade and Pack Conference in 1932, Ben's mother spoke against lowering standards. Dressed in black, her hair black, she was tall, confident, plain-speaking, her eyes a deep, strong blue. It was her contention that even C-grade apples should not be permitted to go out worm-stung, discolored, or pocked by hail. She said that culls sold at $3 a ton should go directly to vinegar plants because the brokers in Spokane and Portland were flooding the C market with high-grade culls, driving prices down. Worse, the price for Winter Bananas had fallen to $1.25 a box, too little to cover picking and packing, not to mention freight and auction. Half the shippers in the industry, she guessed, had gone broke after the stock market crash, and this threatened all orchardists because shipping contracts were the necessary collateral for a bank to cover growing costs. Did everyone grasp this? she asked. Did all support the shippers? She favored a lobbying effort made through the shippers to bring the Great Northern into line at

$1.25 per hundred pounds, and she insisted that apples could be shipped at sea from rail points on Puget Sound as a counterbalance to the railroads. Otherwise, she warned, there would be a lot of orchards out of business within two seasons. There would be a tightening of belts no matter what they did, but the belt would hold and they could endure it and eventually things would improve. In the meantime, she said, picking wages would have to be set at somewhere near 15 cents. The fixed wage for the construction of boxes should be no more than 75 cents per 100; to pay more was worse than folly. She encouraged everybody gathered there to consider the Crop Production Loan Office plan for the purchase of spray and fertilizer. She explained how the Agricultural Credit Corporation could do what the banks had once done. She spoke from the floor, not from the podium, after sitting for two hours beside her sons and husband listening to men joust bitterly, and she announced herself as the wife of Wright Givens, whose grandfather had brought the first fruit stock across the plains, and as the daughter of the founder of the Rainier Delicious apple, and the gathering held silent while she spoke and remained silent afterward. When she was done, she sat with her eyes fixed ahead, fanning herself with a Yakima newspaper, and her husband reached calmly across her lap and took her right hand in his.

Once every month she took Ben and Aidan on her market trip to Wenatchee. The avenues were paved with large fir blocks that froze and buckled in winter, giving horses trouble. The boys accompanied their mother to the bank, the courthouse, and the post office, and to pay the bill at the utility office. They went to the market for bacon, salt, flour, rice, beans, pepper, corn syrup, and sugar. They stopped at the apothecary and the fabric shop on Miller Street, and they visited the nickel-and-dime store. At a fountain shop on Kittitas Avenue, they stopped for a hamburger and ice cream at the counter; the boys sat on either side of their mother, who ate neatly and slowly. When their errands were done, they sat in the city library, combing through magazines and newspapers from Seattle, Boston, and San Francisco. The Wenatchee people spoke to their mother about the progress of the new irrigation pipeline going in on the east side of the river, or asked for her estimate of where prices might fix for Rome Beauties or Stayman Winesaps. She answered everyone in the same way, with confidence but no trace of arrogance. She had attended a boarding school near Boston, had learned decorum there. She had come west enthusiastically, with her parents and her two sisters, in the spirit of an adventure. On coming of age, her sisters went east again, but Lenora Chandler stayed. Now she kept the books for the orchards and told her husband when to plow new land and when to plant new trees. After dinner nearly every evening she sat for an hour at her rolltop desk with a ledger book in front of her. With one hand she held her hair behind an ear; with the other she scrawled neat figures. She worked, generally, with the Victrola playing the music of string quartets. Violins, she told her sons, were in perfect accord with the orchard landscape. She liked to have a half hour in the evening to sit in an armchair with her needlework and with the Victrola playing quietly. The orchard air came softly through the screens, and she would stop, shut her eyes, breathe in the world, and sometimes fall asleep with her feet up and the violin music playing.

In the summer she worked with Ben and Aidan in the packing shed, making apple boxes. They bought box shook from the mill at Malaga and ferried it across the river. They bought a hundred-pound wooden keg full of five-and-a-half-penny nails. The sun filtered in and lit up the pine dust slowly rising on the air. Ben's mother drove nails with a box hatchet, humming while she worked. She wore her kitchen dress with the sleeves rolled up, wiped sweat from her face with the hem of her apron, and hammered with either hand. His father could make sixty boxes in an hour, but his mother could make sixty-five. She held ten nails in her hand at once, as if they were sewing needles. In picking season she wrapped apples in oiled tissue before packing them tightly, nailing down the lids, and loading up the wagon. On each box she glued the label she'd designed: their orchard by the river, hung heavily with fruit, bordered by pink apple blossoms.

Once, at the end of the workday, Ben sat with her in the orchard shade, watching the dusk flight of doves to the river and drinking from a canteen. His mother kneaded the small of her back, sighed and brushed the dust from her hair, then settled back against a tree. "I'd better see to dinner," she said, but didn't get up to leave.

"I'll help," Ben offered.

"I'd rather you read a book," his mother said. "You've got time before dinner."

"There's ditches to clear," said Ben.

His mother watched the doves for a while. "Someday," she said, "you'll grow up and leave. So you'd better get in the reading habit before that day arrives."

"I'll never leave," Ben told her.

"You'll leave. You'll be ready to leave. You'll have your own work, somewhere."

"I don't know what I'd do except apples."

"You'll do whatever is in the spirit of who you are," his mother said matter-of-factly. "Some kind of gift you'll have to give. Whatever God plans for you."

Ben was silent now. His mother was a dyed-in-the-wool Presbyterian who could lecture at length on the life of Calvin, on the sacrament of baptism, or on predestination; she took her sons to church each Sunday, where they heard the minister Joseph Miles declare—when all the congregation was weary of picking apples—that God had ordained their sweat from the outset, on thrusting Adam and Eve from the garden. *Cursed is the earth in thy work,* proclaimed God, *with labor and toil shalt thou eat thereof all the days of thy life. Thorns and thistles shall it bring forth to thee and thou shalt eat the herbs of the earth. By the sweat of thy brow thou shalt eat bread.* His mother, riding home, had revised the sermon, in keeping with her own interpretation of the *Westminster Shorter Catechism:* that work was an expression of love for God, that work was the path toward knowledge of Him, that we are here to do God's work. Our life, she said, was full of worthy tasks to accomplish in accordance with our particular design, in such a way that we are lifted up, to ascend by the work God means for us to do toward a higher love of Him. We know ourselves through the work we do—Ben's mother insisted on this.

Ben was twelve—it was just after Christmas—when he noticed a yellow cast to her eyes. His mother acknowledged noting it too, and said that Ben's father had commented on it, asking her to visit Dr. Williams. She went and was told that her jaundiced condition was difficult to understand and might derive from many sources. For a few days she held to the hope that the problem would simply vanish; then after New Year's she went again to the doctor, and this time he drew blood, collected urine, and concurred with her that the yellowing had grown deeper, pervading the skin around her eyes. By the middle of January her skin was green, and when she cut herself with a paring knife one day—a shallow slice through her index finger—it was difficult to stanch the bleeding. Her blood ran thin, darkly colored. By February she had seen two specialists in Spokane, but despite their efforts she grew more green, gaunt, and hollow-cheeked. She took to bed one afternoon and could not rise to attend to dinner, but lay curled beneath the comforter. The next day she went again to Spokane. She was hospitalized for nearly a week, then sent home with tincture of opium.

After that she lay in a torpor or sat in an armchair wearing her bathrobe, and twice a week Dr. Williams came to dole out more tincture of opium. She had no appetite. The mere smell of food sickened her. She sometimes vomited in the early mornings, battling fever and chills. Her skin was now tinted orange.

On the tenth of April, she turned thirty-seven. That evening blood trickled from her mouth; Dr. Williams came at midnight. He rolled up his sleeves, loosened his tie, and gave Ben's mother a sponge bath. He explained to Ben's father how to move her carefully and change the sheets one side at a time. She was very thin now, and moaned with every breath. Dr. Williams increased her dose of opium. She quieted, and they left her room to sit in the parlor at midnight.

Dr. Williams warmed his back at the fire, a snifter of brandy in his hand, his sleeves rolled up, his face tired. He was a tall man with thick glasses, his jaw long and prominent. He had brought Ben and Aidan into the world, had treated their father for a rattlesnake bite, had stitched up Aidan's hand when he cut it making an apple box. Now he sipped from his brandy and sighed. He set the snifter on the mantel.

Dr. Williams walked to the window and looked out into the darkness of the hills. He paused there with his hands in his pockets. He pressed his glasses against his temples, but then suddenly pried them off, took a handkerchief from his pocket, and began to polish their lenses. "Sit down, boys," he said.

Ben and Aidan perched on the sofa. Their father wouldn't look at them.

Dr. Williams lowered himself to the edge of the rocker and set his elbows against his knees. He held his glasses to the light briefly, then slid them onto his face. "Your father has asked me to talk to you," he said, "because it's hard for him to do it himself."

"That's okay," said Aidan.

"Your mother can't be cured," said the doctor. "That's what we found out over in Spokane. She has a tumor, a cancer of the pancreas. There's nothing we can do to cure her."

"But you're a doctor," Ben said.

Dr. Williams fingered his chin. "A doctor isn't a magician, you know. I wish I was, believe me, Ben. If I was, I'd cure your mother."

"What do you mean you can't cure her?"

"I mean I'm just a man with a little learning and some medicines in an old black bag. I can't stop cancer of the pancreas."

"Yes, you can. You have to."

Ben's father raised his head. He looked gaunt and deeply tired. "There's no point in arguing with Dr. Williams," he said. "You hush now, Ben."

Ben turned his face to the floor. "I thought you were a good doctor," he whispered.

Dr. Williams took Ben by the chin, tilted his head, and looked at him. The light reflected in his glasses. "I'm neither good nor bad," he said, so close that Ben felt the warmth of his breath. "I wish I could make you see that."

"Make her better."

"I can't, Ben."

"You have to make her better."

"I can't."

Dr. Williams went to the rocker. He pulled his black bag close to him and looked inside it, silent.

"The opium," Ben's father said. "There must be some amount that's too much."

"That's for you to decide," said the doctor. "A question of how much pain she can bear, and of when enough is enough."

"I don't know how far that goes. I don't know what that means."

"I know just what you're saying," Dr. Williams said. "That's the hell of it."

Mrs. Emery came to help first, then Mrs. Fisk and Mrs. Elginhurst. At church women organized to help and spelled one another in the day hours. Evenings, after work in the orchard, Ben, Aidan, and their father took over. Ben's mother often lay on her side, looking out over the dark, cool trees stretching down toward the river. In the last light of evening the world looked haunted, as though on the verge of disappearing, solid, into the night.

"Are you scared?" Ben asked his mother once.

"I believe in God," she said. "But yes, I'm scared, to be honest."

He did not know what to say to this, so he said nothing; he waited. "It's the pain I'm scared of," she confessed.

He still had no idea how to respond. He had never heard her this way.

"This isn't any way to live," said his mother. "I miss the world, Ben."

"We could take your bed outside, though. Put it on the porch, maybe."

"It isn't that." She turned to look at him. "It's more that my work on earth isn't finished. Raising you, I'm not done with that. You and Aidan both."

He wished she wouldn't say these things. "Mom," he said. That was all.

"I wanted to see you as men. What you would be like as men. What you would do in the world."

"I don't know," said Ben.

"Do something fine," his mother said. "Do something grand and wonderful. Whatever your heart desires."

"I'll try," he said.

Later that week, her moaning turned into a faint wheeze, and she curled up like a fist, a leaf, curled up like a baby in the end, and died at 6:35 in the morning on the twenty-eighth of June, 1938. Ben, Aidan, and their father were sitting on kitchen chairs brought into the room, their father with his elbows on his knees, his forehead low, close to hers, and then her wheezing came to a stop, and he dropped his cheek to her heart. "Lenora," he said. "Lenora."

They buried her on a knoll above the river, her parents and the Fisks and Coles looking on, and the Robinsons and Knoxes and Elginhursts, and Dr. Williams and the Gilchrists and Cochranes, and the Emerys with their four small children, and twenty-three Givenses from up and down the river—from Kennewick, Wenatchee, Brewster, Kettle Falls—and that evening came a thunderstorm, and the rain beat across his mother's grave.

That summer, nothing was the same. They worked their apples with a hollow feeling, and the orchard fell into a decline.

Wright Givens wandered on foot, hunting birds in the willow canyons. He walked the hills for long hours, carrying his Winchester and following his Black Labs, returning at dusk with his coat pockets full of quail, chukars, and grouse. He'd dump them all in the kitchen sink and sit at the table, smoking. He'd scratch his unshaven jaw aimlessly or pull burrs from the dogs. Finally he'd throw his vest across a chair and stand at the sink with his sleeves rolled up, dressing birds as if in an assembly line. He pinched off their heads, twisted off their wings, severed the tendons in their knee joints, and threw their clawed feet in a metal pail. Rolling the meat in salted flour, he fried it in a cast-iron skillet, which he set on the dinner table. They ate the birds with fried potatoes, the shotgun set in the corner by the door, the dogs curled by his father's boots, asleep with their heads on their paws. All July his father hunted, returning at dusk with dead birds.

The migrant pickers came. They were mostly from Oklahoma and Arkansas, sometimes from Missouri or Texas. Single men and drifters, loners and vagabonds, also families with eight or nine children, they made the fruit run in pickup trucks, hopped freight trains, or walked the roads. In April they picked strawberries in California, then worked northward through plums and pears, arriving in June for sweet cherries and peaches, followed by yet more plums and pears, and finally the apple harvest. The men arrived at the Givenses' place sun-darkened and lean-jawed, bedrolls slung from Manila twine across their backs, unshaven under broad-rimmed hats and smoking hand-rolled cigarettes. In the rows of apples, high in their ladders, nestling fruit into canvas bags slung from suspenders and belted at their waists, they regaled Ben and Aidan with fabulous tales: dust storms, stabbings, arrests, brawls, riding the rails in Arizona or crossing into Mexico at El Paso for the whores in Cuidad Juarez. Herding sheep in the Sierra Nevada, riding roundup in Idaho. The impossible wastes of the Cactus Range, the Amargosa Desert, Death Valley. Condensed milk poured into a radiator to plug a slow-running leak; a crankshaft brought into round again with a shim made out of a bacon rind.

There was a family that came when Ben was fifteen, and one night deep in the rows of trees—they had been with the Givenses exactly a week—he kissed their sixteen-year-old daughter. Her skin smelled of dust, her mouth of apples, and when he pressed against her urgently, the girl wrenched free and ran away. Her name was Nora Ellerby, from Milfay, Oklahoma, and her skin was sun-polished to the color of dark pine wood, and her hair lay long and flat against her cheeks with the tips of her ears poking out of it. Her eyes were shallow and her chin very strong, but her fingers were long, brown, and smooth. Ben watched her hands plucking apples, then spoke to her quietly when no one was listening, and that night she met him in the orchard. They kissed, pushing against each other. The next night they lay beneath the apple trees, where he ran his hands along her waist and touched her breasts through the fabric of her shirt, until Nora, coming to her senses, ran away from him again.

On the following night, the moon rose addled and yellow. They went hand-in-hand to the river secretly and sat in the night shadow of a fine-grained butte pillared along its summit but graced by warm sand at its base. They lay in the sand, holding each other. The girl's breath blew warm against his face, and she spoke with a soft winsome twang. She spoke of a boy in Shingletown, California, who had not kissed nearly as well as Ben and had promised to buy her a brand-new dress if she ran off with him to Canada. She said that she had some money saved and that one day she would live in Sacramento or Chico or Redding or someplace civilized. She would shop in town, live in a house, keep fresh milk in an icebox. She'd been to the county fair in Klamath Falls, to the circus when it came to Yakima, and at a swap meet in Yuba City, California, she saw a man with a tattooed belly swallow a blazing sword. She paid three cents to a fortune-teller there, who told Nora she would have seven children and warned her to be suspicious of men who promised to buy her things. The boy in Shingletown had promised her a dress, but no one else had promised her anything, so what was the point of that prophecy? She had hoped for more from the fortune-teller.

Ben and Nora kissed for a half hour. Then he put his fingers between her legs and touched her where she told him to, until, three times, she shivered breathlessly in small persistent shudders. As if in return, she unbuttoned his pants and clutched him so that he flooded thickly against her arm and fingers. The next day, Nora left to pick fruit in Okanogan County.

School started after picking season. There were fifteen children on the Rock Island Road, and their schoolhouse sat on a knoll above the river a half mile downstream from the Fisk orchards, close to the Palisades junction. It was a small single room built of river stones and heated by apple cordwood. The orchardists up and down the road kept its slope-roofed woodshed filled in winter, and the older children kept the stove going strong by stoking it high when the embers glowed and leaving the draft open. The county ran power to the schoolhouse for a string of lights nailed over the desks so the children could write their assignments and see their maps and primers. The place was tidy and smelled of wood smoke, ink, and wet woolen clothes.

The teacher, Ruth Dietrich, lived with the Cochranes, an elderly couple with children long grown and an extra room to let. She was a lively woman, large, with glasses on a chain, and she peered at her charges over wire frames and then down through swimming lenses to read aloud from *Ivanhoe* or *Alice in Wonderland*. Miss Dietrich wore her gray hair pinned tightly to her head, and a cream-colored lace shawl draped across her shoulders, fastened with a brooch at her breast. Her face was coarse, lined, and thick; two long hairs sprouted from a mole on the left side of her chin. Miss Dietrich collected Wanapum arrowheads, petrified wood, and opals. She knew her medieval history, could recite the chronology of British kings and queens, and could render from memory "Frost at Midnight," "The Passionate Shepherd to His Love," and "The Nymph's Reply to the Shepherd." She was prone to poetry at the slightest provocation, so that the rising of the river breeze was a just occasion for orating an impeccable "Ode to the West Wind," and the various hues of apples on her desk for a rendition of "Pied Beauty." Upon the announcement by a student one day that the Rock Island Dam had been completed, she recited "Ozymandias," then gave a short lecture on the sin of hubris. Miss Dietrich could discourse knowledgeably on the agriculture of Mesopotamia, the habits and mores of the Egyptian pharaohs, and the scientific notions of the Greeks. She knew all about the religion of the Incas, the travels of Charles Darwin to the Galapagos, the Boxer Rebellion, the Potala in Lhasa, and the invasions of the Mongol Khans.

Ben took pleasure in listening to her. He read with zeal the story of Macbeth, *Canterbury Tales, David Copperfield, The Pickwick*

Papers, and *Heart of Darkness*—all loaned to him by Miss Dietrich. He learned the periodic table, the primary theorems governing geometry, and the Latin names for plants and animals as classified by Linnaeus. He learned about the exploration of the poles, the formation of crystals and of sedimentary rock, and the propagation of light.

Miss Dietrich was at home in the orchard country and had an expansive knowledge of apples: the fruit, she told them, *Pyrus malus,* had taken its name from Aphrodite's priest, who was turned into an apple tree after the impaling of Adonis. When her students, in the fall, bobbed for apples, she explained to them, while their faces were wet, that the druids had once done likewise—bobbing—as an act of divination. The apple tree, she told them one day, had been sacred to Apollo and Venus both, and was, of course, the fruit of discord that started the war at Troy. And it wasn't just pagans and pantheists who worshiped apples; in Bulgaria there were paintings of the Virgin Mary with Jesus cradled in one hand, an apple held in the other. When a student misbehaved, she quoted sternly from Chaucer—*The rotten apple injures its neighbors*—or she might borrow from Shakespeare—*An apple cleft in two is no more twin than these two creatures*—in reponse to an argument between the Gilchrist sisters. A student who complained of the burden of homework was reminded that Hercules, for his eleventh labor, traveled to the far western end of the earth in order to bring back golden apples, stolen from the Hesperides, and that he walked a thousand miles for them, and slew a dragon along the way, and if Hercules could do all this, why couldn't they read just ten pages from *Huckleberry Finn*? Once a girl asked Miss Dietrich if it was true that her husband had died at the Battle of Gettysburg, and Miss Dietrich laughed with such sustained force that tears gathered in her eyes, then uttered something about Asgard and apples of immortality. Another girl told her in class one day that a woman who washed her face and hands in water mixed with the sap of an apple was sure to bear a child, and Miss Dietrich smiled and nodded at this and said that a girl in search of a husband should squeeze apple seeds between her fingers: if any struck the ceiling, she was sure to be happy in her quest, for apples were the fruit of love.

One spring Miss Dietrich took ten students on a field trip to identify plants: Ben, Aidan, Billy Lawrence, Willy Griffin, Owen and Clare Goodall, Caitlin and Amelia Burns, and Hannah and Gillon Crichton. The students spread out with their pocket-knives and cut snowberry, wild rose, and boxwood twigs, arranging them in a grid on a square of canvas laid across a slab of table rock. Miss Dietrich showed them the red osier dogwood, used by the Shuswaps for fishing weirs and pipe stems, though she preferred a pipe of elderberry, a wood also good for an elk call whistle, a peashooter, or a drinking straw. She peeled back the layers of a mallow ninebark and explained that where you found this plant, ocean spray could be found, too; the Indians made fishing spears from it.

At noon they moved higher to eat in a meadow, and Miss Dietrich, between bites of her tomato sandwich, extolled the virtues of the surrounding larches: how they were hardier than pines or firs, stubbornly surviving winter weather; how their needles in the early fall turned a brilliant, gilded yellow. She thought of them as inherently old, as dying one small piece at a time but nevertheless showing new leaf each spring, and this in the parched, unheralded places no other tree much wanted. Miss Dietrich was moved to poetry by them and recited Housman's "Loveliest of Trees" and "Far in a Western Brookland."

She held Ben after school one day and told him he was her brightest hope in twenty-seven years on the western plains and a candidate for a good university, should he decide on such a path—a path she urged him toward greatly. A path he should have no fear about; a path he should walk with confidence. Ben answered that his father needed him to work the apple orchard. Couldn't he do that later? Miss Dietrich asked. Wouldn't it be both an adventure and a test? Didn't he owe it to himself? Wasn't the larger world waiting?

He thanked her again and went out to his brother, who was waiting propped against the wall of the schoolhouse, chewing on a stem of wheatgrass. The January wind blew hard off the river, and Aidan had his back turned to it.

"What did she want?"

"She said I should go to college."

"You going to do it?"

"I don't know."

"Probably you're smart enough."

"Maybe, maybe not."

"You ought to go, Ben."

Aidan pulled his hat brim low and rose, still chewing on his grass stem. "Come on," he said. "Let's get on home. We've got horses to feed."

Fifteen months after Pearl Harbor, Aidan was drafted into the Army. He packed his bag three days before leaving and said he wanted one last ride up in the Colockum country.

At dawn Ben and Aidan saddled the horses and crossed the river at Coleman's Landing. They rode on empty stomachs until nine; then they sat at the lip of a spring and ate in the sun from their saddlebags. They turned the horses up Dry Springs Canyon and rode southeasterly through the afternoon, sometimes at a canter over meadow ruts, or at a side-by-side trot over ridges. At dusk Aidan shot a pair of blue grouse from where they had lit on low tree limbs after kicking up before the horses. They made camp just north of Spring Gulch, near a grove of hoary willows. They sat in their blankets with the pair of grouse spitted, the wind railing hard at their backs, the fire's smoke streaming away. It was a chill evening. There were no stars in the sky. The night air was sweet and promised rain: Aidan said he could smell it coming as surely as if he had seen dark clouds borne toward him on the breeze, as surely as if he could see rain just upwind already.

They ate and banked the fire extravagantly, until the flames caused them to sweat. At midnight came a thunderstorm, and they lay with the lantern turned out in the tent to watch the lightning flicker. The rain fell with such fervor that the world disappeared.

They measured the rain's tapering by the quality of its sound against the canvas, and finally there came silence. Out beyond the dripping, dark willows, they took in the stars and the sliver of moon, calm and pale, as if the rain had never happened. "I don't want to go," Aidan said. "You're the one person I can say it to. Truth is, I'm not cut out for the Army. I'd rather be right here."

"I wish you were staying," said Ben.

They were quiet standing wrapped in their blankets in the darkness of the hills. "I don't know nothing but apples," said Aidan, and kicked, hard, at a loose stone on the ground. "What do they want with me anyway? I'm nothing but an apple farmer."

"Anyway, you have to go."

"I don't have to like it," said Aidan.

In the morning they ate the last of the apricots. They rode out onto the ridge top together to take in the long view across the river toward the sage plateau. The high country was March cold, the morning bright, the brush wet. The horses nickered and threw their heads when the riders stood them high on the summit reach by a field of huckleberry. Steam chuffed from their mouths. To the southwest were the big mountains in mantles of snow, and to the southeast the river coiling. "We ought to have climbed those mountains," said Ben. "How come we never did?"

"They're too far off," said Aidan. "They're one hell of a long ride."

"But they look like you might reach out to them."

"They're too far off," repeated Aidan.

They rode back all day to the Columbia, traversed it on the Colockum Ferry, and at dusk came into their orchard tired, on empty stomachs, their hats tipped back, to walk the horses between the rows of trees in a silent kind of processional, and Aidan ran his hands over limbs as he passed them with his horse behind him, the limbs trembling in the wake of his passing, and on, then, to the barn.

A letter arrived for Ben in May from a man named Willard Anderson, president of the Leavenworth Ski Club. Mr. Anderson remembered Ben from the time he'd passed on the jump at Ski Hill and urged him now to sign on with the mountain troops being raised by the Army. The 87th Mountain Infantry Regiment, he wrote, had been activated at Fort Lewis on the day after the attack on Pearl Harbor. There had been much training on the slopes of Mt. Rainier, and various advances had been made. The 87th had been followed by the 10th Mountain Division, and it was this division that was now recruiting, in part with the help of the National Ski Patrol, of which Mr. Anderson was the local chairman, so he was writing to boys of fighting age with an enthusiasm for the high country, in the hope they would find it an honor and a privilege to join the Army's mountain troops at this time of dire need.

Ben's alternative, Mr. Anderson wrote, was to go where the draft took him. Wasn't it preferable, his letter argued, to take matters into his own hands and "meet the war on your own terms, and wearing skis as well?"

Ben's father said that if he had to go, he may as well go as a mountain trooper. "I wish you wouldn't go at all," he said. "I wish you could stay. I need you."

"You'll get along."

"No, I won't."

"You can hire somebody."

"That's not what I mean."

"Well, anyway, I have to go."

"I wish you didn't," said his father.

That June the cherries ripened early, and Wright Givens set the eleventh of the month as the day to begin their harvest. At first light the pickers met by the siding: Ben, his father, and nine migrant workers, the Emerys and their four young children, and finally Mrs. Emery's niece, Rachel Lake from Waterville, Maine, who—as Mrs. Emery explained—had come to stay for the harvest. She'd come, it appeared, not fully prepared, and so wore Mrs. Emery's work clothes, denim pants and a flannel shirt, both many sizes too large.

Ben's father lined them out down the rows, assigning each a set of trees and a picking bucket and ladder. Before long came the sound of cherries striking the bottoms of buckets like hailstones and the voices of pickers beyond the branches. Ben left the woody spurs behind, clearing his bucket of leaves as he went, stripping the limbs of their every fruit, careful to take them with their stems intact, gathering them in clusters. The harvest season lay in front of him now, miles and miles of fruit ahead, ten thousand trees to be gleaned of their yield, days, weeks, and months of fruit, until one dreamed at night of cherries, of apples and pears plucked loose from trees, of moving hands and moving leaves.

When the sun was up and the dew had dried, Ben sprawled in the grass to eat breakfast—three eggs he'd boiled that morning—and looked down the row at the heaped cherry crates waiting under the trees. He could see, not far off, Mrs. Emery's niece, high in her ladder, picking. Most of Rachel Lake disappeared in the leaves, but he noticed that she'd cinched Mrs. Emery's denim pants around her waist with Manila twine. The belt loops in back were tied together. He saw her stand on the toes of her boots to reach into the branches. She stepped up onto a higher rung, and her makeshift belt disappeared.

In the afternoon the heat came up so that the cherries went soft and left their stems behind. Ben's father called off picking for the day, and they loaded the fruit on the flatbed truck, hauled their ladders and buckets to the siding, and lined out the boxes for pickup by the Consolidated Cherry Packing Company. Ben was busy picking leaves from the boxes when Rachel came out of the orchard shade with her flannel shirttail loose. She paused to wipe her face with it. The barest shadow of her belly showed, a dark bar of flesh revealed for a half second. She tucked in her shirt and ran her hands through her hair—neck-length, unadorned, the color of walnut shells. Tilting her head up, shutting her eyes, she drank steadily from a water jug, wiped her lips with the back of her hand, then drank again, pulling hard, the cords in her throat working. He couldn't help noting the shape of her head, her nose, lips, chin. Her face was made of fine bones. She glistened with the sweat of her work. It was hard not to look at her, inside her oversized clothes.

One time they rode in the flatbed together with a half dozen other pickers. The orange sunset glowed in her pores, and her hair was flailed by the breeze. Another time he picked in the tree beside hers. She was fast not because her hands were agile but because she was undistracted. Her forearms emerged from the leaves unscathed, unscratched by twigs and branches. Her wrists were flat, her elbows pointed, her arms brown and long in the sun, her hair flecked with bits of leaf. He had glimpses of her at odd moments—leveling cherries in their crates, perched in a ladder near the top of a tree, bent to drink from a barn spigot with her hair checked by one hand. One evening he saw her at the bend in the river, wearing nothing but her winter union suit, her hair pasted against her head, performing cannonballs from a ledge. Another time he saw her beneath pear trees, weaving dandelion chains with a cousin to hang from the freighted limbs. He saw her one noon at lunch in the orchard, in a contest to spit a cherry pit farthest; she was animated in victory, raising her fists toward the sun. He saw her currying a horse in the barnyard, walking it in the river road, at dusk riding with solitary leisure across the sage-studded ridge tops. She galloped hatless beneath the early moon, easy and still in the saddle.

Later that month came rain showers. They had to wait a full day to let the cherries dry out. Ben took the Black Labs up in a willow canyon to hunt for quail in the wild rose and sumac. It had rained all morning, but now, at noon, the air was fresh and the sun so strong that the dogs worked with their tongues hanging out, stopping at springs to lap at the muddy ground. A game trail threaded in and out of the draw, and the dogs followed it steadily, crashing into thickets now and then without Ben's urging them.

An hour out, they flushed a small covey laying up in bramble and thorn. After that they worked the singles uphill, the birds funneling out across the sage but coiling back into the canyon's cover, seeking the shade of willows. Ben brought four birds to earth in the course of a half hour. In the high heat, he rested at a spring, the orchard country spread out below, the river silver and holding sunlight, the mountains still snowbound on their north faces. Ben lay back to take it all in, as he had many times before. Aidan and he had rested here often. There were the charred remains of the fire ring where they'd sometimes spit-cooked birds.

He rested long in the shade of the spring with his hands behind his head. The ache of the climb was in his limbs, as well as the ache of picking, and it was good to rest in the cool of the willows, the damp smell of the earth beneath him, slightly bitter, alive. He shut his eyes and listened to the wind. He dozed for a while and then turned on his side to look down the ridge.

He saw Rachel there, in the distance, on horseback, riding toward the plateau. A girl at liberty beneath the sun, making her way through the sage. She sat easily in the rhythm of the horse. She climbed to the ridge, turned, paused, and took in the view of the mountains. The horse circled under her, and she worked it around again. Then she disappeared into the east.

They were well into the heat of cherry season when at last he spoke to her. He was unloading cherries onto the siding, and she suddenly stepped in next to him to clean leaves from the crates. Her hands moved through the fruit lightly. The river wind blew against their faces. She'd turned sun-burnished in ten days of picking and had gone to Wenatchee for work clothes that fit— denim pants and a boy's white T-shirt—but they were already stained with cherry juice, as were her teeth and lips.

Rachel said, "What's gotten into the bees today? They're all over the place."

"I don't know. It's strange."

He didn't look at her, just at her hands, swift among the fruit.

"This one's perfect," she said, and popped a cherry in her mouth.

"You're not tired of cherries?"

"I love them."

"Me, too."

"These are the best."

She ate a second and a third. He watched her spit out the pits.

"I've seen you riding," Ben told her. "Up there, toward the plateau."

"That's one place," Rachel said. "But along the river is good too, and up in those little canyons with the willows."

"There's rattlesnakes in the canyons," said Ben.

"I'm not scared of snakes," she answered.

"They're bad this time of year," said Ben.

"I'm still not scared," Rachel told him.

She moved along the row of crates, their conversation finished. He felt certain he'd made a bad impression. A boy living in orchard country, a font of information on rattlesnakes.

The apricots ripened before the cherries were done, and there were two crops to pick. Thirteen pickers lived on the place and at dawn moved out to their ladder sets with their buckets and water jugs over their shoulders, the Emery children and Rachel with them, starting before the heat came up, finishing when the fruit went soft. Ben rose from bed before anyone else, dressed, and went out into the darkness. He laid out crates for the pickers. He put in apple branch props, mowed the quack grass in the orchard rows, and pruned summer suckers out of treetops. Then there was the problem of the codling moth. A man named Kevin Lawrence in Wenatchee, who worked for the Bureau of Entomology, had convinced Ben's father that time and money could be saved with the construction of an elaborate stationary spray system, as opposed to the leaky, wagon-mounted pump sprayer— hauled about by a pair of mules—they'd long gotten by on. Now, at picking time, they were still laboring with laying the base line of one-inch pipe and the lateral lines of three-quarter-inch pipe, driving in the many standpipes, mounting the proper fittings for the spraying hoses, pouring the concrete for the holding tank, and getting in the pump. And then the horses and mules must eat, the windbreak poplars needed water in the heat, more fruit boxes needed working up, and the wire bindings on the wood water pipes were coming loose in the south orchard and had to be replaced. And there was a place where moles were diverting water and no time to see about changing this, and in the evening was the accounting to see to and all the record keeping.

On the last day of June, he spoke with Rachel again. He was standing knee-deep in a feeder ditch, cleaning the weeds from a lateral screen, when she came along with her picking bucket, and he stopped what he was doing and looked at her, weeds dripping in his hand. "Hey," she said.

"Hey yourself," Ben said.

"Is that algae?"

"We just call it ditch weed."

"That isn't any official name."

"I don't know the official name. The Latin name or anything."

"Maybe you know these berries," she said. "Up there growing in the willow canyon. The little red berries you see in the wet places. Not really red but closer to orange. Clusters of them. Little."

"Those are currants," Ben told her.

"Currants," she said. "I've been eating them."

"We used to make them into jelly sometimes."

"I've had currant jelly. It tastes like gooseberry."

"We don't have gooseberry out here," said Ben. "But up in the canyon there's something called serviceberry. They look, sort of, like little purple apples. You've probably seen those, too."

"If I did, I didn't notice." She smoothed her hair, which had turned a lighter shade at the ears since they'd last talked. "I'll let you get back to your ditch weed. Or whatever it's called—ditch weed."

"It could be algae," said Ben.

There was a respite on the Fourth of July, and the pickers lolled through the heat of the day, keeping well in the shade. At dusk they brought out a guitar and accordion, and hollered long across the hills to hear their voices echo. They traded empty curses too, and screamed senseless insults. Ben and his father sat on the porch with the doors and windows open behind them and the Victrola playing the music of violins, which mingled with the noise from the pickers' camp. It was one of Lenora Givens's records, a slow, piercing concerto that her husband played from time to time, though it seemed to Ben an odd choice for Independence Day. They sat and listened anyway. The light fell and blurred the contours of shadows. The stifling air of the river basin cooled, and an evening balminess settled in, the sort that people in orchard country coveted all day.

"You oughtn't to just set here with me," Wright Givens said after awhile. "Whyn't you wander up to the Emerys and see that niece of theirs?"

"Why should I?" said Ben.

Ben's father nodded and grinned. "You waste too much time, she'll be gone," he warned. "Girl like that gets tired of picking fruit, she's going to leave this place."

"Let her," said Ben. "I don't care."

They could see across the way to the Emery Orchard. Most of the lights were on in the house. A pool of light in the glower of dusk overtaking the sage hills.

"She's just right there." Ben's father pointed. "Not any more than a ten-minute walk. And probably thinking on you, too, girl like that, your age."

"Lay off," said Ben.

"It's the Fourth of July. A night natural for festivities. It's reasonable to wander over there."

"She doesn't mean anything to me, okay? I don't care about her one way or the other."

"All right. Sit around here with your old man all night if that's what you want to do, Ben. You damn-fool-greenhorn-wet-behind-the-ears-little-stubborn-lamebrained-mule."

Ben went down toward the pickers' camp. In the dusty clearing in front of the cabins a pair of kerosene lanterns burned, and in their incandescent glare the accordion player and the guitarists crooned, stomping their feet and hopping like puppets, throwing their shadows across the ground, and all about them worn, weathered men shuffled and spun on bandy legs, men who limped and moved gingerly. Men were cursing and jostling, playing cards, rolling dice on the dusty ground, howling like coyotes at the moon. Ben made his way around them to the butte where once he'd lain with Nora Ellerby and run his hand up between her legs. The sand still held the last of the day's heat. The light of the moon illuminated rock faces. Ben sat listening to the hilarity of the pickers honoring the birth of their nation, and beyond it his mother's violin music.

When he returned, his father had a bottle of bourbon on the porch boards beside his chair. His boots were propped on the porch railing, his hat tipped down over his eyes, his hands clasped behind his head. "No luck, sailor?" he said.

"I didn't go over there."

Ben sat down, too, and put his feet up. His father groped on the floor beside him, then took a pull from the bourbon. "Do you know how old I am?" he asked.

"Forty-nine," said Ben.

"Forty-nine's right."

"So?"

"So nothing."

"You ought not to drink that hooch," said Ben. "It just garbles up your mind."

His father took another pull from the bottle. "It's a holiday," he countered.

There were more cries from the fruit pickers. Ululations, mock wolf howls, war whoops, and drunken bluster. "Those men are having a time," said Ben's father. "I just hope they don't go on all night or burn the cabins down."

Ben didn't answer. He looked at the moon. A gibbous moon in the western sky, as bright as though on fire.

"Those men had families, it'd be altogether different," Ben's father said. "They wouldn't be carrying on such. They'd have a different take."

"Probably so," answered Ben.

He heard them long after midnight from his bed, the pickers stuporous but still celebratory, still railing away at the firmament, a passel of travelers who'd stopped in this place long enough to glean it of fruit. Then there was nothing but a scratching from the Victrola. He got up to turn it off. Moonlight over everything. He saw his father out on the porch, hard asleep in his rocking chair, his head tipped back, his mouth open, the bottle between his thighs. He was thoroughly gray now—his whiskers and hair. His face was cross-hatched with wrinkles.

Mid-July, the apricots were done, but the pears not quite ready. They were still hard and green in every tree, and not heavy enough to need propping. Mr. Emery put the pickers to work at making apple and pear boxes, pruning summer suckers from his apples, and scything away at the orchard grass. Ben and his father made progress on the spray system. The evenings were warm and windless. The field crickets resounded at night, and the bats worked over the orchards. In the morning, after the dew had dried, viceroy butterfly larvae fed on the poplar leaves. A red-tailed hawk rode afternoon breezes, languidly circling in a featureless sky. Starlings and robins pecked at the fruit. The coyotes came down at dusk, too. Their calls echoed across the hills, under the wide palette of the stars.

Ben spoke for a third time with Mrs. Emery's niece. He'd gone up into the willow canyon with the dogs and the Winchester 21 and found her with her horse tied, kneeling to drink at the lip of a spring—down on both knees as if to pray with her ankles turned up under her, her hands formed into a dipper. It was early in the morning. The water seeped between her fingers. Her hair spilled past her downturned face; she wore a pair of snake chaps. Ben emerged from between two willows and saw first the curve of her back, her chaps clipped to her belt loops. His dogs paused to consider the horse, then trotted up to drink beside Rachel. "It's you," she said, turning. "Don't shoot me."

"It isn't loaded."

"Supposing it was. Are you saying you'd shoot me?"

"No, of course not."

"That's a relief."

Ben called his dogs away from her, but they insisted on drinking at the spring, lapping at the water vigorously, showing their thick pink tongues. "We had a Golden Lab at home," Rachel said. "She died when I was fourteen."

Ben nodded. "They're always thirsty."

"Well, this is good water. From deep in the earth."

"I like this spring," said Ben.

Rachel drank from her cupped hands. She rose, wiped her lips, and seemed to appraise him and the shotgun broke open across his forearm. He propped it in the brush and looked at her horse, as if that were his primary interest. It was a sorrel mare worn down with the years, swaybacked and scraped and scarred by time, but her cannon bones still straight and clean and her mane and tail well groomed. "Your uncle's horse," Ben observed.

"He lets me ride it," said Rachel.

"He just about sold it last spring, I think, but then he changed his mind."

Ben knelt as she had at the spring, but on one knee only, his elbow against the other, and drank by raising the water in his free hand more than a dozen times. "You're out early," he said.

"It's not that early."

"You're wearing snake chaps."

"They're riding chaps."

"What's the difference?"

"These are longer."

"You always wear them?"

"They're smart to wear."

"I guess so," said Ben.

Rachel turned her back on him and went to her saddlebag. The riding chaps cut across her thighs and were clipped behind her calves. The seat of her pants was worn, dusty. She spoke to him from over one shoulder, so that he saw her face and neck in profile, the fine shape of her chin. "I've got a couple of short-cakes," she said. "Help me eat them, why don't you."

"I won't say no, I guess."

"There's cherries, too, if you're not tired of those."

"I'm not," said Ben.

They sat on the ground, out in the open, where the heat of the sun could reach them. The dogs probed aimlessly along the verge of willows, went their way, and came again. Rachel unclasped and set aside her chaps. She slapped the dust from the seat of her pants and folded the chaps to sit tailor-fashion on them, but then changed her mind and settled instead with her legs folded to one side.

They ate the shortcakes together. Ben pointed to a place in the canyon where she could find serviceberry. "The petals are white," he explained.

"I guess you remember the last time we talked. That time you were standing in the ditch, remember? You mentioned this ser-viceberry."

"That's right," Ben said. "And ditch weed."

Rachel nodded and smiled. "You have a pretty fair memory."

"My memory's bad. I can't remember anything. You're the one with the memory."

"Mine's fair. Close things, I forget. Faraway things, I remember better. I was three when my mom died, but I remember her."

"I can't do that," Ben answered. "I don't know what happened when."

Rachel lay down with one hip against the chaps and propped her head on her hand.

"My mom died, too," Ben told her. "But I was twelve, so I remember it."

"That's worse, being twelve like that. I don't really remember her, so it doesn't affect me like it does you. I'm guessing, anyway."

"It does affect me," Ben answered.

They were silent for a while. Ben ate the last of the shortcake in his hand. Rachel sat up again and reached behind with the ball of her thumb to scratch the middle of her back.

"I'm curious," Ben said. "Why did you come out here?"

"Out here?"

"To your cousins, I mean."

"To help with the picking."

"But you're from Maine, way back east. It's a long way to come to pick fruit."

"September I go to nursing school. In San Francisco."

"Nursing school?"

"The Cadet Nurse Corps."

"You're going to be—you want to be—a nurse?"

"I hope so," said Rachel.

She had one boot crossed over the other, both drumming the ground idly, her free hand resting on her hip. The fingers of her other hand disappeared in her hair, and her long torso rose with her breathing just beneath her T-shirt.

"You'll end up in the war," said Ben. "That's where they're sending nurses."

"That's the plan," answered Rachel.

They followed a cowpath down from the sage hills—Rachel

with her horse on a Manila tether, Ben's dogs ranging far and wide—and he showed her small mats of stonecrop and white stickseed flowers. Beyond rose mountains in the west, blue against the horizon. "I'd like to ride up there," said Rachel.

"You'd need time. After picking's done. Maybe late in October."

"I'll be gone before then, though."

They came down into orchards after ten o'clock. They walked between trees with the sorrel mare and the Labs, apples growing overhead. The light fell soft and diffused between the limbs, and the smell was of ripening fruit. "This is where it's just so beautiful," said Rachel. "This is what really just kills me."

"I feel the same," Ben answered.

A letter came for Ben one afternoon from the adjutant general's office in Washington: an order to report for active service in the 10th Mountain Division. Ben read it closely, twice; his heart began to pound. Then he turned between the trees to find his father in the south orchard, where he was laying new irrigating pipe.

Ben's father read, squinting a little, and scratched his weathered forehead. It was a clear day, windless and hot. The afternoon light fell full and strong, piercing the orchard shade. His father had the Farmall idling—he'd been using it to haul pipe about—but now he shut the motor down and hopped free of the seat. "Well," he said. That was all.

"I'm all accepted," answered Ben.

"I guess you are," said his father.

They leaned together against the Farmall while his father put one boot up behind him and read the letter again. "I don't like this," he said finally. "I don't want you to go."

"I have to go."

"I know that."

"It'll mostly be skiing."

"No, it won't." His father slowly measured his beard stubble. "I don't guess it'll mostly be skiing. But I hope it is, for your sake."

"Me too," Ben answered.

His father sighed, handed him the letter, and beat one heel against the grass.

"Anyway," said Ben, "where could they send me? Norway, or someplace like that. Finland or Sweden, maybe."

"It doesn't matter where they send you. It's still a war, Ben."

"I guess so."

"It is."

His father put a hand on Ben's shoulder and squeezed. "It just doesn't seem like it ought to be, you going off to fight a war."

"Well," said Ben. "I have to go anyway."

"You're seventeen," said his father.

The season of pears was upon them soon, at that point in August when nothing tangible suggests the demise of summer, except our apprehension. They pulled the props from the limbs as they picked, leaning them in the forks of trees, and picked the Bartletts with a steady insistence, easing them out of picking sacks as though pears were delicate as eggs. Ladders stood up and down the rows with the pickers perched in them loading bags by laying fruit on other fruit, the weight of pears gently pulling them forward, their bags swelling deep and low. In silhouette they resembled pregnant women.

On the third day of pears, Ben went with a blade of grass between his teeth and stood under Rachel's ladder. He could see her in among the leaves. She seemed self-contained, absorbed in her silent picking world. "Hey," he called. "It's me."

"Hey," she answered, and stopped working. She turned on her ladder and faced him, her bag of pears against her belly. "What are you doing?" she asked.

Ben pulled the blade of grass from his mouth. "I don't know," he answered. "Just saying hey, I guess."

"Well hey to you, too."

"Hey."

She worked down the ladder, walked past him. She unhooked the ties of her picking bag and unloaded her pears, a slow slide, so that none would bruise or dent. "It's hot today," she said.

"It is," he said. "A day like this, sometimes, I swim in the river after work. Just down there where it eddies."

"I know where it is."

She hooked the straps of her bag into place, then worked the ladder into a new set, in between the pear branches.

"What time will you go?"

"At dusk. In the dark."

"That sounds good," said Rachel.

He met her at the river bend, in the soft sand of the talus butte, to watch the setting of the August sun over the Colockum Hills. In the dark they went down to the edge of the water with the stars spread wide and high overhead, and stood on the rocks together. Ben stripped down to his trousers, Rachel to the union suit he'd seen her in before. She stood with her arms across her chest, her hands in fists at her collarbones, and hesitated with her toes in the river. "There's a strong eddy," she said.

"My brother and I used to come here," said Ben. "Almost every day, after work."

"What brother?"

"He's in the Army."

"What about you?"

"I joined up."

"When do you go?"

"End of October."

"That isn't a lot of time, is it?"

"More than you," answered Ben.

They stood in the river with some distance between them, the water swirling past their legs. "You know what?" Rachel said, pinching the fabric of her union suit. "I'm embarrassed to swim in this thing."

"It's okay," Ben told her. "We don't have to swim or anything. Whatever you want is okay."

"But that's it. I don't know what I want."

"Well, wait until you do."

"Does that point come?"

"I don't know any better than you."

She looked at him, a long gaze, then took her arms from her chest. He turned away and squatted against the shore rocks, looking out across the river so as not to embarrass her further. "I'm going in," she said.

He watched her wade into the river. The union suit revealed her waist and shoulders. The river was running hard for August, and the light washed just where her legs met it in a phosphorescent surge. Then, thigh deep, she dove in and rose a little downstream. She swept her hair back and rubbed her eyes. The union suit clung to her torso now. "The water's perfect," she announced.

He dove in too, and they swam against the current. The water divided and flowed around her. It shone on the skin of her face.

Afterward, still in their wet clothes, they built a fire out of drifts. The drifts burned white and smokeless enough that they could sit close beside them in a bright womb of heat. The world beyond disappeared. Darkness lay beyond the firelight. The stars appeared awash in pale ether. There was a hound, faintly distant, calling. Venus had risen low in the west, as brilliant as the moon.

Ben shoved a limb deeper into the fire. "Why do you want to be a nurse?"

"It's something I think I can do, I guess. Something I can put my hands on."

"I'm not sure I follow that."

"Like Florence Nightingale. Clara Barton. I don't know, maybe I'm stupid. I just have this picture of it."

"It might not be that way, though."

"Probably. I don't know."

She sat with her hands and feet toward the fire. The light played across her face.

"How long do you train for?"

"Nine months. They've compressed the courses."

"Then what?"

"I go to the Army."

"Where exactly?"

"I don't know."

"You could go anywhere."

"I guess I could."

"Me, too," he said.

Ben turned once more to take in her face, richly lit by firelight. While he watched, she pressed the hair at her neck to squeeze the river water from it.

"So you go at the end of October," she said. "Didn't you say October?"

"The twenty-seventh," answered Ben.

"Why are you going? Why do you want to fight?"

"I don't want to fight," he told her. "But I also don't want to be drafted and end up peeling potatoes."

"Well, you shouldn't enlist if you don't want to fight. You should train as a medic or something."

"A medic?"

"Yes."

"First aid?"

"Yes."

"What if everyone wanted to do that?"

"Then we wouldn't have a war," said Rachel.

Ben placed another drift on the fire and worked it into the flames.

"You could die, you know," said Rachel. "You're putting your life on the line."

"I try not to think about things like that."

"You should, though."

"I don't."

He thought about dying, not seeing her anymore. "I wouldn't want any regrets," he said. "So I guess I should just say it."

"What do you mean? You'd better say what?"

"That I like you, Rachel. That's all."

"I like you, too," she answered.

They kissed by the heat of the fire. He was surprised at the human smell of her flesh, the human smell of her mouth. It was not something he would have thought to predict, because for so long he'd imagined her sweetly perfumed—but here she was, mysteriously human, so that it seemed to him, with his lips against hers, that he grasped her mortality. "I don't know," he whispered in her ear. "This might be a mistake."

"I don't think so," said Rachel.

"We ought to think about this," said Ben.

"I already have," said Rachel.

There were evenings together in apple orchards laden bountifully. The apples hung heavy in the late-day sun, the leaves stirred in the wind. The green orchards were cool and inviting against the dun-colored sagelands. Thousands of apple trees gathered light and heat, on every branch a profusion of fruit, so many apples

growing there it seemed an impossibility, a feat of nature rightly
to be met with astonishment and awe. Ben and Rachel took a
picnic basket deep into the coolest rows, where there were trees,
quack grass, and sky. The sun came low from out of the west to
filter in between the limbs, and it lit her face, arms, and throat as
she sat with her legs tucked under her, searching inside their picnic basket—tomato sandwiches, spearmint tea, celery stuffed
with peanut butter, cherries in syrup, walnuts. The light fell and
blurred the contours of shadows. The late summer air of the orchard cooled. They lay on their blanket and stared up between
branches with their hands behind their heads. They watched it
come dark more swiftly than it had the month before. The sky
passed from dusk to night. There were bats about in the orchard
now. The apples in the trees hung black and still, poised above
their heads.

In the darkness, Rachel spoke easily. Her father, she said, was
a farmhand and millwright. She had two sisters, one older, one
younger. They grew up south of Waterville, Maine, in five rooms
heated by a barrel stove, on the property of a one-legged dairy
farmer. Her father's mother cared for them; she was stern and
demanded discipline. Each morning they milked a half dozen
cows and fed chickens, geese, and ducks. Her father acted as
stable keeper; Rachel and her sisters groomed and fed horses and
cleaned out stalls every day. Her older sister had married last
June, to a man who owned a bakery in town; she worked nights
rolling and kneading dough and brought them day-old loaves.
Over the course of the past school year, the dairy farmer's son
courted Rachel. She wasn't interested in him, though. She had it
in mind now to be a nurse. A girl she knew, an acquaintance at
school, had signed up to join the Cadet Nurse Corps—free tu-
ition, she told Rachel, a free uniform, free room and board, and
fifteen dollars a month. Rachel signed up, too.

She saved money for train fare and traveled west with her belongings stowed in a battered leather grip. She got her sleep curled up on a wooden bench and watched the land pass behind her. All of it was foreign and beautiful. She had never really been anywhere before, except to Boston, twice. On the train she decided that nursing was good, that caring for the ill was a worthwhile thing and not merely an excuse to flee Waterville. She began to look forward to the work of nursing, to her training in San Francisco. She felt liberated.

A soldier had flirted with Rachel on the train, and she'd agreed to lunch in the dining car, but nothing came of it. Later she sat with two other girls who had heard there was work in Seattle. The three of them drank from a bottle of gin while crossing eastern Montana. Rachel vomited in the toilet stall, twice. She slept, and when she woke again, they were crossing the Rocky Mountains. The train passed across the wheat plateau and at last came down into the river country, where the apple orchards were in spring bloom, their white blossoms brilliant. Seeing this, she had no regrets, or felt she wanted to be elsewhere. She believed that a better life was starting.

But now it was time for Rachel to leave. They went to the river and stood knee-deep, embracing there in the current. Her skin felt smooth and cool to his touch. "I'm going to miss you," she said.

Her uncle's car idled in the yard. They kissed hidden in the orchard rows, and she promised to write from San Francisco. There was even a telephone in the dormitory, and she left the number with him. "This is it," she said firmly. "Wish me luck, Ben."

"I do," he said. "Good luck, Rachel."

"You too. Good luck."

She brought her fingers gently to his face. "I'm memorizing your features," she said. "I want to remember you."

"Don't say that," Ben pleaded. "It sounds like I'm dead already."

"You do it with me," answered Rachel. "Memorize my face."

Ben left the apple country when the picking was done, the bins and ladders put away, the canvas bags hung up. All the apples had been taken from the trees, the orchards brought to silence now, the transient pickers moving on, disappearing down the river road, leaving the country hushed and lonely: not even an evening breeze.

His father took him to the bus station in Wenatchee. He gave Ben six five-dollar bills and a new pocketknife. They milled about in silence for a while, then sat waiting with their hats in their laps, outside, in the loading bay.

"I'm going to worry," said his father. "Just like I do with Aidan."

"It won't do him or me any good."

"Just the same, I'm going to worry."

"There's too much to do to waste time on that."

"Picking's over," said his father. "I've got time on my hands."

They paused to watch the bus pull in. It came to a stop in front of them. "You take care," said Ben.

"Never mind," said his father.

"You keep yourself away from that hooch."

"I'm not on it."

"Yes, you are."

His father knocked a boot heel against the ground. "No, I'm not," he said.

In the open doorway of the bus they embraced, and Ben smelled his father's hair. "Thanks," he said. "For everything."

His father hugged him harder in reply. "Jesus," he said, "don't go."

Ben rode the bus to Cashmere, where he stepped off thinking

to hitchhike west in order to save on bus fare. He stood by the road with his whole life in front of him. He stood with his thumb out and his duffel bag beside him while a few dry flakes of snow descended from a strange, cloudless sky. A truck pulled over, and he rode to Peshastin, where at noon sheets of lightning crossed the orchards. He sat beneath an apple tree, waiting for the storm to pass, leaning against his duffel bag with the rain beating the leaves around him, his canvas coat pulled tightly against his neck, his hat low on his forehead. When the sun emerged, he went again to the road and took a ride with a farmer from Omak hauling hay to Gold Bar.

He passed the night in a wood of fir trees close to the Skykomish River. It was dense, dark, and silent there, wet and uninviting. But in the early morning he rose from dreams to find the river pale and lovely, mist steaming off its waters, the fog thick on its distant bank, and he went down in the cold dawn light to wash his face at a riffle, where he saw a kingfisher flash by. Then he packed, went back to the road, and got a lift in a log truck bound for Monroe, with a driver who carefully looked him over, snapped his metal lunchbox open, and handed Ben a piece of chocolate cake his wife had baked the night before.

At noon Ben made Seattle. He walked with his duffel bag over his shoulder until he found a diner on Occidental advertising specials in its window. He ate a plate of eggs and toast and drank a glass of milk. He sat with his plate pushed away from him and watched two men sitting low at the counter in hats and city overcoats, slouched over their stools. They drank their coffee and smoked in silence. The waitress stood tipped against the wall with a dishrag clutched between her fingers, hobnobbing with the short-order cook through the glare of the heat lamps in the pickup window. There was the low drone of her city voice, tired and cynical.

After breakfast he walked until he came to the salt water. He set his bag by a creosoted piling crusted with mussels and barnacles and descended a pier-side ladder to dip his fingers in the sea. He tasted it while hanging from the tide-bleached rungs like a sailor from mainsail rigging. Then he rinsed his face in a baptism and looked out over the water to the west.

Ben took a room in Pioneer Square, on the second floor of a flophouse. It was lonely and desolate in his paltry room with its dirt-encrusted window. All night through the lights burned glaringly along the street outside. In the morning, tired, he hiked to the bus station and bought a ticket to Fort Lewis. There was a chance for it while he waited for the bus, so for the first time in his life he used a pay phone, getting help from the operator, stuffing coins into the slot. He had to ask the bus clerk for change and try a second time. But when at last he had Rachel on the line, he told her simply that he loved her. It was easier to say it on the telephone. She told him that she felt the same. The time he had bought with his change ran out, and he hung up the receiver in the Seattle bus station and sat in the hall on his duffel bag, waiting with other travelers now, at the outset of a strange, new life.

FIVE

Tristan nudged insistently: a warm muzzle against Ben's ear, a whining deep in the dog's throat. Ben stirred with the moon overhead—tremulous, improbably large, as though while he slept it had stolen closer to the earth—but with no desire to leave his dreams. The languid serenity of marijuana was preferable, its hallucinatory depths transporting him away from a present in which he was sprawled in the desert, afflicted by a terminal disease. Yet he found himself wakened against his will, and the pain of his cancer, put away for a few hours, became, once more, chief.

Ben took stock. He was in the sagelands, alone but for his dogs, in the deepest hour of night. The cold had entered his long-suffering joints, and his bladder pressed for attention. He was as stiff in his back as if the vertebrae were fused, his left eye was swollen shut, and his fingers were numb and useless. More, his left knee seemed incapable of bending, and his arthritic ankle throbbed. Ben rose on one elbow, put his hand on Tristan's head, and berated the dog for rousing him.

Rex, he saw, was out at thirty yards, head high in the sageland. The dog pranced ahead another five yards, stopped to cast for scent and listen, then turned in Ben's direction, gazed at him, and whined.

Ben didn't know what to make of his dogs or of their present animation. He'd seen Rex and Tristan fidget in the presence of porcupines, moles, skunks, owls, voles, and rattlesnakes, but he could not surmise what bothered them now, out here in the placid desert. There were only the stars and that rich, prominent moon, its surface broken by shadows, pocked by enormous craters. And moonlight silver over everything.

Propped on one elbow, immobilized by doubt, Ben watched his agitated dogs. He wanted to lie down again wrapped in his blanket and leave them to face, without his help, whatever was so disconcerting. Ben recollected hearing somewhere that coyotes sometimes worked in packs to lure dogs to untimely deaths, attacking viciously. For a moment he was certain there were coyotes about, and he peered nearsightedly into the desert as though to spot one against the sage. Then, thoroughly exasperated with himself for indulging his fear of shadows—of shapes that were nothing more than wraiths produced by a marijuana-addled mind—he drank from his water bottle. He hoped no effort would be required, that he might sleep again without interruption if his dogs would only settle down, stem their animal fear of the night. "Pipe down," he told them. "That's enough."

Tristan whimpered louder in reply and came to nuzzle Ben's face again with greater urgency.

Ben rose bitterly, then peed long and hard against the earth. It was satisfying to him here at the end of his days to pee with so much vigor. It was a ridiculous thing to be satisfied about, but still he was satisfied. His stream splashed against the ground. He stretched his back and revolved his head so that the bones in his neck cracked a little. He cleaned his glasses with his handkerchief, and when he slipped them on again, the moon appeared through his one good eye like highly polished marble. Everything it illuminated melted into shadows and was softly, darkly beautiful.

Ben pressed the heel of his palm against his head and hawked spit into the desert. Out to the north, as he stood beside Tristan with his blanket wrapped around him, he heard what he thought was the baying of hounds, a restless din far off somewhere, a chorus of dogs just audible, and he cupped his strong ear to listen. They were hounds all right, Ben decided, and they seemed to be moving closer, coming in his direction, perhaps, though not yet visible in shape or motion, instead a wild singing in the night, a yapping, frantic tumult. "Heel," he called to Rex then. "You get in here now."

He repeated himself more forcefully, until Rex, against his will, fell in beside Tristan, whimpering a little. The dog made several false starts to the north, turned in a circle, and whined. The baying of the hounds, though distant and faint across the hills, was audible now not just as a chorus but as a number of distinct hard-trailing hounds in the throes of heated pursuit. "Stay," said Ben. "Just stay there. We'll let them run right past us."

He regretted, deeply, the marijuana. The world was a viscous dream. He felt inhabited by a listlessness ill-suited to what might be needed. His limbs, he knew, would resist what he asked. He was too numb with cold, too much in ruins, unprepared for a pack of hounds bounding in from nowhere. Ben hoped that nothing would come of them. He hoped they would pass, a night tableau, a spectacle, something merely to be witnessed. He hoped Rex and Tristan would keep out of their way. But his dogs, barking maniacally, bolted into the night.

He called with threat and anger in his voice, but they ran off with a heedless certainty, beyond the sphere of his influence. He thought to call a second time, but they were moved, he saw, beyond his command, and in the next seconds he better understood them—for a shadow slid across the desert, a coyote, he saw, at a full-out run, and his dogs were giving chase.

Ben caught only a fleeting glance: the dark coyote swift in flight, its tail low, its ears tucked back, hurtling along like a ghost in the sage, approximately the size and shape of his Brittanies but with a bottle-shaped tail and longer muzzle. The shadow of motion passed before him and disappeared without warning, suddenly gone into a dip in the terrain, out of his line of sight. A spirit soundless across the desert, his dogs in clamorous pursuit of it, and Ben uncertain if what he had seen was real or a deception of the night.

He dropped his blanket into the sand and took up his side-by-side. He pried two shells from their vest loops, broke the gun open, nudged them in, and snapped the action shut. The shotgun, like the world itself, seemed part of a dope-inspired dream, an object flooded by silver moonlight. It was his father's gun, also the gun he had put in his own mouth earlier that morning. For a moment he regretted every gun he'd ever held in his hands, but he shook off the urge to stand pondering this, rolled his blanket, folded his poncho, and lashed them together with the empty duffel to the bottom of his rucksack. Finally he wrestled his arms through the straps and set off in pursuit of his dogs.

East of the breaks the land flattened out into gentle, unbroken prairie. There was moon and starlight enough to travel by as Ben twined between islands of sage, carrying his gun like the infantryman he'd been in Italy fifty-three years before. The baying grew closer, and his own dogs barked in the distance. He exhorted himself to overtake them, but the back of his left knee soon bound up, and he had to stop to knead it.

He came on a pair of wheel ruts across the sage. Probably they'd been made by rolling stock trucks releasing and rounding up cattle, but they seemed to have no reason to be there, like most human sign in the desert. He followed them for their easy walking and because they tended in the right direction—his dogs were off to the southeast, he guessed, though he couldn't know with certainty. The ruts hairpinned and he followed them for a while, until they hairpinned again. He stopped in their bend to listen for his dogs, but the baying hounds were so close now, their cries mingled with his dogs' barking, and he found himself confused. He stood listening to no avail, and again he regretted the marijuana, its discombobulating effect.

Ben stood as though waiting for the flush of birds, and watched the ridge line a quarter mile north, where the stars disappeared behind crenellated rock, for it seemed to him that from just out there the cry of hounds was gathering. A star plummeted down the length of the heavens, and then a roiling shadow broke over the hill, bursting forth in a duststorm of sorts, hounds pell-mell and hell-bent southward, a sinuous, frenetic pack of them barreling down the ridge. They were too far off for Ben to identify, but he took them to be a half dozen or more, and he guessed from their rolling, leaping gait—gracefully fast, like cheetahs or antelopes—that these were Irish wolfhounds, the coyote hunters of his youth.

A potato farmer up the river road, a man named Dale Saunders, Jr., had run a pack of them when called upon by ranchers whose lambs or calves were disappearing. Saunders was known in the orchard country as a trapper, hunter, and prospector, and also a government bounty man, paid to poison coyotes and to gas coyote pups in their dens. His arsenal included spring-loaded cyanide canisters, leghold traps, and strychnine. Ben had heard Saunders holding forth on coyote killing at the county fair, where he sold his handmade coyote calls, home-welded coyote traps, and a device he called a coyote-getter, which when sprung delivered cyanide to a coyote's nose and mouth. Saunders demonstrated the range of his call, which he claimed mimicked the cry of a jackrabbit impaled on a barbed-wire fence. Any coyote deceived by such a call he dispatched point-blank with his ten-gauge; otherwise he picked them off with his .22-250 Remington, which, he added, was shot from a prone position, such was its immense precision. Still, he said, no method yet devised could match his Irish coursing hounds (which he displayed to fairgoers in a chicken-wire cage mounted on the back of his pickup truck) for pure sport and sheer drama. They were huge, confident, rangy dogs, and capable, Saunders claimed, of leaping twenty feet. Four times faster than a coyote, and also adept at treeing cougars and bringing bears to bay.

It had been fifty years since Ben had seen Dale Saunders's Irish wolfhounds, but he remembered their vaguely terrifying size, their power and lithesome restlessness, and it seemed to him in the desert now, that these shadowy creatures spilling through the night—like wild horses under the moon—had just that sort of galloping height, that equine size and speed. They sprinted across the broken terrain without the slightest hindrance. They killed, Ben knew, for the pleasure of it. They were thought by some to be valorous dogs, desirable as guardians and companions, clever, trustworthy, gentle with children, well-disposed and tolerant, but Ben had no faith in their goodness and didn't count himself among their admirers. They were too much enamored of killing.

They surged toward him—a pack of Irish wolfhounds— though at an angle to miss him narrowly, so that he had time to count their number and note their stride and size. Among the six he saw at least two as large as wild yearling colts, and the pack of dogs in their fury and noise reminded him of desert mustangs. In a panic he raised his side-by-side, his thumb against the safety tang, to kill the lead dog in its tracks should the pack turn full in his direction. He had no reason to believe it would, only an in-choate fear born of nothing distinct.

Time seemed fragmented. The distance between moments was greater than usual, so that he saw the hounds at their close ap-proach with a particular detail prominent—the bubbling slather and foam hanging from the jaws of the lead dog, glistening in the moonlight, strands of silvery mucus flying from its teeth and gums. Then all was a blur until the passing of the hounds re-solved itself into a crystalline frieze: the last hound's high-speed gait broken down into two clear frames of suspension, of airy, springing levitation, the acrobatic feat of touching the ground with only one paw—impossible—at any given moment. Even as Ben made all this out, the hounds went by him as though he was nothing but an apparition in the desert. He lowered his gun and checked the safety.

Then they were gone, fading to the south, their baying squalls still trailing them, and Ben, suspended briefly in their wake, stirred himself into action. He fell in behind and gave chase with as much zeal as he could muster.

It was a matter of proceeding as if on a forced march. He couldn't hear beyond his own breathing, nor could he stop to let it subside, since speed, he felt, was essential, his dogs had inno-cently tossed themselves between these hounds and their quarry. Spurred on by thoughts of the worst that could be, he gave him-self to a fretful haste that magnified his pains. He limped ahead as fast as he could, making his way by the light of the moon and squinting into the distance.

It occurred to Ben that his feverish anxiety made no sense at all. What could it matter to him in the next world if he submitted to the will of this one instead of plunging on against it? Why exert himself painfully to alter the course of things? There was solid ground for apathy. He had no duty to recover his dogs. He was bound to leave them soon anyway. Let them wander where they would; when finished, they would find him again. And if they did not, so be it.

But out of long habit, he pushed ahead. It was not so much his dogs as his conscience that would not allow him to give up. He did not want to be careless, or transgress against his obligations: he wanted to be himself, a doctor seeing to every detail, a man tuned to his duties in life, and he found that even in the shadow of death it was not easy to be otherwise. In this frame of mind, bent on clarity, he stumbled awkwardly in the sage. With only one good eye he had a false sense of distance and caught his boot against a wrinkle in the sand, then lurched to his knees so that his lower back twisted, causing him a sudden pain. He dropped his head against his chest and set the butt of his shotgun down to lean on its length. Ben rubbed his back for a long while, and then, absently, his side. His breathing subsided. Again he heard the cries of hounds. Struggling to his feet, he pressed on.

In fifteen or maybe fifty minutes, he worked his way to the bottom of a draw choked with sumac and willows. The place was mad with the noise of hounds, their guttural fury and desperation, and as he thrashed through the thickets it seemed to him he was in their very midst. He could see no sign of them, only hear, though the full moon poured over everything, illuminating close details. He felt certain the doomed coyote was here, having found a covert where trickery might triumph over speed. The hounds were trying to roust it out, rooting and tearing at the bramble to expose it lying low. Like any animal brought to bay, the coyote had nothing to lose by waiting. It would cling to the earth, deep in its covert, its smallness now its only salvation, while beyond the thorns its enemies thrashed to get it by the throat.

Ben beat his way to the lip of the draw, stood above it in the open sage, then dropped wearily to one knee and called for Tristan and Rex, beseeching each by name. He wished he could catch a glimpse of them. His apprehension was greater now. They should have come at the sound of his voice. He had no trust in the wolfhounds, and the cries emanating from the thickets below were fraught with cruelty.

A dark shape plunged from the sumac thicket not twenty yards from where he knelt, a soundless shadow low to the ground and almost formless in its haste, though Ben noted its bottle-shaped tail, canted left and deployed like a rudder, as the animal became aware of his presence and instantly changed course. He watched it twist off in a puff of dust and disappear into the sage. Behind it, three times as large, with arched loins and pointed muzzle, a wolfhound cleared the tangled draw with as much loud bucking as a lassoed horse, and charged after it. Then four more hounds emerged, and amid them he saw Rex.

Ben stumbled to higher ground. Out in the sage the hounds held moonlight, their flanks shimmering as they ate up ground, their long tails curled. Rex, already, had fallen far behind, while the distance between the hounds and the coyote diminished with astonishing speed. The lead hound surged, the coyote veered in a twisting evasion, the hound found it smoothly. The coyote wheeled to face them all with its teeth bared, snarling.

Two hounds leaped to hamstring the coyote; a third locked jaws between its shoulder blades, while the lead dog spun and drove in low to seize it by the throat. The coyote cartwheeled in a spray of dust but the hounds clung heedlessly to it, addressing its death from various angles, thrashing as though to rend the an-imal, pinning it to the dusty ground. Then Rex drove into the fray.

Ben, struggling free of his rucksack, plunged downhill with his gun. At the same moment, off to the east, he spotted a light on the ridge crest—the solitary headlamp of a vehicle—and then he recognized the silhouette of a dirt bike raising dust in a high channel as it careened in his direction.

He saw the world through his one good eye, through the wire-rimmed glasses from another time, appearing as though underwater as he stumbled down toward the welter of dogs, the dirt bike approaching through the sage. There was no time to ponder anything. The hounds, he saw, had finished with the coyote and were turning their attention to Rex.

His dog seemed astonished to find matters so, wheeling back against the tide of hounds, growling and baring his teeth. The hounds advanced with mad insistence and sent Rex sprawling into the dust, and then one seized him firmly at the hindquarters, another sunk his teeth into his withers, and a third clutched him at the throat.

Ben lashed into their midst yelling, raised his shotgun toward the stars, and fired a deafening warning. Immediately, the hounds desisted, tongues hanging, whimpering, except that one still had Rex by the throat and tossed him left and right.

Ben waded forward and slammed the butt of his shotgun against the ribs of this hound. He saw how desperate Rex was now, pinned by the throat against the earth, his breathing hollow, reedy. Ben kicked the wolfhound as hard as he could, first in the ribs and next in the head, swearing at it under his breath, but it was as though he hadn't kicked at all. And now there was no time for anything else, Rex was dying as he stood and watched, and he had to act without compromise and in a way he had much resisted acting in the years since his war ended. He set his teeth, grimacing, then pushed the barrel of his Winchester home against the ribs he'd kicked before, and squeezed the gun's front trigger.

He had no time to contemplate the outcome or to deliberate with morbid revulsion on the destructive force of his shotgun. Instead, he knelt to look at Rex.

Rex, on his side, twisted slowly in the dust, exerting himself like a drunk man. He meant to rise but could not find the means, and howled a note of pain such as Ben had never heard issue from the throat of any dog. Something like human suffering was in it—a high, piercing wail. The dog's hindquarters were clearly ravaged, and Ben feared his spine was broken. "I'm sorry, Rex," he said.

He tried to put a hand on Rex's flank, but the dog writhed, his howl surged higher, and Ben thought better of it. The wolf-hounds leered at him uncertainly, keeping a respectful distance. Ben swore at one, and it loped away.

The dirt bike stopped in front of him, throwing sand from under its tires, and the rider, whom he could not see—he had his headlamp aimed in Ben's direction—cut the low-throated motor. Ben caught a glimpse of one heavy boot as it came to rest against the sand, its steel toe protruding through the leather. He threw his free hand over his forehead and tried to make out the face of the rider, but to no avail: he was jacklighted. He was as blind and incapacitated as a deer in a car's high beams.

"Supposing you put out that light," he said. "The thing is blinding me."

"It's my coyote spotter," the rider called.

The light stayed on, blindingly. "Your dog looks pretty torn up," said the rider. "But mine there looks plain dead."

Rex howled, but the tenor of it had changed, as if he'd made an adjustment.

"I had to shoot him," Ben explained. "He was tearing up my dog."

"Whyn't you just kick him off?"

"I tried that. It didn't work."

"Always works with me," said the rider. "I don't know why it wouldn't."

"Your dog had mine by the throat," Ben said. "He was strangling him. I didn't have a choice."

"Well, you're too damn fast to use your shotgun," the rider admonished him. "I've kicked every one of these dogs before. You give 'em a kick, they listen."

"All right," said Ben. "Turn that light out."

"Hey," the rider answered firmly. "You don't have a right to be out here, so you don't have any leg to stand on, do you, asking me to put out my light. Not while you're on private property, out here trespassing, damn it."

His voice was that of the country around them, flat and laden with certainty and an intention to get things done. Ben recognized it as the voice of men he'd known in his youth and childhood, the voice of the farmers and ranchers of the basin, and he knew there was no arguing with it.

"I'm sorry," said Ben. "It shouldn't have happened. But like I said, I didn't have a choice."

The rider seemed to contemplate this. "Damn," he said. "Listen here. You pick up that gun of yours. Carefully."

Ben did so, holding it by the breechblock, in his right hand, away from him.

"It's a side-by-side," the rider said. "I believe I can see that from here."

"You're right," Ben answered. "It is."

"Well, you fired two shots," the rider said. "So unless you reloaded after shooting my dog, the barrels are empty right now."

"I didn't reload," Ben said. "Why don't I break the gun open?"

"No," said the rider. "I don't want that. I want you to toss it out in front of you. With one hand, as far as you can. And I want you to do it now."

Ben hesitated. The Winchester had been his father's gun. "Look," he said. "Throwing it that way might damage it. What if I just put it down?"

Again there was a pause from behind the light, the disembodied voice gone silent. "All right," the rider said at last. "You set it down there in front of you. I'm watching. You go ahead."

Ben set the gun down gently. "There," he said. "That's that now. I'm going to see to my dog."

"Hold on," said the rider. "I want you to go on over there and get beside that dog you killed and take a look at him for me."

"What?"

"Get over there and take a look. Just go on now. Do it."

"Listen," said Ben. "I'm sorry he's dead. But it's my dog who needs attending to, if—"

"That dog's going to be all right. You get over there."

"Listen," said Ben. "I—"

"Look," the rider said firmly. "Just you do like you're told. I got my gun pointed at your head and I want you over there."

"All right," Ben told him. "I'm going."

He stumbled to the dead wolfhound. It lay on its side about five feet off, where the force of the shot had thrown it. Its midsection, its withers and flanks, were bright with viscera and bits of white bone, and its head lay tilted at an unnatural angle, as if it had been severed and then reconnected incorrectly. "Okay," Ben said. "Now what?"

The rider adjusted his dirt bike slightly so as to throw a full light on Ben. "Read his collar there for me," he demanded. "The tag's at his throat. Read it."

Ben dropped stiffly to one knee and took the slain dog's collar. He worked it around until he found the tag. He squinted for a long moment. "Jim," he said. "I think it reads Jim. I can't tell. My eyes are bad."

"Jim," said the rider. "Damn."

"I'm sorry," Ben said. "I am."

The rider again fell silent. "Jim," he said after awhile.

"He had my dog by the throat," Ben explained.

"You shouldn't have done it," the rider said. "I don't want to hear about it."

"Fine," said Ben. "You won't."

"Damn," said the rider. "Come out in front now. And keep your hands up high."

Ben rose and stepped around the dog, his face averted from the light.

"On the ground, now. Face down, go on. And spread everything out."

"What for?"

"Just do like you're told."

"I have to look after my dog now."

"He can look after himself, damn it. You get down on the ground."

Ben lay down on his belly. He rested his cheek against the sand.

"All right," said the rider. "You turn your head. Look off toward the west there."

Ben did so.

"Just so you don't get nervous," said the rider. "I'm going to take a walk out here and pick your gun off the ground."

"Go ahead," said Ben.

"And this coyote here," the rider said. "I'm going to take his tail."

"All right," said Ben. "Go ahead."

He waited while the rider went about his business. One of the wolfhounds sat in Ben's view, dour and bored-looking. Ben listened to Rex's whimpering and the sound of the rider's boots. Then to the sound of his shotgun broke open, the metallic snap of the action. "Say," said the rider. "A regular antique. And some fancy looking engraving."

"It's a Winchester 21," said Ben.

"What do you figure it's worth?" said the rider. "Because replacing Jim'll cost me some. A dog like that isn't cheap."

"I don't really know," said Ben.

"Anyway," the rider informed him. "I can't exactly leave this here. You're liable to shoot me in the back with it. So I'm going to sell your shotgun off and get myself a new hound."

"Now wait a minute," Ben said. "That's highway robbery."

"Shut your mouth," said the rider. "You just shut your mouth now." He snapped the gun's action closed again. "Smooth," he said. "You just stay right there. Don't you move a muscle."

Ben made no reply.

The rider whistled his hounds in about him. Ben heard the soft trotting sounds of their feet. "I ought to make you bury Jim," the rider announced bitterly. "I ought to make you paw out a hole and give Jim a decent grave."

"I didn't have a choice," Ben said again. "Jim was strangling my Brittany."

He struggled to his feet, brushed the dirt from his jacket. "Shoot me if you want," he told the rider. "I'm looking after my dog."

"Shooting you'd just be more trouble," the rider answered him. "If shooting you could bring Jim back, I wouldn't even think to hesitate."

"It couldn't be helped," Ben said. "He was killing my dog, like I told you. I didn't have a choice."

"Well, now you don't have a shotgun," said the rider. "So it can't happen again."

"Go to hell," Ben said.

In the nimbus of light around the rider his remaining wolf-hounds milled. Ben could see them in silhouette, turning restlessly.

"I'll tell you what's got me worried," said the rider. "Maybe while I'm tearing out of here, you'll try'n plug me in the back."

"With what?" said Ben. "You stole my gun."

"With whatever else you got on you. Hidden down your pant leg."

The rider started up his bike with a hard shove that registered beyond the light. "I'll tell you what," he said above its roar. "If you can draw that fast and hit a moving target, 'specially blinded the way you are, you deserve to get your gun back."

He spun out suddenly in a spray of sand aimed in Ben's direction. The dirt bike turned, gathered speed, and found its way between clumps of sage, the pack of wolfhounds following it as though on a casual training run, the rider intentionally veering to and fro in an effort to dodge the bullets he imagined Ben was aiming at his back. But, of course, there were no such bullets. Ben had already turned away to kneel, a doctor, beside his dog.

SIX

Rex had ceased to struggle. He seemed languid in a way that suggested shock, yet his breathing came neither rapid nor shallow, nor did he heave with a racing pulse, nor did he seem submerged in a torpor, but merely patient with the state of things, containing his distress in some private space, yielding himself to fate.

Ben rose and located his rucksack, uphill in the sage. Then he knelt beside his dog, and with his medical kit propped open beside him, his headlamp fixed just over his eyes, took stock of Rex's wounds.

"I'm sorry, Rex," he whispered.

Using moist towelettes from his kit, he scrubbed his fingers thoroughly. He unraveled a length of sterile gauze and draped it over one shoulder. Gently he put one knee on the dog's head, the other in his rib cage. Rex lurched with a feeble resistance, growled, and lurched again. Ben formed the gauze into a hanging loop and maneuvered it over Rex's muzzle. "I'm sorry," he said. "I know it's not pleasant," and then he snugged it moderately tight, crossed the ends beneath the dog's chin, brought them up behind his ears and tied them off at the top of his head, so that Rex looked like a soldier with a head wound dressed on the field of battle. "There," said Ben. "We're done now."

Lifting his pinning weight from the dog, he lay a hand against Rex's flank and stroked him soothingly. "You're all right," he said. The dog whimpered through the makeshift muzzle. He did not seem entirely resigned; there was a hint of anxiety in his voice.

"You're all right," Ben said again. "I'm just going to look."

Under the headlamp, working through the fur, following the evidence of blood matted there, he took account of Rex's wounds: the left hamstring, between the hip and stifle, was punctured and swollen from hemorrhage; from shoulder to shoulder, low across the withers, a long run of skin had been ripped open, a gaping tear he could retract with his fingers to reveal the transparent fascia, the blunt tips of the spinal column, and the neat bone of the shoulder blades; and finally a broad tearing of the skin at Rex's throat, exposing one jugular.

For many years Ben had played, informally, the role of climbing expedition doctor, and his kit testified to that. He carried Compazine, erythromycin, butterfly bandages, roller gauze, Telfa and adhesive bandages. He also carried a scalpel with a set of blades and suture material in packets. Ben had field-stitched pocketknife cuts and an ice-ax laceration. He had, in the field, set a fractured arm, had reduced both shoulder and hip dislocations, and had seen to the construction of makeshift litters, transport slings, and crutches. Yet he had never field-stitched a dog before, and that was needed now. Rex had a desert journey in front of him. He would need his wounds closed first.

There was plenty of downed willow on the bank of the draw, and Ben dragged out what he could in ten minutes and with his spearpoint blade cut shavings. His cigarette lighter sparked sluggishly, so he squeezed it inside his armpit. He lit one of the paraffin fire starters and built, quickly, an extravagant blaze. The wizened willow burned hot and clean. He heaped long branches of it on, then sat by Rex, watching him, one hand brushing his coat. He hoped Tristan would smell the blaze and come to it soon, unharmed.

Ben drank again from his water bottle. He had not passed a night so physically taxing since the assault on the tunnels at Lago di Garda and the counterattacks the retreating Germans made against the town of Torbole. He sat close to the fire's heat, his body seeking to balance itself after the surges of marijuana and adrenaline that had coursed through it these past hours. His exertions and the tension of confronting the shotgun thief had been at war with his drug-induced reveries, the dream world he'd inhabited. But he felt at last that he was coming loose of his addled, soporific haze. He had entered a place of tired clarity. He was alert in some enervated, worn-out fashion, with the kind of acuity one arrives at in the aftermath of fever.

After awhile, when the dog seemed calm, he washed his hands a second time, drew out his suture needle, opened a packet of two-ought nylon suture—the only sort he had on hand—and rinsed the needle in antiseptic.

"All right," he said. "It'll hurt a little, Rex. A lot less than what you've been through, though. We'll just go at it carefully."

He pulled up his coat sleeves, adjusted his headlamp. He pinned Rex again beneath his knees, and held him down firmly with his left hand, which seemed the only workable position. He would have to throw stitches in a one-handed fashion, in a continuous pattern, like a seamstress. "Here we go," he whispered.

Rex heaved beneath him when he threw the first stitch and again when he tied the anchor, but after that the dog surrendered. He was braver than Ben had anticipated, more patient in the face of pain. Rex had always seemed too brash, too headlong and imprudently eager, but now he acquitted himself with a decorous restraint, and endured nobly. Ben felt a grudging admiration.

When the dog had been sutured at the throat and back, he slept as though to obliterate the truth of the various insults he'd suffered. Ben worked the muzzle free and caressed Rex's flank while examining his handiwork. The stitches, he concluded, were not too bad, given the conditions under which they'd been thrown. They gave him a curious pleasure.

He banked up his fire. He was hungry now, hungrier than he'd been in a long while, and he pulled the chukars out of his rucksack and skinned each in the light of his headlamp, cutting the backs and viscera out along with the second joints of the wings and culling the small legs and thighs. He skewered the breasts and the dark meat on willow sticks; the rest he buried in the sand. He drew himself up to the fire, into the smoke and light and heat, and with a slow care not to burn the meat, grilled it much as he'd done long ago, camping in the sage hills with Aidan.

Ben ate indulgently. He devoured the birds to the bones. They tasted better than anything he'd eaten in weeks, many weeks. He drank a little water, with an eye toward conserving; Rex, he knew, would need some. There were the blond girl's pumpkin seeds, and he ate them too, and thought of her with a distant ache and a faint trace of desire. It was not so much her as the thought of her, of having been once young himself, of Rachel's skin against his own, the smell of Rachel's mouth and throat—everything he could not replace or easily let go of. And why couldn't he detach himself from this earthly, mad desire? Why did he go on wanting a woman who no longer lived in this world? Her hold on him was still great, a need with roots in his core. To die, he thought, was to escape passion's grasp, but that was the last thing he wanted. Instead he wished to be seized by passion and pinioned, held in its palm forever—he could not imagine any other existence as embracing any real happiness.

Ben reserved some meat for Rex and limped to the draw for more willow branches. He worked slowly at the gathering of wood. It was important now to marshal his energies. A long journey lay ahead of him.

He stumbled onto the corpse of the coyote, its neck distended by the whiplashings of the hounds, its tail cut off by the dirtbike rider who'd stolen his father's shotgun. Then he remembered the dead wolfhound and went to it, his headlamp a grisly spotlight. The picture before him gave him pause, inspiring a stab of regret. The dog's abdomen was an abraded pulp of raw muscle, splintered bone, and purple, glistening viscera smelling of half-digested food. It was an unkind thing to look on, but worse to consider that he himself was the agent of this destruction. Ben dropped to one knee, penitent.

He took the chain from the dog's neck and read the tag's inscription. The dog's name, JIM, was in capital letters, but underneath it, in smaller type, was the name of his owner, the rider in the sage, and his address and telephone number. William C. Harden. He lived out of Malaga on Joe Miller Road. Ben squeezed the tag in his fist and raised his head to look into the east, where the sky now showed a paler hue, a cerulean tint on the horizon, the stars fading away. Dawn, he understood, was imminent, and he'd survived to witness it.

With the light he knew there was no choice left but to go in search of Tristan. He walked the rim of the willow draw, crossed at a swale of low wheatgrass that wet his boots with morning dew, and reconnoitered up the farther side with the steam puffing from his mouth. Twice he stopped to call into the silence, and in the heightened stillness that followed, he listened carefully. No answer came from any quarter, nor did he really expect one. For hours, now, he'd sensed the dog's fate, and it angered him to imagine it, this dog he had known for ten full years as a placid, sober, sensible companion, this dog he had brought home at seven weeks, not to hunt birds—he was not hunting then—but because he had wanted a dog in his life as a vestige of childhood. He'd seen Tristan through ringworm, coccidiosis, cherry eye, yeast otitis, then through a series of old-age maladies—gastroenteritis, a perineal hernia, a dislocating kneecap. He'd observed the dog's steady decline, his need to sit whenever possible, his waning zeal to cut up cover or pound his way through heavy brush, his great thoroughness everywhere to make up for an advancing sloth. That was when Ben brought home Rex, in the hope that the young dog might learn what he could in the seasons before Tristan died.

Another twenty minutes passed before Ben found Tristan at the base of a willow, sprawled in the position in which he slept, so that at first Ben hoped it was only sleep, until he saw Tristan's broken neck. The dog's head had been wrenched and distended, the skin at the throat torn open, the jugulars both severed. A penumbra of blood surrounded Tristan's head and stained the ground under him. Already his upturned eye had clouded, entirely obscuring the lens.

Ben carried Tristan up into the sageland, and at a little distance from his willow fire dug up the ground with the entrenching tool he carried in his rucksack. The grave was shallow and imperfect, but he had no strength to give Tristan more, and he laid him to rest with a little less care than he might have mustered at better times. Nevertheless, it was a grave of sorts, and the dog deserved at least that. He knelt beside it for a moment, then pressed the dog's eyes closed and shoveled the sand back over him.

It was that odd morning hour when clouds roll over after a clear fall night has passed, clouds that would douse the sage for an hour before marching eastward across the desert toward the Selkirk Mountains. Sitting beside his willow fire, Ben noted them, first and foremost, as a transformation in the texture of the air and a subduing of the morning light, as something imminent to be felt in all things, a sensation he remembered from childhood. He watched the sky and then, a third time, tucked his fingers under Rex's right hindleg to press against the femoral artery, measuring the dog's resting pulse, which seemed satisfactory enough. Then, his back warmed by the flames, he turned to watch the clouds come. They were high, dark plumes, fully massed in vertical columns like the ramparts of battleships, their lower reaches dense with rain. Ben, in the face of them, stirred himself and urgently loaded his rucksack.

He stood with his compass in his palm and estimated that in three miles of walking, shading slightly northeast, he would hit a piece of section road, or perhaps the reclamation project's West Canal, and then he could follow the roads or the canal another five miles into George. It was shorter, he guessed, than the walk into Vantage, and while he could not outrun the rain, he could get a jump on it if he set out now, and with luck he might even hail a ride, though chances were slim, in the Frenchman Hills, that many cars would be on the roads. George, Ben decided, might be ten miles off, which in his state of health and with the dog to carry meant the better part of the day ahead. His work stood starkly cut out for him.

He spread his blanket on the sand and, after a moment's hesitation, put one hand on Rex. The dog didn't move except to lift his head—but as if this were part of some bird-hunting dream—nor did he move when Ben took him by the forelegs and right hindleg, worked him gently into the center of the blanket, took up the corners in a jury-rigged sling, and devised himself a thick carrying knot against which to settle his hands.

He drank the last of his water. He would have to find more water soon, somewhere in the sage. He slipped his arms into the rucksack, hoisted the dog over one shoulder, and adjusted Rex's weight carefully, so as to not cause him pain. Bent under his burden, Ben doubted he could endure it. But he set out anyway, an old beleaguered man in the desert shuffling along on a cold fall morning with the rain clouds bearing down from the west, his back straining beneath his load. His chin was gray with stubble, his left eye swollen shut. He felt himself a node for travail, a gathering up of suffering into a single point. It was something he'd known long ago at war and on steep hard windy glaciers, where endless meditation on pain served only to deepen it. In desiring always not to suffer, one only heightened suffering. So now he employed the climber's trick, which was also the slogging infantryman's trick, of working to detach his mind from his body, of standing aside as best he could, observing his labored, torturous progress instead of enduring it. Yet he found, at his age, no relief in this. He was too downtrodden, beaten to the core. He stopped beside the next willow draw, eased the dog into the sand, and collapsed beside him, defeated.

Ben lay staring up at the sky, fiddling with the Italian carabiner. He worked its hinge aimlessly. He deliberated for a long time, until he came to a solution. Then, with his folding saw, he went down into the draw and cut two willow poles. He brought them out, smoothed them patiently, then lay one on either side of the dog, drew them into the shape of a V, and lashed their ends together. It took time to adjust things to his standards, but eventually he tied in Rex's blanket sling at the carrying knot he'd made earlier. Finally he ran a loop from the pole ends, clipped the Italian carabiner in, and slung the webbing over his shoulder to use as a makeshift harness.

It was a travois of the sort once used by Indians to move loads over the plains. As Ben pulled it, Rex swayed where he hung, snared like so much cargo. Still, it worked acceptably. The lashings held up sufficiently. The ring-angle piton, threaded on the carabiner, bobbled as Ben hauled his dog across the desert, and his travois scored the sand.

He felt a damp wind blowing at his back, and the first large raindrops began slapping hard against his shoulders. He remembered the poncho in his rucksack, but it seemed impossible to wear it and pull Rex without overheating. Ben was already drenched in a sweat that turned cold whenever he stopped, so he pushed on under the rain, pausing often to catch his breath with his elbows against his knees. The cold rain soaked the crown of his head, his neck, back, and ears.

Sometimes, journeying, he thought of other things, but mostly his mind was returned to the present by his agonized discomfort. He was worn-out, utterly exhausted, and at times his discipline fragmented and he felt himself begin to cave. The rain moved east, leaving the morning dour, the desert sand darkly stained with water, the sagebrush dripping wet. Ben's periods of rest lengthened. There was a rhythm to his thoughts when he struggled forward—panic alternating with redoubled efforts to cultivate detachment. Finally he rested on his back for so long that he had to quell the urge to rest permanently before setting out once more.

In two hours Ben left the sage behind and entered into a vast, dreary field, turned to lie fallow for the cold season. He crossed its unbroken, sodden expanse, traveling toward a line of power pylons and carefully keeping the big river bluffs over his shoulder to the southwest. Tucked under a ridge stood a stack of moldering hay bales five times as large as any farmhouse and covered with black tarpaulins. Ben came down into wheel ruts and a sign—HUNTING BY PERMIT ONLY—nailed into a fence post, and another that said LEASED HUNTING. The weeds at roadside had been burned off. It occurred to him that yes, he had trespassed last night, as the rider in the sage had indicated. He cleared a rise and south, toward Royal Slope, lay blond, sweeping, dry wheat fields and north toward the Caliche Lakes grew trellised apple trees stretching geometrically across the plateau reach.

He came down out of the Frenchman Hills, tortured beneath his burden. Below stretched big fields all disced under, and standing fields of grain corn. On the slope grew Gala apples trained on spindles in the European fashion, and a broad neat swath of Red Delicious trees in umbrella form, with centers open. The branch props were stacked by the orchard. There were no bins in sight.

At last he found a branch canal, which he knew to be laden with pathogens and the excreta of cattle, water he would never imagine drinking at any but desperate times. Now he filled his bottles with it, dropped into each an iodine pill, waited for the crystals to dissolve, and drank with steady greed. The taste was abhorrent; he spat it out. He untied Rex's traveling hammock, let him lap water from his palm, and fed him the remaining chukar meat.

Ben stroked the dog's coat softly. Rex sat on the blanket looking about, pawing tentatively. Finally, he pushed into a standing position, and keeping one foot free of the ground, hobbled forward on the other three.

"You're looking good," Ben called after him. "You're looking better, Rex."

The dog limped off about twenty yards, and with considerable trouble, whining a little, defeated in the sand. He tried for a time to lick his wounds. He turned, hopping, ran his tongue along his hamstring, poked his nose into folds of his coat, then hobbled off another ten yards and urinated feebly, stumbling in the midst of his stream. Licking his wounds again, he limped to the blanket, where Ben was already dismantling the travois. "Looks like you can walk," Ben said.

He looped the carabiner once more around his neck. It bounced against his sternum as he walked.

They limped on, two invalids, two lame wanderers in the desert. They hobbled across the plateau reach and at noon came out on a section road. They passed a pile of rubble in a ditch—stone, bricks, slab concrete—and then a draw strewn with worn-out tires and the rusting hulks of appliances—refrigerators, freezers, dryers. There were dusty side roads, irrigation pumps, the canal water drifting lazily in its course of half-round concrete. A sign sat mounted on a metal post, PURPLE LOOSESTRIFE HARMS WETLANDS AND WATERWAYS, and a few cattails grew here and there where the irrigating water spilled over. They'd come into true farm country. There were mobile homes with satellite dishes. There were lines of poplars, irrigated fields, and newly planted orchards. They came to an intersection with a paved two-lane that Ben guessed was the Beverly-Burke Road as it cut north from Low Gap Pass back in the Frenchman Hills.

They traveled on across the plateau, past mailboxes, newspaper flutes, and big aluminum silos. They surprised three coots on a brackish pond, who began to swim as Ben and Rex approached, paddling silently around a corner. The plain lay broken by shade trees and silhouetted farm buildings far into the east. There were no cars anywhere. Some time after two o'clock they passed what remained of the George Feed Store with its window frames devoid of glass, a mobile-home park laid out behind poplars, a gravel yard full of irrigating pipe, and finally a street of unkempt homes with ragged squares of lawn. They passed the Church of the Assembly of God and the George Community Hall. There was a sign in English and then in Spanish: WARNING NEIGHBOR-HOOD CRIME WATCH. ALERTA SE ESTA VIGILANDO LE VECINDAD. They limped on into the town of George, the doctor first and behind him his dog, and when they came across a boy behind a chain-link fence who was changing an excavator's hydraulic hose—a boy dressed in a mechanic's grease suit, haggard-thin, his hair worn long, a cigarette hanging from his lips—Ben asked in a weary voice if there was a vet somewhere in town. The boy replied that he didn't know, cast an eye briefly over them, and then, adjusting his cigarette, went back to his labors.

At the Colonial Market, Ben selected a can of dog food, a gallon of spring water, a quart of prune juice, five bags of salted peanuts, a banana, and a Winesap apple. It was warm inside, and he lingered; there were no other customers. One clerk worked the checkout stand and another the video counter. All the shelves seemed a quarter stocked, as if the place was going out of business. There were mostly canned goods and little that was fresh—two heads of iceberg lettuce, a clutch of bananas, a few tomatoes, some apples, a handful of pears. A glass case displayed cheap souvenirs—spoons, mugs, postcards, American flags, painted plates.

The checkstand clerk, a teenage girl, was unfriendly in a neutral fashion, offering nothing in the way of pleasantries when he approached her with his armload of goods, though she gawked at his swollen eye. "Is there a vet in town?" he asked.

"Quincy," she answered. "Eleven miles."

"I don't have a way to get to Quincy," Ben explained to her. "You don't have a vet here, do you—someone right here in town?"

"Only on Tuesdays," replied the girl. "The vet comes Tuesdays, runs a clinic."

He paid with a twenty-dollar bill, and she grew more comfortable. "It's a doctor you need, not a vet," she said. " 'Cept we don't have one of those, either. Closest doctor's up in Quincy."

"I don't need a doctor," Ben said.

He found Rex where he'd left him, splayed out in front of the store. They made their way to a copse of willows, where there were two hubcaps just behind a log, among desiccated roof tiles and rotting sheaves of particleboard, and here he opened the can of dog food and dislodged the meat into one of the hubcaps with the length of his spear-point blade.

The dog choked the food down instantly. Ben watered him and thought of Tristan buried out there in the sage. The night previous seemed unreal. Except that his shotgun and Tristan were missing, it might have been only a nightmare.

Examining the stitches he'd put in Rex that morning, he decided they'd held together sufficiently during the desert crossing. He rinsed them a little with the spring water, then sat on the ground with his back against the log, sighed, and drank long and hard.

Ben ate a small bag of peanuts. The salt and oil tasted good, and he ate a second bag. He drank half the prune juice, but it didn't slake his thirst, so he followed it with long draughts of spring water. He ate the banana and the Winesap apple. It was a good apple for store-bought, sweet and properly ripened. He ate it to its core, happily, and wished he had another.

A farmer passed in a mud-splashed pickup and gaped at him through the side window. Another truck rumbled by and the people in it, a boy and a girl, leaned forward to gawk at him. In his dishevelment, Ben understood, he cut a disconcerting figure, a transient pauper, a graybeard drifter, a derelict or vagrant. A rootless old bum who had wandered into town to die in a corner or sleep in a barn, piss against the tire of a car, eat an apple squatting on the ground, feed his dog from a cast-off hubcap. He knew what he looked like suddenly, and for a moment he wanted to laugh.

Sitting there with his jug in his lap, he thought of those Hindu wanderers he'd seen on a public television documentary, mendicants abroad with begging bowls, dressed in rags and clutching staffs, divested of all other property, seeking to meet the world unencumbered, aspiring, always, toward—what did they call it?—atman, the self, God. They had a better chance when liberated from possessions, moving freely through the world. There were no distractions in this way of life, everything pared to the barest essentials: food, water, rumination. It wasn't the life he had chosen to live, but it seemed more comprehensible now, as he sat on the ground reduced by exhaustion to an appreciation of simple pleasures. He recalled reading once that the Hindus saw life in four progressive stages: twenty years a youth, twenty years a fighter—one needed nothing martial to pursue this phase—twenty years as head of a household, and twenty in the cultivation of the spirit. It was part of this final stage that he was going to miss by dying of colon cancer, as if the last movement of a symphony had been truncated, rendering all before it pointless, stripping it of fundamental meanings and preventing it from achieving its effect of harmony and completeness. A few more years of twilight, melancholy perhaps, but beautiful.

Ben and Rex shuffled on. They hiked along Montmorency Boulevard with its median grass and poplar trees. They passed a sign for a Lutheran Church declaring its membership in the Missouri Synod. The leaves had come down everywhere, and the wind had whisked them into the gutters, where they were ground to an auburn paste.

Out by the interstate, at Martha's Inn, a stock truck sat in a parking lot of dark, wind-rippled puddles. Underneath the highway sign, starkly gargantuan up on its pole—

MARTHA'S INN

CAFE, FAMILY DINING, LOUNGE

CREDIT CARDS ACCEPTED

—sat two more gaudy tractor-trailers, one inscribed with the name *Glory*, the other painted pearl-black with jaunty purple roof faring. Ben crossed in front of them, tied Rex near the inn's doorway, and settled him on the blanket. "Wait right here," he said softly. "I'm going to get you to a vet."

He pushed into the foyer with its Pepsi machine and inert, still video games. He pressed on through to the heat of the place—a snug, agreeable cookstove heat—and holding his rucksack at his side, waited in front of the glass cashier's counter where a painting of a black Lab was displayed for sale, another of three elk poised in a field, a third of an iridescent waterfall.

Ben drew off his cap and entered the dining room. A mother and daughter were playing cards and eating a plate of onion rings. A man with a gray high pompadour scrutinized Ben with what looked to be a casual ill will for strangers. A wind-furrowed farmer in a flannel shirt trembled over his coffee cup and worked on a wedge of pie. At a table nearby sat a crowd of young people eating hamburgers and french fries. One was swellingly pregnant. She pulled on her soft drink, then on a cigarette. A name was tattooed on her shoulder.

Ben washed in the bathroom. A vaultlike dispensary sold glow-in-the-dark condoms, the directions for their purchase inscribed on a decal in both Spanish and English. Ben combed his hair, brushed his teeth, and cleaned the lenses of his glasses. He dried his face and hands on paper towels, then paused to look at himself. His eye had blackened obscenely now. He looked, he thought, horribly old, as smashed and bruised as a boxer.

It was difficult to accept that the face in the mirror belonged to him and could not be altered, the ravages of time reversed. But he gathered himself, pressed his hair into place, and tried to appear presentable. He dried his neck with a paper towel and examined his face in profile. His clothes were still wet from that morning's rain, and in the heat of the place he felt chilled.

He strode onto the restaurant floor, set his rucksack against his leg, worked his wallet free of his pocket, and holding three twenty-dollar bills high, announced in the firmest voice he could muster that his dog waited, injured, outside, that he needed to get him to a vet right away, and for anyone willing to take him up to Quincy there was sixty dollars in it.

A man stood up. Tall, thin, and hollow-eyed, he wore pointed, black sideburns. He wiped his lips with a napkin as he rose, then dropped it on his table. "I'll do it," he said. "Let's go."

His name was Stu Robinson. He shook Ben's hand in his tall lanky way. He wore cowboy boots and a tight red windbreaker with the name of a saloon in Arizona printed in white across its back. "What happened to your eye?" he asked.

"I was in a car wreck," Ben explained. "Up in Snoqualmie Pass."

"Christ," Stu Robinson said with a wince. "Don't even tell me about it."

They went outside. It was late in the day now. The light had begun to fade.

Robinson was interested in Rex's wounds and in the story of the dog fight. He listened to Ben's brief, colorless account with no sign of questioning its omissions. He took the story of the dusk chukar hunt and the desert camp and the coursing hounds at face value, it appeared. Then he bent over Rex on his storklike legs to examine the stitches more closely. "I had a German short-hair fell off a cliff once and broke one of his hind legs. Out hunting quail."

"Where was this?"

"West Texas."

"Is that where you're from?"

"Montana."

"Rex is a pretty good quail dog and adequate on pheasant, too."

"I always kept shorthairs," Robinson said. "But I know Brittanies to be good dogs. I was just partial to shorthairs."

He knelt a moment longer beside Rex, fingering his pock-marked chin. Robinson was acne-scarred in a raw, infected, graphic way, his face broken out in virulent eruptions of scarlet, blue, and purple. "I'm driving that tractor-trailer," he explained. "We can put him up in the sleeper, maybe. He'll ride comfortable there."

"I appreciate that," said Ben.

The truck's refrigeration was running—overworked, rattling compressors. "Restaurant salad," Robinson said, when Ben asked him about it. "Twenty-pound sacks of restaurant salad I'm taking to Calgary."

He had christened his truck the *Sweet Dreams Express*, a Freightliner painted freshly blue, loud racing stripes across its flanks, immaculate, pristine.

Robinson scrabbled up the passenger-side steps and pulled back the door to the sleeper. He set Ben's rucksack inside, then took the dog bundled up in the blanket. Rex gave no fight.

They climbed into the cab—it smelled faintly of diesel fuel—and Robinson pressured up the air brakes. The cab had the look and feel of a sarcophagus constructed out of gray plastic. It was high off the road and efficiently compact, like the cockpit of a jetliner. The roof and walls were covered with gray fabric, and everything seemed fastidiously kept, except that the windshield was much bug-bitten for this late in the fall.

Ben turned to survey Rex's situation. The dog lay staring back at him, as though these circumstances were dubious, beyond all understanding. The sleeper unit was like a motel room, clean, sterile, claustrophobic. A neatly made bed, a refrigerator, a closet, and a television set mounted in one corner. A remote-control channel switcher lay squarely in the middle of Robinson's plumped pillow. "This is something," Ben said. "I've never seen this before."

Robinson shook his head, rubbed his jaw, and picked at the tip of one sideburn. "What you see back there is my home," he said. "This is where I live."

"All year round?"

"Just about."

"You don't have a house?"

"This is it."

"You don't have a family waiting somewhere?"

"This is it," Robinson repeated.

"Well," said Ben. "I've never seen this before."

"It's a good rig," said Robinson.

Ben's heart recoiled. The lean, spare life of the wanderer, which had held some attraction an hour before, held no attraction now. It was time, he thought, to head home, defeated. What in God's name was he doing out here, beaten the way he was? He tried to embrace some other end than the one he'd chosen for himself— he thought of dying in a hospital room, imagined languishing in one. He fell silent and stared out the window. There were no good answers to important questions. He tried to picture the shape of Stu Robinson's final days, but he couldn't even begin.

Robinson shifted gears, let out the clutch, and teased his truck from its spot. He turned to the left, then leaned to his right to check his rearview mirrors. The *Sweet Dreams Express* bounced over deep potholes and onto the Frontage Road. They passed a field of wind-blown corn, beyond which cars flew by on the highway, toward Vantage and Moses Lake, toward both Seattle and Spokane. Robinson ground patiently through the gears, and the truck crossed over the interstate and onto Highway 281, the way north to Quincy.

The road made a bend just after the interstate, then straightened to run through fields of seed peas, potatoes, alfalfa, peppermint, and wheat. There was a stand of low bare walnut trees and a feed lot thronged with cattle. It was not familiar as the country of Ben's youth, because it had been so deeply alchemized by the coming of irrigated water. What he recalled as wastes of sagebrush broken by coulees and willow draws was now fields and orchards. The river of his youth had been diverted and poured out broadly across the land to seep through dirt to the roots of crops instead of running in its bed. The river was no longer a river, and the desert was no longer a desert. Nothing was as it had been.

He knew what had happened to the sagelands. He himself had helped burn them. Then men like his father had seized the river without a trace of evil in their hearts, sure of themselves but ignorant, and children of their time entirely, with no other bearings to rely on. Irrigators and fruit-tree growers, they believed the river to be theirs. His own life spanned that time and this, and so he believed in the old fast river as much as he believed in apple orchards, and yet he saw that the two were at odds, the river defeated that apples might grow as far away as Royal Slope. It made no more sense to love the river and at the same time kill it growing apples than it made sense to love small birds on the wing and shoot them over pointing dogs. But he'd come into the world in another time, a time immune to these contradictions, and in the end he couldn't shake old ways any more than he could shake his name.

He was coming into the place he'd sought when he'd set out on his journey. From Quincy it was six miles to the Columbia. Over the crest of Babcock Ridge and across the mouth of Lynch Coulee, beyond the trading post at Trinidad, and then upriver toward Rock Island. Northwest of Baird and Willow Springs, but southwest of Moses Coulee. Southwest of the Burlington Northern Line and the road to Palisades. It was the place Ben wanted to end his life, if he could only get to it. A surcease from living where his life had started. A neat, uncomplicated end.

SEVEN

Just before dusk they pulled into Quincy at the junction with Highway 28, the Ephrata-Wenatchee Road. Robinson asked a boy at a gas station where a veterinarian might be found, and the boy, without any hesitation, gave elaborate directions. Then they drove west down 28 until they were opposite the Quincy cemetery, not far from a cold-storage warehouse as cavernous as an airplane hangar. Robinson pulled into the parking lot of a low building made of cinder blocks, the Quincy Veterinary Clinic. Its lights were out, it was late on a Sunday, but posted on the window just left of the door was the after-hours telephone number, which Robinson wrote down. "We'll get this thing licked," he said.

They found a phone booth at the Quincy Deli-Mart. Ben climbed down the ladder steps while Robinson sat with the engine running, clawing his chin and cheeks. In the parking lot Ben drew his hunting coat close and looked across at the cold-storage warehouse, then at the gate of the cemetery. The October wind blew east across the headstones. Darkness was settling in.

He dialed the after-hours number, but it gave him only a recorded voice instructing him to call a cellular phone number or a second number Ben took to be the veterinarian's home. He dialed the latter, and a woman answered; he asked for the vet and she said, flatly, "I *am* the vet. Is this an emergency?" Ben said it definitely was, he was standing in front of the deli-mart, his dog was severely wounded. "How severely is severely?" asked the vet, and he explained to her that he was a doctor and detailed the nature of the dog's wounds, the treatment he'd administered, and the distance he and the dog had traveled, from Vantage to George, on foot. "Go back over to my office," said the vet, "and wait for me, right out front. Give me fifteen minutes."

"All right," said Ben. "I appreciate it."

"Fifteen minutes," said the vet.

Robinson drove Ben back to the clinic, and they sat in the cab with the engine running while the darkness deepened outside. The *Sweet Dreams Express* hummed extravagantly: its cab felt snug and warm. Ben gave Robinson the sixty dollars, which Robinson said would buy enough diesel fuel to get him five miles up the road, maybe ten if the price of fuel hadn't gone up in the last three minutes. They laughed at this and drank Robinson's coffee, thick and overly sugared. Holding plastic cups in hand, they turned together to check on Rex, who looked content to be where he was, asleep sprawled on the floor. Robinson tuned in the radio traffic and lit a cigarette. He said he'd come up north from The Dalles on Highway 97, but at Ellensburg he'd headed east in order to avoid Swauk Pass. It was all the same to him, he said, if he hit the 97 at Wenatchee or followed the 28 to Soap

Lake and caught the 17 to Brewster. He could make Wenatchee or Ephrata for the night or drive on up into the Okanogan and pass the night at Omak. He could stop anywhere, he said. It didn't really make any difference. He had a bed and enough food— salad to feed two armies. Sitting here didn't mean anything, twenty, thirty minutes either way.

"You're not on a schedule?"

"There's leeway in it."

"How many years have you been driving like this?"

"Sixteen. I quit for a couple once."

"What did you do?"

"I tried out a day job. Down in Texas."

"How was that?"

"Not so good."

"You didn't like it?"

"I don't know. It wasn't the job so much, I guess. It was being married did me in, put me back on the road."

Ben looked at him. "Married?"

"Not even for seven months. If you want to call that married."

"I don't know," answered Ben.

Robinson picked at a sideburn. He adjusted the heat in the cab.

"I was married for fifty years," said Ben. But he couldn't think what he might add to this. He didn't even know why he'd offered it.

"*Was* married," Robinson said. "Now you've moved along?"

"No, I haven't," Ben replied. "My wife died nineteen months ago."

Robinson nodded and held a respectful silence. "How's your eye?" he said finally.

"It's doing all right."

"Dog seems comfortable."

"I'd just as soon see the vet show up. He needs attending to."

"We can wait," Robinson assured him. "However long it takes."

"You don't have to," Ben said.

When the vet pulled in, Robinson helped; from the door of the sleeper unit he lowered the dog's blanket-sling as though from a helicopter cable. Then he looked down on both of them, rubbing his ravaged face. "All right," he called, with an air of finality. "The best of luck with everything." And he cast his eyes in a far-off direction, as if something there drew his attention.

"How far is it up to Calgary?" Ben asked.

"Not too far. Maybe five hundred miles."

"All right," said Ben. "Good luck with it."

"All right," answered Robinson. "Same to you."

The veterinarian was a solid young woman with the sturdy hands and face of a farmgirl and thick, soda-bottle glasses. She spoke in the direct, firm way of the country, with the vigorous practicality and certainty that had remade the sage desert into fields. Kneeling in the parking lot, she examined Rex, and Ben guessed she was not yet thirty, even though her professional manner suggested years of experience. There was something irrepressibly young in her, some vague crack in her doctorly demeanor through which her private self seeped as she introduced herself as Dr. Peterson and made note of his blackened eye without commenting on it. He had the idea she was shelving small talk until some later, less critical time, after the dog was treated. There were Petersons, he knew, up and down the plateau, from Manson south to Royal Slope—more Peter*sons* than Peter*sens*— and he guessed that she was a daughter of this clan, born and raised in the river basin amid the builders of the dams and farms and the fruit and potato growers. He guessed she rode horses from an early age and had decided as a child to become a vet, staunchly sticking with her girlhood plan even as the romance wore off and she found it to be hard work. She must have been admired for her perseverance, praised by her grandparents, aunts and uncles, her church pastor, Bible class instructor, the leader of her 4-H group—all, perhaps, had smiled on her pursuit of a profession both honorable and useful. Now there was no hint of hesitation in her as she turned the lock to the clinic door and held it open wide for him so he could haul Rex inside. He found, despite her youth, that he trusted her. She was just the sort to do well by Rex. She communicated proficiency, as all good doctors must.

"There's a registration form on the counter," she said. "Go ahead and fill one out, and I'll get things started back here."

She left, and Ben collapsed on a bench, where he massaged the ache in his side for a while before filling in the form. Rex lay sprawled at his feet.

On the counter he found her business card: ILSE PETERSON, DVM, DEDICATED AND CARING. A bubbling aquarium full of angelfish, an orange canary in a spacious cage, pamphlets on canine parvovirus and enterotoxemia in sheep, copies of *Cat Fancy* magazine. The room was orderly, efficient, well lit, with a pill dispensary behind the counter and notices posted high on the walls: *Does Your Pet Have Bad Breath? Ask about Our Dental Program. Tired of Getting Scratched? We Have Safe Pet Carriers. Member Quincy Valley Chamber of Commerce—Promised Land of the Columbia Basin. Please Keep Your Pet Leashed.*

Ilse Peterson hurried around a corner and opened a file cabinet. "You can bring him in," she called.

Ben took Rex up in the blanket sling and followed her into a warren of rooms, past an office with shelves of neat veterinary texts, past a tiny operating theater, finally into an examining room—an anesthesia machine on wheels, a stainless steel table with a drain hole and bucket, a bright, adjustable light overhead, and an electric razor poised high, hung from a retractable cord.

"Good, then," Dr. Peterson said. "Let's take a look at him."

Ben set Rex on the stainless steel table and assessed, critically, the equipment on hand: a blood cell counter, a blood chemistry unit, a high-powered tissue microscope, an X-ray machine with folded lead drapes, a pair of sealed plastic bins for the safe disposal of waste. "Just relax now," the vet said to Rex, one hand stroking the top of his head, the other patting his dusty side. "We'll find out what your problem is and see what we can do about it."

There was no condescension in her voice. She did not pretend the dog was a child or a difficult human being. She pressed her glasses against the bridge of her nose, pulled her light closer. Then she checked Rex's feet for warmth. She pressed on his gums, pinched the skin at his forehead, palpated his chest, stroked him. "So you're a doctor," she said.

"I was a doctor," Ben told her. "I've been retired for a while."

"Where at?"

"Over in Seattle."

"General practice?"

"Thoracic surgeon."

She nodded a bemused assent. "I hate to say it," she said over her shoulder, "but you don't much look like anyone's idea of a surgeon just now."

"It's a long story," Ben said. "I was in a car wreck yesterday."

"You can tell me later," Dr. Peterson said. "In the meantime, I could use some help. There's a lot of resuturing that'll have to be done. I'm going to have to put him under, set up his IV support. And you're going to have to sign a consent form. We're looking at two or three hours here—a hundred fifty to three hundred dollars."

"I'll stay," said Ben. "I want to."

"It'll get him off the table quicker."

"Whatever I can do," said Ben.

He unbuttoned his field jacket, peeled it off, and set it on the floor in a corner. It had been nineteen months since his last surgery—repairing a human heart in trouble, not this work of assisting a veterinarian in sewing up a dog. Nevertheless, he felt a twinge of excitement. He rolled up his sleeves and washed his hands. He had not expected anything like this. Strange and stranger still, he thought, that at a moment in which he'd intended to be dead, rotting and eaten by flies in the sage country, he was instead scrubbing for surgery as he had thousands of times.

Dr. Peterson asked Ben to hold Rex down while she administered ketamine and Valium, leaving the needle in the dog's cephalic vein and taping the catheter to his foreleg. They watched while Rex succumbed to the Valium and fell into a wide-eyed haze. Dr. Peterson set up an IV; Ben held the dog's maw gently open while she fed in an endotracheal tube, inflated the cuff to tighten it, and tied it securely in place. She pulled the anesthesia machine closer, opened the valves to the oxygen and isoflurane canisters, then hooked up Rex's tube. Watching the meters, she made her adjustments. She leaned in close, adjusted her glasses, and finely tuned the valves. Rex went under swiftly, sagging low against the beanbag mattress, his eyelids fluttering closed. Peterson checked the valves again. "All right," she said. "Now 500 milligrams of Keflin by slow injection in the access port of the IV tube, if you want to do that."

"I'll take care of it," said Ben.

While he administered the antibiotic, Dr. Peterson injected a painkiller, butorphanol, subcutaneously. Then she plunged into a thorough evaluation, bringing a strong light close to her work and cutting away the field stitches. "These are very well done," she said. "They kept most of the dirt out."

"I had to throw them one-handed," said Ben. "Otherwise, they'd be better."

"They're good," she said. "They're excellent."

She palpated the ligaments and tendons of the left hamstring, then pulled the razor on its retractable cord and shaved away the hair. Ben ran the hand suction for her. The skin looked badly punctured and hemorrhaged. She palpated everything one more time. "I'm looking for laxity in the joint," she said. "It seems all right. It feels pretty good. I don't think there's serious damage."

"That's good," said Ben.

He brushed the stitches down the drain hole. At the vet's direction, he eased the blanket free, and replaced it with a thick padded mattress of polystyrene beads. Peterson flushed the punctures with saline and scrubbed them with an iodine solution, painting the skin a garish orange. She retracted the largest hole—a true laceration, not merely a puncture—and peered inside, blinking.

"I'll tell you what we've got here," she said. "The semitendinosus muscle is pretty badly torn up, but there's no damage to the Achilles tendon. He's a lucky dog on that score. This is something that will heal."

"Which muscle?"

"The semitendinosus."

"The tendon is all right?"

"It seems fine."

Peterson doused the wound with more saline and applied a wet dressing of sterile gauze. Then she addressed the other wounds. "Skin-deep," she assured Ben. "There's no problem anywhere here. It's a sewing job, and we're done."

She asked Ben to do the skin prep. He lavaged copiously with saline and scrubbed the wounds with the iodine until the skin gleamed brightly. Peterson took the dog's pulse and listened to his breathing. "All right," she said. "We're moving into my operating room. Why don't you carry the dog and the mattress? I'll wheel the anesthesia and bring along the IV bags."

They settled Rex in the operating room and hooked up the heart monitor. Peterson applied the final Betadine prep and filled the lavage basin with saline. Then they opened the sterile surgery packs, the gown packs, and the lid to the cold tray, scrubbed up, put on cloth caps, and wrestled into masks, gowns, and gloves. Peterson laid blue drapes over Rex, framing the hamstring wound. From the cold tray she selected the Metzenbaum scissors. Then she went about debriding the skin, laying it asunder.

Ben assisted with the retractors. There were bits of sand and strands of hair inside, and the vet picked at them methodically, with her fingers first and then with tweezers, breathing roughly through her nose. "In a minute here I'll irrigate," she said. "Sixty cc's at a time will do. And a 14-gauge needle."

"I'll put it together," Ben said.

He set it up for her. She made sure he'd done it right, and after that seemed to settle on a basic trust in him. She irrigated, watching for debris, then flushed the wound again. "It's plenty clean," she concluded. "I think we've doused the road dust here from all the way back to Vantage."

"It looks good," Ben agreed.

Peterson selected a sterile packet of single-ought suture material. They discussed the merits of two stitching approaches and settled on a mattress pattern. Then he watched her take the stitches, with pleasure and no small admiration for her precise and vigorous work. She threw them with adroit small turns of the wrist and took up the tension smoothly. She was accomplished in a plain and steady way. Her fingers were strong but surprisingly fluid. She didn't flag or grow restless, and she paid attention to the lay of each stitch, making fine adjustments, leaving no dimples or wrinkles.

Ben assisted in the placing of the Penrose drain. She irrigated liberally while he opened a packet of three-ought suture for her to use subcutaneously. Standing back, she checked the meters on the anesthesia canisters. "The hard part's over," she said.

"You're an accomplished doctor."

"It isn't heart surgery."

"It's not that different."

"Not technically." She pushed, again, at the bridge of her glasses with the back of her wrist. "But I imagine it was probably more difficult for you to face whoever was out there in the waiting room when you had to deliver bad news."

"I never liked that very much," said Ben.

"I don't like it, either," said Dr. Peterson. "But I would guess it's harder for a doctor than a vet. As much as people love their dogs."

She used three-ought suture to bring together the subcutaneous tissue and closed the skin with a stapler. She moved on to the shoulder blades, scrubbing again with iodine, debriding the wound to leave clean edges and irrigating with saline. She closed the shoulder blades and then the throat, while Ben watched and rubbed his side. He admired the patient tidiness of it. Dr. Peterson, the last staple inserted, surveyed her handiwork critically. Then she gave Rex a half cc of butorphanol and a dose of acepromazine, disconnected the heart monitor, backed down the valves on the anesthesia machine and, when Rex began to blink and swallow, slid the tube from his throat. Prying open an eyelid, she looked at the dog's pupil. "He'll come around soon," she said.

They dropped their caps and gowns in a bin, and Dr. Peterson gave Ben a ten-day supply of an antibiotic, and five days' worth of a pain reliever. Then they washed and went to her office. She sat at her desk writing copious notes and spoke to him in a preoccupied fashion, her glasses low on her nose. The dog would stay overnight with her. She recommended thorough rest for the leg. The staples could be removed by his vet in Seattle, after he got home. Ten days later, limited exercise. The drains were due out in forty-eight hours, something Ben could do himself, unless he wanted his vet to. The antibiotic should run to the end, he shouldn't stop it short. Eat and drink as normal, but rest, no hunting for a while. Perhaps, with luck, come Thanksgiving, Rex would hunt birds again.

"The dog lives to hunt," Ben told her. "It's all he ever wants to do."

"Well, six weeks or so and he'll be doing it. But maybe you're anthropomorphizing. Maybe you live to hunt."

"Not really," said Ben.

Peterson slid off her glasses, rubbed her eyes with the palms of her hands, and massaged her eyelids with her fingertips, the pen still between her fingers. "So what happened to you?" she asked.

"I just about killed myself. In Snoqualmie Pass."

"You what, now?"

"I hit a tree. Right at the summit. Some kids in a Volkswagen van came along and took me down to Vantage."

"You and the dog."

"Me and two dogs. I lost the other. I was hunting chukars out on the breaks. They ran off with some coursing hounds, and my other dog was killed."

"Coursing hounds?"

"Irish wolfhounds, a pack of them. They were coursing coyotes on the river breaks."

"Irish wolfhounds," Dr. Peterson said. "That'd be Bill Harden's dogs. He's the only one around here who keeps Irish wolfhounds."

"Bill Harden. Rides a dirt bike?"

"I don't know. Could be. But anyway he's got a pack of wolfhounds. I've seen them out at dog shows."

"He's breeding them?"

"I'm not sure. Used to, I think. They have a good-size orchard, the Hardens, out back of Malaga there. Wolfhound Orchard, they call it."

"Wolfhound Orchard," Ben said.

She slid her glasses back into place and finally put her pen down. "Wolfhounds," she said. "That makes a lot of sense. The way your dog was ripped up—exactly what I'd expect to see from a run-in with Irish wolfhounds. That or a broken neck."

"That's what happened to my other dog," said Ben. "He was too old to fight back, I guess. It might be just as well."

"I don't know," Dr. Peterson answered. "Better old than dead."

"Maybe," said Ben. "It's a question."

She rocked back in her desk chair. "So you walked up here?" she asked.

"I stitched up Rex and carried him to George. Most of the way. He walked some."

"It's a long walk."

"I didn't have a choice."

"The whole thing sounds crazy."

"It is crazy."

"This is what you get for killing little birds. Maybe you should take up golf."

"That's a lot of walking, too, from what I understand."

Dr. Peterson smiled. "You're up a creek," she said. "Do you have any kind of plan?"

"Sleep," said Ben. "My plan is to sleep, like a dead man."

"Sleep," she repeated. "Your best bet's probably two doors east, the motel just down the street over here." She pointed at the wall as if it meant something to him. "You take a right, and you're there."

"That sounds perfect," said Ben.

"Come by here when you wake up. It'll be two hundred and fifty dollars. And I don't take credit cards."

"All right," said Ben. "Two fifty."

"Two minutes' worth of open heart surgery is two hours' worth of dog surgery," Ilse Peterson declared. "That's one difference between dogs and people we didn't talk about."

"Malpractice is bigger, too," said Ben.

She nodded and smiled. "I'll drive you over to the motel," she said. "You look like you're ready to collapse."

She dropped him off, and he thanked her for it, and by way of an answer she advised rest and no fretting about the dog. When he stepped from her car, a wind from the mountains struck him in the face, dry and carrying the smell of apples and of alfalfa fields put to sleep for the winter. It was a smell Ben remembered from childhood.

He went in and set his rucksack on the floor. The boy at the front desk greeted him crisply. Young, pudgy, manicured, he moved bits of paper about with a flourish, conducting the ritual of a motel check-in as though its details were pleasurable. He took pains to angle his stapler, and laid the strips from the computer paper neatly in a plastic garbage pail. "Free coffee," he told Ben, "is right behind you. Help yourself, anytime."

He put the room key on the counter. "What happened to your eye?" he asked.

"I'm a boxer," Ben told him. "The senior circuit. We had a tournament in Moses Lake. The other guy looks worse."

"I never heard of that," said the motel clerk. "Senior-circuit boxing."

"It's a new sport," Ben told him. "Just got started a couple years ago. Everyone who does it is crazy."

"It sounds like it," the clerk agreed.

In the room the alarm clock was off by an hour, as though someone had forgotten about daylight saving's time. A Gideon's bible had been left on the side table, beside a placard listing local churches. On the wall behind the bed hung an oil painting of seagulls, shells, driftwood, and dunes, from the other side of the mountains.

Ben turned the heater as high as it would go and sat on the bed in front of it. It made an enormous, clattering din, then blew cold air into the room. He still had his field jacket wrapped tightly around him, yet he felt the cold in his bones. Bent to work free of his hunting boots, their laces festooned with sharp burrs from the desert, he was suddenly aware of how much his feet hurt, of how much he wanted to get out of his boots, and he pried them off with considerable effort, then stripped off his wet socks. His feet, ghastly white, were chafed at the arches and red where his boots rubbed his heels. His toenails looked rotten.

The heater began to work better. Ben peeled off his glasses, rubbed his eyes, and massaged his side for a while. He worked his bad knee and his arthritic ankle, took the measure of the pain in his hip, touched the cut above his eye. Every muscle felt bound up, seized, his range of motion limited, and he considered simply collapsing on the bed without a shower or food. Instead, he found the remaining bags of peanuts and the half-empty bottle of prune juice, and sat by the heater eating and drinking. When he'd finished, he looked in the double cupboard, the drawers, and the two-shelf refrigerator, but there was nothing left behind or forgotten, only a small box of baking powder and a near-empty bottle of vinegar.

Ben ran the shower, switched on the heat lamp, and struggled out of his clothes. He took the Italian carabiner from his neck and set it on the counter. Without meaning to, he caught his image in the mirror: his naked form, at seventy-three, was not a kind thing to look on. His eye was a darkly swollen mass, the lower lid distended. His forehead, when he pulled free the bandage, looked almost as raw as it had when he'd cut it, the ruptured blood vessels still visible, the surrounding skin a sickly gray.

He was ghostly, pale, old. The hair sprouting from his chin and head was gray and as stiff as brush bristles; a few wisps, paltry and listless, sprouted from his rounded shoulders. He was bent forward, slack-heavy in the chest. His many moles showed dark against his skin. The tautness in his muscles was gone.

Ben stepped into the shower. The water felt so intensely hot, he stopped breathing for a moment. Yielding, he shut his eyes and let the stream wash over him. A simple, ordinary pleasure. He stayed that way, the water running down his chest, and then he washed indulgently, shampooing his hair three times.

There was some minor key of redemption in cleanliness Ben had noted before. When he was done, and dry, his teeth duly brushed, he sat on the toilet with his head between his knees, made use of the hemorrhoid cream, and lathered his cut with Neosporin. Fearing leg cramps, he took his calcium gluconate. He slid into his long underwear, switched off every light in the room except the one beside the bed, and lay down beneath the covers with a sigh.

It was good to be there, clean, revived, but still, at the core, he felt chilled. His side hurt, and he cursed it silently—a burning, prodding sensation. He drew up his knees to temper it and warmed his hands between his thighs, but the pain persisted despite his manipulations, and after awhile he rose. He peed and ran a fresh towel through his hair. He was suddenly occupied with the thought of his daughter, of how she might contemplate his sudden death on the arid side of the mountains. He saw her examining his credit card records, discovering that his car had been towed on Saturday, October 17, the transaction posted from North Bend, Washington, and finding that on the following day he'd taken a motel room in Quincy, 125 miles to the east. She would wonder how he had covered those miles. She would wonder what had become of his dogs. She would contact the Grant County coroner and sheriff and the man who had towed her father's car. Renee would piece together his final hours, the way in which he'd lived them. She would hear about his swollen eye and ask questions of Ilse Peterson, who would relate the story of the wolfhounds and of the death of Tristan and the recovery of Rex, and certainly it would all seem strange. Eventually Renee would want to see the place where her father had entangled himself in barbed wire, and perhaps she would even visit William Harden, to get his view of things. Everyone would recollect a similar image: a man in dust-bitten hunting gear, filthy, hauling an overloaded rucksack on his shoulders, as smashed up and broken as a vagrant or boxer, stinking of sweat and sage. Renee would feel troubled. Something in it would not add up. The county sheriff might become involved, and suspicions might fall on Harden. They would ask questions of Bill Ward. The truth of Ben's cancer might emerge.

So the thing to do was call her now and tell her what had happened. That all had finally settled down, that he was safely ensconced in his motel room, the long night of Tristan's death behind him, the car wreck details seen to. That he intended to hunt blue grouse west of the river—something he could do without a dog, allowing Rex time to convalesce. In a day or two, he'd tell Renee, he would bring Rex home in a rental car, they'd be back Tuesday or Wednesday. He would tell her, too, about his one good eye, how the other was swollen shut, and this would figure in her postmortem conjectures as the source of his error in spatial judgment while negotiating strands of barbed wire. His vision had been skewed, truncated, and as a result he'd bungled the fence crossing.

Dishonesty was his policy now; but dishonesty on behalf of the living, not for his own advantage. He lied in order to leave this world as quietly as he could. Yet at the moment—more than a technicality—he had no shotgun with which to exit. He thought of buying one up in Wenatchee, but this might seem curious to his daughter: her father dead with a new gun, his old Winchester missing. That would be a mystery to her, and it certainly would be to the county sheriff, and the investigation into Ben's death would deepen, and Bill Ward might be prompted to speak. Ben understood that he needed his Winchester, mainly as a prop for his suicide. But also because it had been his father's; he did not feel right losing it.

He picked up the phone to call Renee, but his grandson answered after one ring, and Ben wasn't ready for that. "Chris," he said, "It's you."

"I'm over here studying. My apartment's no good. People play music all the time."

"How is everything?"

"They're piling on homework."

"Merciless pedants."

"It isn't that bad."

Ben thought of the purpose of his call. But he didn't want to lose his grandson yet. "I remember the beginning of my third year," he said. "I don't think I slept very much."

"I get four or five hours when I'm not on night duty."

"That isn't enough."

"I'm doing all right."

"But you don't get outdoors."

"Not like you."

"So what are you going to do about it?"

"You and me. Silver Peak."

"Cakewalk for you, Chris."

"You, too. A tune-up."

Ben sat rubbing his temples, eyes shut. "You ought to go without me, somewhere. The Stuarts, maybe. Mount Stuart."

"Why couldn't you go?"

"Too tough these days."

"So what?"

"I'm out of shape, Chris."

"Work on it."

"My legs aren't under me."

"Yes, they are."

"Do Stuart without me."

"I've been up Stuart."

"Do something else, then."

"We'll do Silver Peak together."

"All right."

That seemed a note to end on. He didn't want to end on small talk. "Is your mother around?" he asked.

"Mom's at a meeting."

"Tell her I called."

"You want to leave a message?"

"I'll call in the morning."

"Where are you anyway?"

"East of the mountains."

"Any birds out there?"

"Chukars. A few."

"You've got legs for that, Pop."

"It's not uphill."

"So what?" Chris asked. "You're fine."

Afterward, Ben sat in his long johns, perched on the edge of his motel bed. He wiped his good eye with a fingertip, but the bad one leaked water onto his cheek. He dried it with a corner of the bedsheet.

EIGHT

Ben switched off the bedside lamp and absently massaged his side, as if to knead away the cancer. There was the din of the heater but no other sound. A rim of light showed around the curtains. The heat and darkness were just what he yearned for, but the pain in his gut was sharp, severe, and despite his weariness he couldn't sleep. Acquiescing, he turned on the light and dug in his rucksack for the marijuana cigarettes the drifter had given him at the river crossing. Ben thought of the night before, of the dysfunction of his mind through it, and it seemed to him a mistake to risk again that kind of folly and befuddlement. Yet in his motel bed, what could go wrong? What use here for a clear, sober mind? He needed relief from pain.

He slid one of the cigarettes between his lips and sat back

against the pillows, his lighter between his fingers. After the third deep inhalation, he recognized the feeling from the previous evening—a busy, relentless current of thought, a confusion about the meaning of things—and after the fifth, he felt paranoid. When he had smoked the entire cigarette, he worried that the room was thickly noxious with a sweet green pall that would seep outside to indict him as a criminal. Perhaps a guest in an adjoining room would catch a whiff of marijuana and call the Quincy police. There was no way to judge if this worry was valid—there was no way to know, now that he'd smoked—so he decided that, to cover himself, he should open the windows and run the bathroom fan. Then he remembered the carton of Himalayan incense the young people in the van had given him.

In his long johns, breathing roughly through his nose, he lit one of his parrafin fire starters, blew it out when the wax softened, set it beside the bathroom sink, and pierced it with a stick of lit incense. A fine line of smoke unfurled from the tip, rising in a fragrant helix. The smell of what he took to be saffron mingled with the marijuana, and he thought of the Himalaya Range, mountains he had never seen. It seemed profound that this incense had traveled from Tibetan monks on the Sikkimese border to a motel in sagebrush country. Its convoluted journey here seemed evidence of God's vast reach.

Ben crawled into bed, unhinged, dazed, and switched off the bedside lamp. The pain in his side felt bearable, but his mind traveled restlessly, and the fact of his death seemed pronounced and heightened, more real and more frightening. His limbs began to tremble. He felt neither awake nor asleep but, rather, in a curious limbo, a third form of consciousness. In this state of mind, ineluctably, he found himself thinking of his war. He tried to put it away, ward it off, but here it was again. For years he'd struggled with his memories of it, wishing they would go away, but here they were, unleashed by marijuana, welling up on the cusp of sleep.

At Camp Hale, in Colorado, he'd trained as an infantry rifleman. He'd arrived in a snowstorm on the Denver and Rio Grande Western line with six per diem dollars in his pocket and presented himself, his duffel bag on his shoulder, to the sergeant on duty at the train station at two-thirty in the morning. The sergeant passed him into the keeping of L Company, in the Third Battalion of the 86th Mountain Regiment, and Ben spent his first night sleepless in the barracks, fully dressed beneath two blankets, curled up with his hands in his armpits, thinking of Rachel Lake.

That first morning, the company assembled on the parade ground with the late fall wind driving down from the mountains, sodden snow underfoot. The cold seized Ben's face and hands and rose through his boots. The drill sergeant announced to the new recruits that in this place it was every man for himself, and then they began calisthenics. On the snow-covered drill field they stripped off their shirts to perform jumping jacks, knee bends, and push-ups at seven in the morning. They marched for three hours at 10,000 feet, on the Continental Divide, north of Leadville. They marched over Tennessee Pass in the coal smoke rising from the barracks stoves, and before noon it began to snow, a pelting snow, like rain. The new recruits buckled and wavered. Three went down and were left on the ground while L Company traveled on.

Ben suffered from a dull nausea, and his hands and feet grew numb. He marched in a stupor, short of breath; blood trickled from his nose. In the evening he was sent to the camp hospital. He could not get warm or stanch his nosebleed, and his temperature rose overnight to 103 degrees. In the hospital barracks he lay on his bunk and considered going to Denver, AWOL, as soon as he was sufficiently recovered, but for now he had cotton balls stuffed in his nostrils and a hacking, expectorating cough. A doctor assured him he would soon get better and explained that scores of men in the regiment had preceded Ben in altitude sickness— asthma, respiratory collapse, fever, nausea. "Things could be worse," the doctor said. "You could be fighting a war."

After three days his health improved, and Ben returned to training. He was a private first class and infantryman who served in L Company's Second Platoon, and as with everyone else at Camp Hale his lips were cracked, his eyes stung, and he wheezed with every breath. The camp air reeked of coal smoke, not only from the barracks stoves but from the locomotives in Tennessee Pass, striving up the basin's grade in great black plumes of exhaust. At taps the men sloshed water underfoot for the humidity it might provide. By dawn the floorboards were sheets of ice, and the men arose to reveille in the dark with the windowpanes frozen from their breath. Under stars they went in silence to the parade ground for shirtless calisthenics and close-drill marching, the wind blowing in their faces.

Ben was transferred to N Company for no apparent reason. They assigned him to a weapons platoon, perhaps because he'd scored high at firing the .30-caliber light machine gun. The sergeant placed him among the machine gunners, but then the company commander transferred Ben to a rifle platoon, where the lieutenant handed him a BAR to carry—the Browning automatic rifle—assigning him two ammunition bearers, Bill Stackhouse and Kelly Lastenpole, to haul the extra clips. Carrying this weapon in training, on top of his field pack and his own extra clips, Ben floundered in the snow.

After two months, the regiment embarked on winter field maneuvers. They started in the dark, shouldering ninety-pound packs, skins on their skis, steam chuffing from their mouths, and herringboned into Tennessee Pass, then toward Ptarmigan Peak.

They traversed uphill in single file, the mortars lashed on toboggans, the mules hauling artillery. Ben carried a canvas mountain tent, white felt boots, camouflage gear, pile jacket, and double sleeping bag. At dark the company made rough camp in the lee of a ridge at twelve thousand feet and ate K rations from boxes: cans of veal loaf warmed on gas stoves, bouillon, and powdered coffee. Ben passed the night with his socks, insoles, and canteens of water warming against his belly. Between the linings of his sleeping bag, he kept his boots and bindings.

In the morning it was twenty below. They ate a frozen biscuit each and broke camp wearing chamois masks, the air stabbing their lungs. No one could remember cold like this—it was cold on a mythic scale. A corporal removed his glasses from their case, and the frames shattered in his hand; another man's eyelashes froze solid and pulled free in white shards. The batteries in the field radios turned to ice. The M1 rifles wouldn't fire.

On the third day out, the temperature fell again, and those who felt too ill to push on were lashed to toboggans and hauled back to camp like so many frozen corpses. On bivouac that night, Ben heard around him the explosive frost-checking of the mountain birches; in the morning fresh snow had inundated the tents, whisked over them like sand. A radioman closed up his tent with two cookstoves going inside, and for a moment he had a working radio to call for tracked Snow Weasels. None came for them.

A blizzard was general to the mountains now, but no one of rank would call off the maneuvers, and the company fumbled toward Ptarmigan Peak on empty stomachs, sleepless. Ben's feet bled from the gusseting of his shoepacs. His fingers cracked open inside his gloves and the blood froze against his nails. Welts formed along his back from the pressure of his pack straps. Yet he slogged on through frozen trees, snow roiling under his skis, clouds of white suspended dust. That night, at Ptarmigan Peak, the hoarfrost grew like mold on the tent he shared with Bill Stackhouse. Their own breathing melted it.

They were ambushed that night—their guards having burrowed themselves into snow caves—and taken prisoner. Ben was lying in his sleeping bag with the drawstring pulled around his head when the hypothetical enemy attacked in the quiet hour before dawn. One of them tore open the tent door and knelt there pointing his M1 at Ben, telling him to sit up cautiously and do nothing to inspire an itchy trigger finger. Ben was in no mood for war games. His Browning rifle had frozen solid, and the pistol he normally kept between his thighs had been left, overnight, in his field pack.

The air warmed to 35 degrees that day, and Ben's clothes grew wet with melting snow, but at dusk the temperature dropped again, and his pants and shirt froze against him. A heavy snow fell fast in the darkness, and there was nothing left to eat or drink but snow scooped up with a mitten, and no fuel left to melt it. In the morning they followed the order to dig out and with packs loaded marched through a pass, under an armed guard. Sidehilling on their sealskinned skis, they made a bitter ascent.

On the open slope, flailing in new snow, the wind tearing off the mountain summits so that he couldn't look any place but down to where his skis disappeared altogether, Ben came to understand what it meant to freeze to death. There was nothing to it but to wait in one place, and he saw that by doing nothing he could escape from all the suffering of the past interminable days. He paused to get the feel of it, this death by default, this seductive surrender, and then shrugged off his attraction to it and flailed grimly in the snow again, with a new and desperate resolve.

To live, Ben felt, was to be on fire, lest one turn to ice.

In the summer they left the mountains behind to inhabit the flatlands at Camp Swift, Texas, a land of chiggers and copperheads, poison ivy, cockroaches, dust, and scorpions. There was no explanation as to why mountain troops should be stationed in such an arid place, and they languished there unhappily. Ben wrote Rachel about army life, confessing that the imminence of war filled him with the fear of an awful death, or worse, of permanent wounds. She wrote back to say that in her training she had seen much that was terrible and disturbing. She had seen men legless, armless, and blind, their faces seared beyond recognition, their backs riddled with shrapnel, their feet blown off by land mines. She did not wish by describing these injuries to inspire in Ben a hindering fear, but on the other hand she thought it wise to tell painful truths. And she asked him bluntly to reconsider—couldn't he serve as a medic? Did he want to participate in killing? Ben replied that they'd made him a gunner, that from this there was no turning. On the issue of war they traded letters, Rachel insisting that the work of healing was better than the work of killing, Ben replying that his feelings compelled him to fight the war directly.

In the middle of June, Rachel finished classes and was sworn into the Army Nurse Corps. She volunteered for overseas service and despite her inexperience was accepted. She wrote Ben again from Fort Devens, Massachusetts, where she'd been transferred for an eight-week orientation in the art of military nursing. Once she wrote from Waterville, where she'd gone on leave to visit her family, and once she sent a card from Manhattan, where her unit was on standby, awaiting orders to embark. By mid-August she was on a transport ship, headed for the coast of France.

In the fall Ben's orders came, too, and in late November, after Thanksgiving, the Third Battalion of the 86th went by train across the South, living in Pullmans for three days, eating standing up in the kitchen cars, washing mess kits in cavalry cans in which the dishwater sloshed and churned as the steam engine negotiated bends. They passed through Arkansas and Mississippi,

Ben staring vacantly at fields turned fallow and at bleak, drab pine forests.

They passed through Norfolk, Virginia. At Camp Patrick Henry, they slept in tar-papered barracks, played rounds of five-card draw, and read dog-eared novels borrowed from the camp's library. German prisoners manned the chow lines, and in the camp stockade, sequestered behind a high double fence, were draftees who had refused their orders to board ships for Europe.

Ben sailed aboard the SS *Argentina*, a converted luxury liner. It was part of a convoy of troop transport ships escorted by destroyers through Hampton Roads and out into the winter swells along the Virginia coast. The destroyers took gunnery practice with their aft-mounted antiaircraft guns, shooting at enormous gas-filled balloons ascending into winter skies—as deafening an exercise as Ben had been party to, setting up a ringing in his ears. Within a few hours men fell ill who had no stomach for rolling seas. That night they lay in bunks six deep, thousands of men in the hold of the ship, many of them retching, the floors slick with vomit. Ben could keep nothing down, either, and lined up in the gangways for seasickness pills that didn't solve his problem. At night he stood guard with a life vest on and leaned over the rail heaving, salt spray dashing his face. There were sudden, irrational submarine drills, and drills to determine if all knew their lifeboat stations, and at dawn more deafening gunnery practice while the convoy plowed through twenty-foot swells, over waves boiling with sea spume. It was a fogbound crossing, sunless. Soldiers played craps and blackjack in stairwells, in companionways deep in the hold of the ship, or lolled in their hammocks morosely, meditating on private omens.

Word was that they would land in Naples, and on the seventh day out they saw in the distance the green coast of Africa. They were detained briefly at the Strait of Gibraltar while an escort of four destroyers assembled, supported by a phalanx of PBYs, blister-gun ports aft of their wings, transparent gun turrets in their bows. Passing into the Mediterranean, they stood on deck in an African breeze, the water placid off their bow and blue in a lushly textured way that reminded Ben of the sky at home on certain midsummer afternoons. He leaned over the rail. Bill Stackhouse appeared beside him and said he'd won almost five hundred dollars playing craps in the hold.

"I'm spending it all," Stackhouse said, "as soon as we get into port."

"It's a lot of money," Ben said.

"I'm buying Italian women," said Stackhouse. "I might not get another chance."

"Yes, you will."

"I might not."

"You're not going to die."

"We might, Givens."

They passed close to the Isle of Capri, and on the ninth day, in dismal weather, entered the Bay of Naples. They were directed to anchor on the south side of the harbor to wait their turn to disembark, and from there they saw sunken German ships resting on the harbor mud, their superstructures and upper decks breaking the surface like reefs. Some of the harbor buildings had been bombed and stood windowless with gaping walls, rubbish piled against them. Between rain squalls the air freshened; beyond the city sat Vesuvius. On the dockside street milled young women Stackhouse took to be prostitutes. Kelly Lastenpole explained to Bill how appropriate it was that here the sirens had lured wayfarers of antiquity to a death on distant shores.

The *Empress of Australia* anchored beside them, at such close quarters as to block their view; they saw only the curve of its hull. That night Ben tossed sleepless in his hammock, and in the morning felt weary as he packed his rucksack and hauled his duffel topside. No military band hailed them, like the band at embarkation in Virginia, playing "Over There." Instead there was rain and a throng of beggars, Red Cross girls in overcoats cheerily handing out stale doughnuts, and a line of army trucks waiting in the street to take them God knew where.

Ben made his way down the narrow gangplank and was disgorged into Italy. The day before Christmas, 1944. Bailey bridges spanned the pier's bomb gaps, a catwalk crawled over a capsized ship: the docks at Naples were a giant staging area choked with newly arrived soldiers. Ben deployed into a quartermaster truck that had been refitted to carry troops, and from it saw the wreckage of Naples with its streetcar tracks bombed loose and twisted, the facades of apartments dropped away. A girl squatted in the street to defecate, half-concealed by her coat. At the edge of town Stackhouse threw a small boy a chocolate bar, which landed at his feet.

Christmas Eve they staged at Bagnoli in the remains of a bombed-out orphanage the Germans had earlier occupied. Ben's company was assigned to its school, a cold building with no lights or furnishings, where the rain slanted through the broken windows and spattered against the stone floors. Ben wore his trenchcoat and beneath it his field jacket, wrapped his blankets tightly around him, and tried to sleep sitting up in a corner, like fruit pickers he remembered who'd slept against tree trunks on nights the ground was too cold or damp for sleeping in the grass. Sleepless, bored, and shivering, he thought of home and Rachel Lake.

At noon they ate turkey and potatoes from their mess kits in celebration of Christmas. The next day they boarded the SS *Sestriere* and debarked in darkness at Livorno. They went by convoy northeast to Pisa to bivouac at a muddy staging area where the sound of distant artillery was audible, the flash of it visible at night. They encamped in the Tenuta di San Rossore, which had once been the picnic ground of kings, a place to hunt wild boar. Now under handsome poplar trees, men played five-card draw.

Ben shared a pup tent with Lastenpole, who came from Syracuse. Ben told him about the orchard country, and Lastenpole remembered picking apples in orchards along Lake Ontario. Every year, his father made cider.

They lined a #10 can with sand, poured it full of gasoline, and tossed a lit wooden match inside to make a lantern of sorts. Then they lolled in their pup tents, while the rain beat hard outside. Lastenpole drew on a hand-rolled cigarette, at rest with an arm behind his head, blowing smoke toward the tent canvas. He insisted that the real action was in Belgium and France: the goal here was to force the German military to divert resources southward. He'd read in *Stars and Stripes* that a German offensive had been repelled in Luxembourg, that the Russians were closing on Warsaw and Budapest, that at Bastogne the 101st Airborne Division stood face-to-face with the German Fifth Army—but there was no mention of hill towns in the Apennines, or even of Italy. The war, said Lastenpole, would be won when the Rhine was crossed, when the Russians pushed their way into Berlin; the smart thing to do in the meantime, he argued, was to keep out of harm's way.

They convoyed again out of Pisa to the south and made a fresh bivouac at Quercianella, putting up tents by the coastal road along the Ligurian Sea. In the new year the *Stars and Stripes* reported that the Germans had been halted and routed in the Ardennes; it ran photographs of Montgomery and Patton, and one of Eisenhower in Paris. Lastenpole pronounced the war all but over; everything that happened hereafter, he said, was a mere denouement. Montgomery was about to cross the Rhine.

A bag of mail was distributed, the letters in it weeks old and full of Christmas salutations. Rachel wrote to Ben from Revigny, where she was billeted in a concrete barn: she and twenty-five other nurses were huddled in the servants' quarters with a charcoal brazier and an array of candles, cutting snowflakes and stars from tin cans in preparation for Christmas. They were stringing red berries, cutting out angels, and making paper snowflakes for children convalescing in the hospital. There were plans afoot for a talent show. They'd salvaged foil wrappers as tinsel, and they were going to eat turkey and fruitcake.

Arriving that summer in Normandy, she reported, they'd bivouacked in an apple orchard throttled by swags of mistletoe and inundated by hornets. Their camp covered sixty acres, a city of tents laid out in muddy rows, German prisoners of war watching them from behind a barbed-wire stockade. They lived in floorless ward tents and slept on flea-ridden straw. They killed field mice with their GI shoes and ate C and K rations, Spam, hardtack, tins of cheese spread, fruit bars, raisins, canned corn. Their luggage had been lost en route from England, so they had no change of clothes. They had their musette bags and dungarees, but not their class-A uniforms. They sampled the brandy of that region, made from windfall apples. Rachel couldn't stomach calvados, but other nurses were fond of it.

The hospital ran on kerosene lights. Its first patients were two village children who'd strayed, at play, into land mines. Women came in for difficult births; farmhands appeared with blistered feet, jaundice, and tuberculosis. Soon soldiers from the front arrived. Rachel saw cases of trenchfoot, hepatitis, pneumonia, and gangrene. The burn cases were terrible; at night dark moans could be heard from the ward that made Rachel feel helpless. She was pressed into surgery service and had learned to administer a blood transfusion, start an IV, suction a lung wound, and perform a secondary skin closure. She'd also learned to dig a foxhole and shoot a carbine rifle.

Paris was liberated while she was stationed in Normandy. The rains began, their tents collapsed, and all were perpetually soaked. They bathed in their helmets, worked double shifts. They chlorinated their drinking water in Lister bags and tinctured it with lemon crystals. Soon it grew cold enough to coat their tents with a thin film of ice. They warmed themselves at coal burners. They could no longer get the *Stars and Stripes,* but there was the BBC on the radio and a movie tent with leaky seams.

Late in the fall, they were transferred. They moved closer to the war. During the fighting near Bastogne, Rachel was evacuated—she climbed into the back of an ambulance that soon mired itself in mud, and had to cling to the rear of a half-track all the way to a clearing station in the town of Malmedy. Now here they were in Revigny, her post for the foreseeable future. At the hospital, they were inundated: men lay swaddled in blankets on the floor, in the hallways, even in the boiler room. It was so cold, the morphine froze, as did the plasma supply. There were men in the wards with their spinal cords severed, others who had lost their arms and legs, others whose faces were wrapped in gauze with no holes for their eyes. Rachel remained in the surgery service. She thought of Ben all the time, she confessed. She remembered her summer in the orchard country. Those days seemed like a dream to her now. She missed him very much. She loved him.

Ben's company practiced digging foxholes, despite the fact that a foot beneath their boots lay an immense slab of marble. They were ordered to remove their insignia, cut away their stripes of rank, and were forbidden to salute outdoors anymore, in order to minimize the exposure of officers to potential sniper fire. This, said Lastenpole, was an ominous sign. It meant they were going into combat.

It was raining hard on January 8 when they set out for the front in quartermaster trucks and battalion supply vehicles. They traveled through uplands far to the northeast, into the Apennines. The rain became snow settling slowly over fields, and it was cold and still in these gentle, low mountains broken by fallow farmland.

Higher up, the roads were more difficult, filled with heavy, wet snow. Snow fell steadily out of a still gray sky, as heavy and fast as spring rain, and by afternoon the hills lay shrouded, there was no way to see any distance. They heard muffled artillery as the road wound up through forests, its sharp bends rising steeply through fields and quiet hill towns.

They came to the village of San Marcello. Ben's rifle platoon was billeted in an abandoned primary school for girls. They slept on a concrete classroom floor and burned slabs of pine on the portico. Overnight, more snow fell, and in the morning the valley opening below sat beneath a foot of it, with vineyard trellises showing. Children waited with wooden pails near the tent kitchen set up in the town square. The muffled, distant artillery had stopped. The world was tense and silent.

For three nights they patrolled the hillsides. Stackhouse complained about the weight of the BAR clips, since not a round had been fired. Lastenpole smoked his cigarettes and made entries in his journal. Ben went with Stackhouse to drink grappa at a tavèrna. As promised, Stackhouse had spent all his money on whores, so Ben paid for both their drinks and for a bag of figs as well. They ate them looking out over the country, their helmets in their laps. Stackhouse was from Baltimore. He hadn't finished high school. He had begun training to be a machinist and had worked delivering ice. Stackhouse confessed to hating the Army. He was drunk from the grappa and wanted to go home. The whores had been bleak. In Pisa he'd found one who spoke English and paid her to talk with him all night.

Orders came, and they moved north, first to Lizzano in Belvedere, then toward the town of Querciola, traveling in the dark under heavy loads, working uphill through snow-blown vineyards, fields, and apple orchards. Querciola lay deserted by its citizens because it sat in range of German shells, and the company established surveillance there and probed the countryside. On their fifth night in Querciola, a German patrol in white camouflage penetrated the foxhole perimeter. Ben lay on the ground with other men while the telephone operator called for reinforcements, and in ten minutes reserves came up from positions to the south. They, too, lay on the ground while the telephone operator called for artillery, but the reserve unit sergeant grew impatient and ordered his squads to fight. They spilled out toward the German fire, and a Private Zwickert was shot in the back by a BAR man of another rifle squad who had not understood the reserve's intentions and had assumed Zwickert was a German. This was the first of Ben's company to be killed in Italy.

Afterward, the sergeant of the reserves railed long at them, calling out the name of the dead man, telling them all it was John Zwickert they'd killed in their cowardice and stupidity. Then the perimeter fell quiet. They set up trip wires to deliver flares in case the Germans tried again, and they manned their foxholes by the book. At dawn they were shelled by 88s that cut through the trees like scythes. In a lull they were replaced by other men and withdrew to Vidiciatico, where they passed long hours in coal-heated rooms, sleeping or lying about. It was damp in Vidiciatico, the wind coming down from Riva Ridge, the snow melting at the height of day, turning the roads to mud. The jeeps traveled up to their axles in mud, and the men coming up from back of the lines reported that southward it was nearing spring—in the lowlands the air smelled of lemon blossoms.

Ben was shaved by an Italian barber with large, callused hands. He acquired new woolen underwear and a new helmet liner. With Lastenpole and Stackhouse he went to a trattoria and ate polenta and farina of chestnut and drank the wine of the country. A boy of twelve in a jersey of sheep's wool followed them to where they were quartered, until Bill gave him cigarettes. At Ben's request the boy named trees—the abete, the pini, and the castagno, which Ben recognized as a chestnut. In pidgin English the boy explained that the clay of the region made excellent plates, that the wild pears tasted sour, and that the berries growing in summer on the ginepro were especially good for one's digestion. Bill gave him more cigarettes, and the boy showed them the biancospino bush, whose berries, he made theatrically evident, were a chore to gather but delicious.

The weather turned sharply cold thereafter, and the snow fell hard overnight. Powder settled in the ravines and defiles, and the cliffs turned to ice. Ordered to patrol, the men went out in mattress covers sewn into snow tunics and in creepers made of tightly knotted rope. In darkness they crossed the Dardagna torrent and climbed by way of gullies and buttresses onto outcroppings of crumbling shale, searching for a route up Cappelbusso to serve as a supply trail. Lastenpole complained of frozen fingers. He insisted that their endeavor was useless, until the sergeant told him to shut up.

In the second week of February, the snow began to melt. The south slopes of hills were laid partially bare, and the air felt comfortable, balmy. At night a fog rose thick from the earth and concealed the movement of troops. All along the roads now, behind turns and under banks, lay stocks of rations, gasoline cans, and crates of ammunition. Ben and Stackhouse were sent to the rear on a mission to retrieve white phosphorus grenades, rucksacks, K rations, and mountain jackets. In the curves above Lizzano-in-Belvedere they encountered trucks and men moving up, mules driven slowly by Italian alpini sporting jaunty Tyrol hats, more big guns being hauled toward the front, and tractors sent by engineers to scour out the road mud. Farther to the rear, the boxes of materiel—rations, wire, ammunition, GI cans of drinking water—were stacked openly along the roads, where they resembled a kind of wooden hedge too high to see over. In the fields below were the encampments of the engineers, the signal corps, the truck companies, and the armored infantry. By the following night Vidiciatico was thronged with concealed soldiers and munitions, and there were new gun emplacements hidden in the hillside facing the long-entrenched German positions on the ridge from Spigolino northeast toward Mount Belvedere. Ben and Stackhouse sat with an infantry map, memorizing the names of promontories—Mancinello, Serrasiccia, Cappelbusso, and finally Campiano, where the ridge fell away toward Rocca Corneta, a hamlet occupied by the Germans. Through field glasses they watched the place: stucco peeling from the stone walls of a barn, willows hanging over a road, red roof tiles fallen from a house, a shutter dangling against a wall of crumbling white plaster. Bare earth showed in the pockets of snowmelt, and the hillsides were covered with leafless chestnuts. The main road, now that the snow had cleared, revealed last year's layer of fine white sand where it wound downhill to Lizzano.

On a frigid night of low-lying fog, Ben's company left Vidiciatico and traveled in refitted quartermaster trucks to the foot of Mount Belvedere. From there they hiked to the line of departure, and in the dark they dug slit trenches in the rocky earth. Fresh snow had fallen earlier that day against the steep rock faces. The valley was a bowl of darkness. The wind from the ridge bore down on them.

After one o'clock, Ben heard the far-off crack of gunfire and the detonations of mortars. A blister on his left heel troubled him, and he treated it with Mercurochrome, bandaged it and adjusted the boot, tightening the laces a little. He drank long from his canteen. Stackhouse chewed on his fingernails, checked his watch from time to time, and sat on his knees to relieve himself.

At first light, word came down the line that Riva Ridge had been taken. Yet they stayed in their slit trenches all day long, stiffening in the February cold, hearing the German counterbarrage and the artillery fire to the north, which finally quieted at dusk. Ben field-stripped and cleaned his BAR, then ate the tinned cornbread and peaches in his pack. In the dark he defecated on his entrenching tool blade and flipped its contents into the night; later, Stackhouse did the same.

The sky was lit by brilliant flares, and the German artillery began firing. Stackhouse directed the light from his headlamp on the face of his watch and timed the rockets fired down Belvedere by the Germans on the summit. They were smoke throwers, he said—six rounds every ninety seconds—and later in the night he announced with a curse that the Germans had gone to 88s, which traveled hard for twelve miles and weighed twenty pounds.

They stayed in their trenches while tracers behind them lit the slopes high above. The 88s arrived without warning, roaring directly overhead, while the grinding rise and fall of the smoke throwers—screaming meemies, Stackhouse called them—caused Ben to hold his breath. Later, shards of hot steel fell out of the illuminated sky, and beyond the dark silhouette of limbs, trees toppled and settled against other trees, into the forks of branches. Ben blew into his numb fingers and felt himself drawn tight. Stackhouse held silent beneath his helmet, but whenever the long low moan of a shell grew ominously loud in their direction, he swore under his breath.

At dawn, P-47s roared over, shadowy bombs beneath their wings, which they dropped on the summit of Belvedere. Ben's company was ordered to move up the slope and secure itself behind the front. The men did so and hunkered behind chestnut trees, and at 0700 the company commander issued the news that Mount Belvedere had been taken by the 85th, and shortly thereafter Gorgolesco, and the Third and First of the 85th had been ordered by General Hays to defend these new gains at all cost against counterattacks. The Third of the 86th, Ben's unit, was to move up through the lines at the front to take Monte Della Torraccia.

They came out of the pines in single file and slogged toward Mazzancana. On the trail they met a party of mules with dead GIs lashed across their backs, driven by Italian alpini. As the mules picked their way down the pocked, hard slope, the corpses pitched and settled. The line of infantrymen moving to the front slowed to watch the procession. The dead were skewed and twisted unnaturally on the backs of the silent mules.

Ben's heart beat harder. He climbed upslope past trees sheared high where 88s had slashed through them, then under chestnuts where wounded men sprawled, some of them smoking stuporously, others prone with their heads on their helmets, awaiting escort to the aid station by litter-bearing squads. Later they passed a dead German sitting upright, his back against a tree, a neatly rolled cigarette in the corner of his mouth; then a GI with his left foot, inside its boot, severed from the rest of him. When someone turned him over to have a look, it was Gavin Neiderhoff. He'd tripped a mine, plainly; he lay in a perfectly round depression, his helmet tipped to one side. At midday they found Leonard Campbell, whom Ben knew from chess at the Camp Hale Service Club: he'd been hit in the throat and chest by mortar fire, and the snow around him, pierced by artillery, was strewn here and there with pine twigs. Leonard had bared his wound to the sky and died with his dog tag twisted.

They passed through beeches ravaged by mortar fire, some splintered, cracked, and toppled, others sheared of prominent branches, which speared and festooned the ground. They passed through a snow-covered pasture, always climbing steadily. In the trees beyond, men were digging in, and the company paused behind them to check orders by telephone lines laid up the mountain. They sat waiting in the damp woods, where Ben changed the bandage on his foot. The blister had opened and oozed a clear fluid. He dressed it carefully, laced up his boot, and examined the sear on his BAR.

The platoon leader, Lieutenant Daniels, told them that at dusk they would proceed across the shoulder of Hill 1018 and onto the slopes of Della Torraccia, where they were authorized to hold until daybreak in the thick pines there. The front lay directly forward, he said. There were no more troops between them and the enemy. In the morning they would make their assault, but only after artillery fire had prepared the way for them. The Second of the 85th, previously covering the ground before them, had taken considerable casualties; now their unit composed a second wave aimed at the defended crest. They would move up at dusk and dig in for the night. It was advisable to go deep, if possible; otherwise, to dig a slit trench. The BAR men should be prepared for the task of providing heavy fire in full support of a frontal attack, and the ammo bearers should stay close, since the guns were useless without them.

Ben rested against a tree, watching the light seep away. The pines all stood in silhouette when Kelly Lastenpole sat down beside him and tilted back his helmet. The dark humor was gone from his eyes. He smoked with his hand cupped around his cigarette. "This is crap," he said.

"Have you seen Bill?"

"He's back that way."

"He's supposed to be here."

"Forget about that."

"Come on, Kelly."

"It's crap," said Lastenpole, and flicked his cigarette away. "I'm not going to put myself out there."

In the night they took over foxhole positions from the men of the 85th. At dawn Lastenpole squeezed shut his eyes while mortars sailed overhead toward the German positions. When the order came to advance upslope, he vomited on his knees in the hole. Strands of it hung from his mouth.

Ben heard the sound of his own breathing as he vaulted out of his foxhole, struggled into his field pack, and took up his Browning rifle. While he shrugged his pack higher into place, he heard the whine of a shell hurling by just to the left of his face. It came so close that he felt the wind from it.

For a moment he stood behind a tree, Lastenpole on his knees beside him, and then he moved into the open, hurrying uphill with other men. Lastenpole stayed until Ben called, saying he needed the extra clips, and then Lastenpole, gathering himself, dashed up the hill.

They stepped over bodies, some of them from the Second of the 85th, others in German uniforms, but there was no time to ponder the nature of the wounds or how the dead had met their ends, since more 88s were raining in. Some men clung to the shell-pocked ground, others scrabbled on their hands and knees to dig into the hillside. Ben moved unthinkingly, because other men were moving. He ascended a ridge but at its crest was met by machine-gun fire. A radioman sprawled beside Ben to report their position through his headset but received only static for his efforts and swore incessantly, the side of his face against the earth. More 88s slammed in at their left, canceling out all sound. Ben, in a pause, set up his BAR and began to fire at nothing in particular, simply forward of his position.

P-47s came in low and sought to clear the way for them with fragmentation bombs. Men ran wildly down the slope while the planes passed closely overhead, and Ben, hauling his BAR along, followed them into a north-facing hay field still ankle-deep with snow. He moved into sheltering pines, advancing along the edge of the field—the snow hard in the shadows here—set up his BAR a second time, and fired into the trees. Again it was indiscriminate;

he fired merely to fire. No one from his squad was near. The ammunition bearers had not shown up—Lastenpole or Stackhouse. There was no sign of Lieutenant Daniels.

Sheltered by trees, he held his ground until a staff sergeant came along who was organizing the company for an assault on the German line. Spittle hung from the sergeant's mouth, and he'd lost his helmet and sidearm. Ben advanced behind other men, following a mule path etched into a side hill; and as he climbed it in a long traverse, an 88 blew two soldiers off the trail in a plume of smoke. Ben abandoned the mule path and scaled the ridge in a direct ascent, where he found Lastenpole and Stackhouse, stopped by a tangle of trip wires. They passed through it under fire and staggered down into beeches, where they lay breathing hard on the ground, struggling out of their packs.

Ben heard only the ringing in his ears. Stackhouse, rolling onto his back, put his canteen to his lips; the water ran across his face and down into his shirt. He wiped his forehead a couple of times, twisted over onto his belly, and lay one cheek against the ground. "Goddamn," he breathed.

"Where is everyone?" asked Lastenpole. "What the hell is going on?"

He slid on his elbows between the trees as if to survey their position. With the first shot, a sprig of pine needles dropped on his back. With the next, he clutched his shoulder and twisted onto his side. The third entered behind his ear and passed through his skull below the eye. Lastenpole brought his hand to his cheek, turned on his back against the ground, and lay facing the tops of the trees, blood between his fingers. "Oh, Goddamn it," he said.

He died quickly, shuddering. Blood ran out of his mouth.

Stackhouse lay low, staring. Ben crawled to the cover of a tree, lodged himself between two roots, and stayed there for over an hour. Three Germans passed, one waving a white rag tied to a pine branch, the other helping a comrade whose intestines were falling out of his abdomen; he held them in as best he could, but purple loops slipped between his fingers and slithered against the snow. It occurred to Ben to shoot all three in return for the death of Lastenpole, but Stackhouse counseled strongly against it, and when one of the Germans looked at them, Stackhouse waved them toward their rear.

Later there came another German, limping through the woods without a helmet, a bloody bandage around his forehead. A tall, gangly man in glasses, he appeared thoroughly dazed. Bringing his hand up to press against his head, he grimaced and closed his eyes wearily, then staggered forward ten more steps and stopped nearly in front of them. He wore fingerless gloves and a stained, tattered field jacket—a German in his middle thirties, perhaps forty, gray stubble on his chin. His field pants were tucked into his boots. The lenses of his glasses were misted by vapor, flecked by damp green needles. The canteen at his belt was missing its top, and beside it was a pistol in a muddy holster.

Ben set his finger against the BAR's trigger, hoping that Stackhouse would decide matters. He felt frozen, unable to act. The German doubled over beside a tree, one hand against the bark. Head hung, he steadied himself, hawking spit on the ground. Then he turned to look to his left and squinted through the interstices of bramble—one end of his bandage coming loose—where Stackhouse lay fumbling with his rifle, trying to pull the safety back, the German noting this commotion in the brush and saying something in his language, at the same moment scrabbling for his muddy pistol, clawing to pull it free of its holster, with Stackhouse screaming at Ben to shoot the man—*Shoot him! Shoot him! Goddamn it, shoot him!*—and Ben still paralyzed while the German brought his pistol up and fired three rounds into the underbrush. Stackhouse groaned, and Ben shot, squeezing down hard on the BAR's trigger. He severed the man at the waist.

The German's legs pitched forward, but the rest of him toppled backward and lay twitching against the ground.

Ben pulled his hands from the BAR and moved away from it. The German was still alive. The eyes behind the glasses met Ben's. He lurched and shuddered, and a whistle came from his throat. His legs shivered; one foot trembled. "Christ," cried Bill Stackhouse. "I'm shot up. Christ."

Ben pulled Stackhouse's field jacket up, ripped his trousers open at the hip, and found a gaping bullet wound flecked with splinters and shards of bone, dark blood spilling from it. "I'm sorry," Ben said. "Jesus."

"Goddamn," said Stackhouse. He spoke wincingly, his teeth set. He grunted each time he exhaled. "My shoulder, too," he said.

"We need litter bearers," Ben said.

"The guy goddamn shot me."

Ben pulled the first-aid kit from his pack, opened it, and hesitated. Eighty-eights sailed over the trees to crash on the slopes behind. He mopped the blood with a compress, then poked a sulfa pill into Stackhouse's mouth and tried to make him swallow it, but the water leaked between his lips, and the pill would not go down. "I'm sorry," Ben repeated. "Jesus."

He put the compress over the hip wound and yelled, without hope, for a medic. He passed a roll of gauze around Bill's hip to hold the compress in place and watched it darken with blood. There was no point in merely watching. Watching didn't change things. Ben hurried out onto the open slope and yelled again for help.

He saw himself from a distance now, or as if at some watery remove. A loud hum echoed inside his head he could not shake or stop. He was aware in some detached way of the trembling in his shoulders. He couldn't keep from trembling. A mortar sailed overhead, then another, and a third, and all the while he screamed for a medic, hearing his own strained, high-pitched voice, which seemed to come from elsewhere. The air smelled of gunfire.

In the end he carried Stackhouse toward the rear draped across his shoulder. Stackhouse grunted with each step as Ben labored through the pines, sweating hard beneath his load. Soldiers passed him in both directions. When he saw one with the Red Cross brassard, he lay Stackhouse at his feet.

The medic cut holes in the arm of Stackhouse's jacket, shirt, and long underwear. Then he stuck him with a morphine styrette, poured sulfa powder into the wound, stuffed a compress tightly in, and bandaged it—coat and all—to stem the flow of blood. He tore open the gash in Stackhouse's field pants, tossed the blood-soaked gauze aside, and mopped the blood before pouring in sulfa powder and applying another compress.

"Hey," he said. "Are you there?"

"Nnn," Stackhouse answered, ashen. His face glistened with sweat.

"You're all right," the medic told him. "We're getting you out of here."

There were no litter bearers anywhere in sight, and they could not wait for any. The medic slipped a wound tag around Stackhouse's ankle. They knotted a blanket over either end of a pine pole and carried Stackhouse in the hammock it formed, the medic leading the way downhill, Stackhouse slung between him and Ben something like a ceremonial pig slaughtered and spitted for the fire.

The battalion aid station was at a place called Carge, which was no more than a solitary farmhouse at the far end of a tree-studded meadow. The chestnuts beyond it were bare of leaves, and the whole area was strewn with shell crates, discarded K-ration boxes and cans, a muzzle snow-cover left behind, an infantryman's forgotten ammo bag, an empty first-aid dressing carton, a stack of litters, an entrenching tool, a pair of muddy tin cups. A netted helmet with a wet leather liner, the strap frayed off, top down in the snow. Beside it, a shooting mitten.

Litter bearers sprawled near the aid station with their hobnailed soles propped on rocks, beside a trail of boot prints etched raggedly through the mud and bloodstained snow. Next to the farmhouse with its tile roof, a chestnut tree stood starkly outlined against a sky of cirrus clouds and against a lofty ridge to the south dusted with sparse new snow. There was hay put up in the animal pens, dark and dense as peat. The upper reaches of the farmhouse had been shelled, but its thick stone walls remained intact. Its windows were blacked with tar paper.

Inside, the wounded slouched against the walls, some seated with their heads hung, others prone on the dirt floor. Medical technicians worked among them, carrying flashlights and kerosene lanterns, and none took note of Ben and the medic as they hauled Stackhouse inside and lowered him onto a vacant litter. While the medic caught his breath, Ben cut the blanket free with the scissors; then they hefted Stackhouse's litter and set it down on crates and bins arrayed beneath a gas lamp to serve as an operating table.

The light here shone fierce and glaring, a hard, garish cone of light, and the battalion surgeon stood in it, a broad-faced man with a salt-and-pepper mustache, fresh blood on his hands. He was bent over a soldier's Adam's apple, and the soldier was coughing bright blood.

The surgeon turned to look at Stackhouse; the medic exposed the wounded shoulder for him and ripped Bill's pants open. The pants and blankets were saturated, and the shoulder stained with blood. Stackhouse's eyes were open but glazed, and he didn't move at all. "I gave him morphine," the medic explained. "The guy's going fast."

"Does he have a pulse?"

"I think so."

"Don't think, know," said the surgeon. "And get a blood-pressure cuff on him. You," he said, across the room. "Get some saline in this guy. Start him on an IV, quick. And get some plasma going."

He looked at Ben, then turned away. He seemed both angry and tired. He went back to working on the throat of the other soldier, whose head was held down by a medical technician Ben recognized from Camp Hale. "Put some pressure on that hip for him," the surgeon said without turning. "Otherwise, get out of here. There's too many people around."

"You mean me?" Ben asked.

"Put some pressure on it for him, soldier. Go to it already."

"Okay," said Ben. "All right."

They cut Stackhouse free of his field jacket, combat shirt, and T-shirt. They cut away his pants, too, so that Stackhouse had on only his filthy underpants, muddy boots, and socks. The technician couldn't get the IV started, because Stackhouse's veins had collapsed: his blood wouldn't keep them open. The surgeon turned from his other work and with a scalpel cut through the skin and fat at the inside of Stackhouse's elbow. While the sergeant retracted the skin for him, he isolated the vein with a hemostat and passed a suture under it. Then he nicked the collapsed vein open, ran a large-bore needle in, and fixed it in place by tightening the suture. "There," he said. "Now tie off that vein. And put a stitch in when you get the chance." And abruptly he went back to the soldier with the wounded throat, taking a clamp in his hand.

The surgeon pushed his glasses snugly against the bridge of his nose. "Listen," he said to a medical technician, in the same direct, emphatic tone he used for everyone in the room. "I've got to work on this new guy over here. He won't make it if I don't. So I want you to watch this clamp I've got until I can get back to it. Just make sure he doesn't work it loose."

The technician took hold of the clamp. "I've got it," he said.

The surgeon turned again to Stackhouse, and gave orders to all in the room. "Move," he said. "Let's get moving. Get that plasma I asked for brewed in the next two seconds or so."

The sergeant technician ran saline through Stackhouse with the valve cock turned all the way open and started a new bag immediately. "It's going right through him," he said.

"I'll do a second cut-down," said the surgeon. "Get his pulse again for me. And take a pressure reading."

He cut through the flesh in Stackhouse's other arm and again isolated a vein with a hemostat, ran a needle into it, fixed it, and tied it off. "I don't have a pulse," the sergeant said. "I don't think he has one anymore. Not that I can find." But the surgeon continued with his work. Ben watched his hands move swiftly. He kept his own hand against Stackhouse's hip, which looked stark white in the light of the gas lantern hissing overhead. "Plasma," the surgeon called. "This needle's ready and waiting here. Fill the poor bastard with plasma."

The sergeant technician hooked up the plasma, which had been reconstituted by a medic in the corner who was busy reconstituting more. The sergeant opened the valve fully. The surgeon placed two fingers against Stackhouse's neck. He moved them around, stopped, moved again. "I'm on the carotid now," he said. "Not a thing. Nothing."

"Jesus," Ben said weakly.

The surgeon made no reply to this. "You," he called to a second technician, "get into that crate and find the epinephrine." He paused over Stackhouse, whose chest and belly had turned a sallow blue. The face was empty, the eyes wide open, the pupils enormously dilated. "This guy's dead," said the surgeon.

He hit Stackhouse in the chest with no small violence. Nothing happened, and he hit him again. He hit him a third time, harder still, and Stackhouse bounced a little. A medic handed him the epinephrine, and the surgeon filled a syringe with it. Aiming deliberately between two ribs, he plunged the needle through Stackhouse's chest, and with no hesitation drove it forcefully, using his arm and shoulder, into Stackhouse's heart.

"Nothing at all," said the surgeon.

The surgeon struck Stackhouse's chest twice more, as if it were made of wood. "Zero," he said, with his fingers at Stackhouse's neck. "I can't get anything."

"No," said Ben. "Please."

The surgeon ignored him. "Sergeant," he said. "You let Waterman man the IVs and ventilate this soldier for me. Can you do that for me, no matter what?"

"Yes, sir," said the sergeant.

"Just keep him ventilated," the surgeon ordered.

The sergeant tilted Stackhouse's head back, pulling him by the chin. He slid an airway into the mouth to hold back the tongue. He laid an anesthesia mask over the lower half of the face, wrapped his lips around the blow tube, bent low, and went to work. He blew forcefully.

The surgeon turned to Ben now. "There's a packet of sterile gloves behind you. Hand them over to me."

"All right," answered Ben.

"Hurry up," said the surgeon.

Ben found and opened the packet. While the surgeon worked his hands into the gloves, he went on giving orders. He asked that the surgical retractors in the equipment chest be doused thoroughly with alcohol and brought to the operating table. He told

Ben and the medic to stand by until he showed them what to do. He said he was going to cut the man open and would need them to manipulate the retractors.

Ben felt a tremor in his shoulders. The idea of opening Stackhouse's chest as he lay before them dead on the litter with his eyes blank and his face blue was horrible to contemplate. But the medic brought the retractors, and the surgeon with his gloved fingers counted the gaps in Stackhouse's rib cage and plunged in his scalpel. He swept it gracefully along the shadow of a rib, cutting slightly longer than a hand's width two inches below the left nipple. Contrary to what Ben expected, there was no blood to speak of, only beads of it. The surgeon handed his scalpel to the medic. "Give me the retractors," he said.

He inserted them into the lips of the cut, against the exposed ribs. Ben saw the pink of a lung. It deflated while he looked at it, and then it rose again, swelling and glistening, when the sergeant exhaled through the blow tube. The medic took one retractor in hand and Ben took the other. "Pull hard," said the surgeon. "Open him up."

They pulled, and the surgeon turned to face Stackhouse's head. With his left hand he reached through the incised gap so that his palm and wrist disappeared. It seemed to Ben a kind of illusion, one man's forearm disappearing inside another man's chest. The surgeon rotated his arm to the left, until it slipped a little farther in, and then rotated it back again, wriggled, and bent even lower. "I'm there," he announced. "I've got it now. You keep that plasma coming fast, run plasma through both arms, take him off the saline. Sergeant, stay with that blow tube."

The surgeon turned to Ben next, his forearm pumping rhythmically. "Pull a little harder," he said. "It's biting into my arm." He nodded when Ben put leverage on Stackhouse's rib and pulled it out of the way. "This is much easier for left-handed guys," the surgeon said matter-of-factly. "I don't have the same finesse."

"Is he dead?" Ben asked.

"He's been out for less than a minute," said the surgeon. "I'm trying to compress his heart and get him started again."

"You're doing what?" Ben asked.

"I've got his heart in my hand," said the surgeon. "It isn't too much of a trick, really. You just want to make sure you palm it correctly, don't try to do the work with your fingers, and especially not with the ball of your thumb, which is very tempting and seems right, but what you want is to cup the thing and squeeze it hard and evenly, as if you were wringing a sponge."

"So he's not dead," Ben said.

"He was dead," the surgeon said. "I don't know right now."

"This is a helluva thing," said the medic. "I haven't seen this before."

"It's the last resort," said the surgeon, the muscle in his forearm still working rhythmically where it disappeared between the retractors. "It's a relatively basic thing. I'm pumping his heart for him."

"Yeah, but still," said the medic.

"Sometimes," said the surgeon, "this actually works. If everything goes just right."

He was true to his word in this regard. Stackhouse's heart began to beat again, quite irregularly for more than two minutes, but then with a racing, regular rhythm, so that the surgeon slid his hand out, pressed it hard against the incision, and with the other checked the carotid artery. Stackhouse's pulse ran thready and wild; his blood pressure was coming up. The sergeant pulled away from his ventilating work, and they all looked at Stackhouse's eyes. The pupils had constricted again, and the surgeon immediately ordered more morphine, lest the patient, stirring toward consciousness, find himself with his chest cut open on a litter in an Italian farmhouse.

The surgeon did not stop his work, slow down, or relax. Keeping his hand pressed against the incision, he commended the sergeant for his endurance in ventilating the wounded man and urged him to continue for a while longer until he could sew things up. He ordered a urinary catheter and told the technician to cut openings in it and douse it with alcohol. He asked the medic to find a can and half-fill it with water. Without hesitating in his delivery of commands, he told Ben to rinse the scalpel, and when he had it in his free right hand, he made a hole in Stackhouse's chest and plunged a hemostat through it. A technician took over compressing the incision, and the surgeon fed the catheter in, trapping it in the hemostat's jaws in order to draw it out. He tied it off with purse-string sutures, attached a length of IV tubing, and ran the end to the floor. "Tape this in here," he told Ben, pointing at the can of water. "There's some tape in the crate over there. Tape the tube against the inside of the can so the end of it stays in the water."

He took a deep breath, checked Stackhouse's pulse again—it was racing still, in frantic fashion—and urged the technician with his hand on the incision to apply a sealing pressure. "Just a little longer," he said. "Then we'll sew him up."

The surgeon leaned over Stackhouse's hip and removed the medic's dressing. "This guy took it in the femoral artery," the surgeon observed, adjusting his glasses. "He took it right in the bone, too—opened the marrow cavity."

He turned his attention to Stackhouse's shoulder, pulling the dressing aside. "Same kind of problem here," he said. "The subclavian vein has been torn."

A litter team hurried into the room and deposited another

wounded soldier on the bins and crates behind the surgeon. The soldier's left leg was missing below the knee. A tourniquet had been applied, stained red with blood. The doctor turned to examine it, then ordered the medic to twist it tighter and returned his attention to Stackhouse.

"All right," he said. "We have to turn this man on his side and get this wound taken care of."

They pulled Stackhouse's right arm over his head so that the side of his face lay against his bicep, and they passed the IV around the sergeant technician, who knelt, red-faced, at the blow tube. The surgeon ordered a rolled blanket placed beneath Stackhouse's neck and head to free the right arm for the passage of plasma. Then he swabbed clear Stackhouse's hip. The blood welled up immediately. "This guy's down to no clotting factors," the surgeon observed, compressing the wound. "He's bleeding out pure plasma here. There's nothing left to coagulate. He's just lost too much good stuff."

He opened the hip a bit more with his scalpel, to drain the accumulated blood. He took a closer look inside, made a tamponade of gauze, tucked it firmly into the wound—packing it tightly at the edges—and taped a compress over it. Next he did the same with the shoulder. "Like sticking your finger in a dike," he said. "That should work for a while."

He turned his attention to the boy behind him, whose leg had been blown off. He tightened the tourniquet and swiveled again. "Okay," he said. "Tell you what. I want this guy"—he pointed at Ben—"to wash his hands over there. Then he can keep a seal on that incision while you"—he pointed at the technician—"get this new man an IV."

"All right," the technician said.

"You get this soldier in shape," said the surgeon. "Get him some plasma, take his pulse, get a blood-pressure reading."

"Yes, sir," the technician said. "The problem is, I'm stuck right here until this man"—he gestured at Ben—"gets his ass in gear. You're just standing there, Private."

Ben washed his hands and took over the technician's job of sealing Stackhouse's incision. It pushed against his palm a little each time the sergeant blew into the tube. "How is he?" Ben asked. "Will he live?"

"His heart's beating," the surgeon said. "But he won't coagulate anymore. He needs real blood, quickly."

"Well, I'm his friend," Ben said. "Maybe he should take some of mine."

"You O-positive?"

"I am, yes."

"Okay," the surgeon answered. "Right now we'd better sew him up. Then we'll draw a pint out of you and drop it into him."

"Take more," Ben told him.

The surgeon used sutures of heavy black silk, working rapidly. He pierced the skin and looped around the ribs to draw the incision together. "This is dicey," he said to the sergeant. "If you don't sew things good and tight, you end up with an air leak."

"Hey," the sergeant answered, pulling the anesthesia mask aside. "The guy's breathing again."

The surgeon anchored the catheter to the skin with three sutures around it. "Air-tight," he announced. He called for a fifty-milliliter syringe, attached it to the catheter, and suctioned air from Stackhouse's thorax. He broke the syringe free and attached the catheter to the IV tube snaking into the bucket. "Take a look," he said to the sergeant, rubbing his face with the back of his wrist. "We've got air coming out of the chest now. See those bubbles in the water?"

"My God," said the sergeant. "What a miracle."

He drew a blanket over Stackhouse, tucking in its edges. "Christ," he said. "It's a miracle. It's a goddamn resurrection."

"Call it what you will," the surgeon said, still rubbing his face and scratching his nose with the back of his hairy wrist. "But you could learn to do it, too. It isn't something from a Bible story. You go to med school, you can do it."

"Look at that," said the sergeant. "The guy's back from the dead."

"It's a miracle," Ben agreed.

"We'll talk about it after the war," said the surgeon, turning to the boy behind him with the tourniquet on his leg. He checked his pulse, two fingers at his throat. "In the meantime, sergeant, I again need plasma to throw at this other poor bastard."

They drew two pints of Ben's blood, and he sat in a daze while the technician disconnected the plasma line and started Ben's blood into Stackhouse. A third soldier was hauled in on a litter, but Ben didn't look at him. Instead he cradled his head in his hands and stayed that way until they passed him into the keeping of Father Carr, the Third Battalion chaplain. Father Carr consoled him a little, but seemed himself at a loss. Then they went into the night, down the hill with other men, toward the rear, away.

For three days Ben stayed in the rear, wrapped in blankets on a cot. The division psychiatrist interviewed him twice to determine if he was fit for service, and in the end they put him back in the line with recruits brought in from the replacement depot. Ben spoke to none of them. It was better that they remain nameless—they would leave less of a wake.

He made no pretense of fighting as the regiment advanced over the plain of the Po to liberate Bomporto, San Benedetto Po, Villafranca, and Verona. Fortunately, he was not much called upon except in the fighting to liberate Torbole, and there he squatted behind a wall and didn't participate. When the surrender came, they sent him to Bolzano, where men from his company commandeered shotguns and pistols from the Beretta factory, and guarded a warehouse in which the Germans had hidden paintings plundered from the galleries of Florence. In the distance rose the Dolomites.

On the train to Livorno he had nothing to say, though other men were loud and raucous in expectation of going home. They steamed down the spine of Italy in boxcars, and men drank wine, leaned from the cars, and waved to the peasants in the fields. It was July-hot and oppressively humid, but nobody seemed to mind very much and the general atmosphere was one of mirth. They passed fields of battle, towns shelled, farmhouses shattered, the plains strewn with burned tanks.

Ben sent a letter to Rachel in Marseilles, and she came to Livorno aboard a hospital ship on a leave of twenty days. He looked for her in a makeshift encampment of army tents by the Ligurian Sea, just north of the city. It was midafternoon, a day of still heat, and he was sweating, unshaven, and filthy, dressed in military issue khakis and a military tank-top undershirt, his skin darkened from his days in Italy, his lips chafed by the wind. He asked around and was told by a nurse that Rachel had gone down to the sea to swim, and he went in search of her.

He found her wet, her hair in flat strands, wearing a plain blue bathing suit. A lean woman with amber skin, older than he remembered. But the smell of her mouth was as he recalled. She wept a little, looking at him. She, too, was harder, darker. She held him tightly and stroked his hair. "Never you mind," she whispered to him. "Never you mind now, Ben."

That night they took a room in town, over a bakery. The toilet stall was two flights down. There were mice about, and from the street outside came the clamor of wee-hour drunks. Without a fan, they flung open their window, and yet there was no relief from the heat, and the mattress beneath them was soaked. The noxious smell of the town's sewers, the exhaust of cars, the smell of the bakery, the lamps in flats across the narrow way, the clattering passage of motorcycles over the ancient cobbles. They dragged the mattress onto the floor. Ben lay on his back gazing up at her face, held lightly in his hands. Very close, her hair falling into the space between them, the girl he remembered from the orchard country, a woman now in a foreign country, her long arms on either side of his head, Rachel sweating over him at five A.M., at dawn.

They were married the next morning by an army chaplain glad to dispense with regulations. No blood tests required, he said, nor did he care that the bride was an officer, the groom an enlisted man. There were many such weddings afoot, it seemed, and the chaplain performed them with a generosity consistent with the circumstances. The end of the fighting, he explained to them, had inspired many couples with love, and who was he to thwart them? God worked in strange ways, he droned: out of the cinders of ten million deaths were born the seeds of marriage. And how to explain that except as God's will at work among us in this world? The divine hand lay in it; God used the attraction between two people to further the unfolding of His scheme. The chaplain wished them the very best, bade them exchange vows of mutual fidelity in good times and bad, in all such conditions as the years might bestow, instructed them in signing the documents, and sent them on their way. Ben and Rachel, once outside, requisitioned the chaplain's jeep, in which he'd left the keys.

They bought two bottles of chianti and took the road to Florence. They passed a night in Pontedera. In Florence they left the jeep with a motor pool in front of the Palazzo Strozzi. They rode a train north into forested valleys. It was on the train to Bressanone that Rachel thought of roses: their ashes, she said, should lie side by side, his for a red rose, hers for a white, until with time they merged into one, a soft and delicate pink. It was a story she'd read, of two lovers, the final flowering of their passion. She could not remember their names now, it was something from very long ago, a book of tales from the library, illustrated: she might have been ten years old. Ben had wondered in teasing fashion if in fact it worked that way. Did the two roses mingle into one pink bush, or did their blooms tangle and intertwine, red and white, for eternity? There was no guarantee of pink, they decided. Who knew the outcome of such a thing? They would have their ashes interred side by side, leaving the rest to fate.

They disembarked, rode west in a supply truck, then set off on foot into the mountains. He told her about the German he'd killed, the man's eyes, his legs in front of him, the twitching, rattling death. "I didn't think," he confessed.

"It's difficult in a situation like that."

"It didn't have to be that way."

"It's done now," said Rachel.

They were resting in a rock-and-timber hut where a rough-framed painting of a beneficent Christ had been hung in one corner. Ben sat back with Rachel against him, looking out at wooden ladders bolted to a cliff.

"I wonder who he was."

"That makes things worse."

"I think about him."

"Try not to, Ben."

"Maybe he had a wife. A family."

"It's in the past," said Rachel.

That afternoon they came to a hamlet of Ladin homes and barns. They hiked uphill past potato patches and rested under a plum tree. A farmhouse stood open to travelers, and they presented themselves to the woman there, who wore a green apron and a hat of plaited straw and was busy lofting hay over racks. She led them through a low door, into a room made of pine boards. The floor had been painted in a floral pattern wearing away underfoot. They sat by a window in hand-hewn pine chairs, at a table painted in wildflowers—calendula and edelweiss—and looked out over long hay slopes falling away to the south. The woman brought a bottle of wine, diluted and chilled by spring water. She brought dumplings flecked with chives, polenta, and roe deer goulash.

Ben told Rachel about the field surgeon who had saved Bill Stackhouse's life. "You were right," he said. "I should have been a medic. I should have listened to you."

"This place is a dream," Rachel said. "A fairy tale or a dream."

"You warned me. You tried to warn me."

"There's green onion in the dumplings, too, mixed in with the chives."

"I want to be like that surgeon," said Ben. "A person like that, a doctor."

"I'm with you all the way," answered Rachel.

NINE

Ben opened his one good eye to a still and empty October morning in a motel room in Quincy, Washington. A nimbus of light,
a gray corona, formed a halo at the curtains. The heater fan made
a terrible racket, and outside, in the parking lot, someone was
warming the engine of a car by repeatedly revving it. The air
smelled of saffron, and from the bathroom the toilet sang. Ben
felt mired from the marijuana, his limbs immovable. He couldn't
rise with his war still in him, and he lay there feeling troubled by
it as he had for fifty-three years. He'd returned home from Italy
to the news that Aidan had died at Peleliu, hit in the neck by
mortar fire. That fall, the apples rotted on the ground. Ben's father sold ten acres to the Fisks before Christmas. In the spring,
he sold the rest to a Wenatchee man, young and starting out,
and moved into a cabin on the outskirts of town. He did odd

jobs, hired on with the railroad. He moved to Spokane, then Yakima.

Ben thought of the miracle of Stackhouse's heart: Bill had come away with a limp and a shoulder that ached in cold weather; was retired from a position in sales at an office-supply company in Bethlehem, Pennsylvania; and had, to date, eleven grandchildren, photographs of whom he'd sent to Ben with letters over the years. Ben had seen him three times at reunions of the Tenth Mountain Division. They'd spoken at length about what had happened. Stackhouse was slowly writing his memoirs, so that his progeny would know about it, too.

Ben thought of the hearts of other men and women in all their naked, exposed truth—muscles about the size of fists, pulsing at the center of living forms. The heart that was for poets and priests the seat of all things beautiful, the house of love, the host for God, the chamber of sadness, rage, discord, envy, despair, glee. Ben knew the heart as a muscle first, designed for the work of pumping blood, not so terribly intricate that it couldn't be duplicated. Parts of it were replaceable: a heart valve could be made from titanium, or lifted from a hog. In knowing the heart in this cold way, he had lost all innocence about it. It was not that he didn't believe in love, but first he was a scientist, a physician, and a man of reason. He had manipulated the hearts of human beings, and he thought he understood that when we speak of love, we speak of something transitory, something gone when we go. The heart, for Ben, was tangible—and nothing tangible remains.

There were few things more depressing he could think of than to be alone in a cheap motel room, dying of cancer at seventy-three, the smell of fallow fields outside, gruff voices in the parking lot; a bleakness grew in him he couldn't face, couldn't abide or accept. He rose from bed, limped to the bathroom, and sat on the toilet with his head dropped between his knees, noting his thin and flaccid thighs, but nothing passed from his obstructed bowels except for a foul dark squirt of water that antagonized his hemorrhoids. An old man, terminally ill, thoroughly humbled on the toilet. An old man fallen from grace.

He was driven out before eleven by hunger, and walked toward town with his hat pulled low, his hands deep in his coat pockets. The sun rode high and pale in the east, but a hard wind gusted from the mountains. A train whistled, gaining speed, churning toward the Rock Island crossing. The grit in the gutter rose and boiled whenever a truck flew past at high speed, and he was surprised once by the hiss of brakes when a freight truck slowed alongside him to turn at the Central Bean Company. To the south stretched a long row of mobile homes and trailers, some with windows broken and patched with duct tape and cardboard. In a packed-dirt yard of sparse weeds, a school bus dispensed kindergartners—the children of fruit pickers, Ben guessed—raising dust as they went. A mangy dog, yellow and slat-ribbed, came out to fend off Ben as he passed, stopping warily at thirty feet, its tongue spilling from its mouth.

Ben had no desire to face the world. He longed to be in bed again with the heat turned high, the sheets pulled close, his head resting on a pillow. But hunger urged him forward. He limped toward town, barren fields to his right, past the cemetery, a fruit warehouse, a nursery full of apple-tree rootstock, a ditch full of roadside cattails. The night had settled the wounds of his journey into a general soreness. He felt, as he walked, each of yesterday's miles, carrying them in his bones.

At Akins Foods, a chain-link fence kept the firewood out front from the hands of sneaks and thieves. A dozen cars were parked near the double doors, but the rest of the lot was littered with beer cans, food wrappers, broken bottles, a pair of overturned shopping carts, a brown paper bag ripped apart by dogs—the refuse of the previous night.

Inside, at the automatic teller machine, Ben withdrew two hundred and sixty dollars to pay Ilse Peterson's bill. It was warm in the store and smelled of donuts and of the bread for sale in the bakery. There was a rug-cleaning apparatus for rent and a Lotto Scratch Ticket machine beside it, bags of bulk-size dog food, toilet paper in cut-open cartons, a pyramid mound of Presto-Logs, and a display of canning jars. There were sunglasses, cigarettes, bags of ice, and a rack of romance paperbacks: men with oily, puffed-up bodies, women shorn of half their clothes, grappling together on sunny beaches or posed in front of palm trees.

At the end of the aisle of Mexican food—pozole, mole, yucca root—a girl gawked indiscreetly at his eye as he fumbled past with his shopping cart: the bruised and swollen violence of it, he saw, aroused her curiosity and disgust. Padding about uncertainly, deliberating on what he might stomach, he selected a can of chicken soup, a box of rye crackers, a pint of vanilla yogurt, a liter of prune juice, a half gallon of spring water, a bag of fig bars, two Winesap apples, and a ripe-looking mango. He found a plastic spoon at the deli counter and hauled everything to the checkout stand, where the cashier glanced at his eye twice before asking him about it.

"A game of croquet," Ben answered. "It got out of control."

"What a crock," the cashier said. "Hah, hah. Very funny."

"These people take it seriously," insisted Ben. "I got cracked with a mallet."

"I always know when somebody's lying."

"Croquet," said Ben, "with the wrong people."

"If you say so."

"All right. I'll confess. I walked into a door."

The cashier, a girl of twenty-five, laughed derisively. There was a splotch of red between her eyebrows, and her hair had been stiffly frosted. "Oh, my God," she said to him. "You should have opened it first."

"You're right," said Ben. "Next time."

"It's not that hard, opening a door." The cashier shoved his things aside. "$12.78," she said.

He limped out into the cold again with his shoddy plastic bags in tow, one in each hand. They felt heavy, heavier than they should have: his shoulders ached from carrying Rex, as did the tendons in his forearms. He passed the forlorn trailer court and a placard urging dieters to call a toll-free number for the secret to loosing thirty pounds a month. MAGIC! it read. GUARANTEED! The sky was cloudless across the broad plain, tender with morning sunlight. Beneath its expanse, Ben felt alone. The cashier had been devoid of compassion, and he took her heartlessness with him. But how was she to know of his condition, his need for kinder treatment? He felt like going back to tell her that she ought to be careful about what she said, but he could not summon the strength it would take, and at any rate it would cause a scene: a crazy old man with a black eye ranting away in Akins Foods, embarrassing everybody.

There was no way to explain himself. He felt removed from the world. Suffering suffused everything. The sadness in the October wind was also the sadness in the cashier's mouth—different notes struck from the same chord.

Ben hung the DO NOT DISTURB sign on his door and choked down the overripe, dripping mango in an excess of appetite. He wiped his chin and, still ravenous, devoured the vanilla yogurt. Next he poured the chicken soup into the plastic ice bucket beside the sink and warmed it in the microwave oven. The bucket melted and warped slightly, but he saw no reason to worry about it and sat down in front of the television. Rifling through stations aimlessly, he ate the soup, blowing at his spoon and dropping crackers in. He tried to take an interest in something, the midday talk shows with their amicable hosts, but none of it appealed to him, it was all puerile gibberish, and he muted the sound with the remote controller and picked up the Bible on the bedside table left there by the Gideons. He had not read the Bible for a long time. He turned to the Book of Job:

> *Days of affliction have taken hold*
> *upon me.*
> *In the night my bones are pierced*
> *and fall from me,*
> *And my sinews take no rest.*
> *By the great force of my disease*
> *is my garment disfigured;*
> *It bindeth me about as the collar*
> *of my coat.*
> *He hath cast me into the mire,*
> *And I am become like dust and*
> *ashes.*

It struck him how Satan and God conversed with such indifference and arrogance about their experiment. It was disturbing, too, that God punished Eliphaz the Temanite, Bildad the Shuhite, and Zophar the Naamathite—all come to comfort Job—simply for misunderstanding Him in the course of delivering comfort. That Job himself recovered his health and lived a hundred forty years more, with fourteen thousand sheep on hand, six thousand camels, a thousand yoke of oxen, a thousand she asses, three new sons—not to mention the fairest daughters in the land—seemed too much of a happy ending, until Ben came to the book's final passage, where Job died.

He looked up from the pages of the Holy Book to find the television still on. He fumbled for a moment with the remote, then turned the volume up. A married couple sat on a stage, ordinary

people, overweight, the man with a handlebar mustache and sideburns, the woman's dress revealing the cleavage of slack, pendu-
lous breasts. They were swingers, the man was saying. They were
twenty-seven and had no children. They had sex with members of
a swingers association at weekend conventions and get-togethers.
There were also weeknight rendezvous. They were happily married, said the man. He enjoyed the thought of his wife that way.
She, too, liked the arrangement. She thought about sex all day at
work. He did, too—the coming of evening. He was in marketing
with an auto parts company, she a receptionist for a floral distrib-
utor. They labored, he said, to pay their bills—their real lives
were all about swinging. They saw no need to change this. They
saw a future of endless sex, so why should they change anything?
They were the happiest people they knew of. It seemed to them
they shared a secret. In restaurants full of ordinary people they
groped each other under the table, as randy as seventeen-year-olds.
Why would they want to be any different? Why would they want
ordinary sex, the garden variety most suffered through? They held
the key to living, said the man. Sex, said the woman, was the heart
of things. What else was there as wonderful?

Chewing on a Winesap, Ben changed the station. A pale man
near his own age was bowling, and Ben watched him toss his ball
down the lane with as much force as he could muster. The man,
poised, watched the course of the ball, anguish creasing his face.
For a moment the world was brought to a halt, the bowling
ball arresting time, the bowler wholly unaware that elsewhere
swingers were pawing each other with a desperate, blinding passion. For the bowler there were no swingers, the course of the
ball was everything. He followed it with a yearning heart. Ben
switched off the television.

He called the Greyhound 800 number to get the schedule for
the bus run upriver, then a Wenatchee company to reserve a
rental car. His plan was to drive to Malaga, find William Harden's

Wolfhound Orchard, and try to pry his gun, somehow, out of Harden's hands. After that, he would walk for grouse in the Colockum country, find a barbed-wire fence somewhere, and shoot himself in the neck.

Ben sat mulling the difficulty of retrieving his gun from Harden. He could not present himself at the man's door and expect a hospitable reception. If he pressed his case for rightful ownership, made an entreaty invoking fair play, or apologized again for the wolfhound's death, he would only be turned away. He couldn't just ask for the gun's return, though the notion of acting in some other fashion—as a burglar or thief—was beyond imagining.

Ben thought through what he had to say, then called his daughter in Seattle. "I thought you were hunting," she said.

"I am," said Ben. "I'm over in Quincy. What are you doing, dear?"

"Nothing, really. Working on my screenplay. Chris said you called."

"Working on a screenplay isn't nothing," said Ben. "What's this one about?"

"It's a children's movie."

"What's it about?"

"It's complicated."

"In a nutshell, then."

"A boy on a journey."

"What happens to him?"

"He loses his dog and goes after it. A lot of things. It's complicated."

"Well," said Ben. "What a coincidence. That's the reason I called."

There was a pause on the other end of the line. He could hear Renee breathing into the receiver. "What?" she said. "I don't get it."

"I had an accident," Ben told her. "Saturday morning. I crashed the car."

"You what?"

"I crashed the car in Snoqualmie Pass. But I'm fine, I didn't get injured."

"You crashed the car? Your four-wheel-drive car?"

"That's the one," said Ben.

"You're kidding, Dad. Did you hit anyone?"

"I hit a tree. In the summit exit. The road was wet, and I lost control. It could have been much worse."

"You didn't get hurt?"

"One eye is swollen and bruised a little. Other than that, nothing."

"You ought to have it checked, Dad. You don't want to take a chance."

"It's fine," said Ben. "It's nothing."

"Wait a second," Renee said. "How did you get up to Quincy?"

"Some people stopped and gave me a ride. A couple of very nice people."

"You hitchhiked?"

"No."

"Who were they, then?"

"Two kids in a Volkswagen van."

"You're kidding me."

"What's wrong with that?"

"That's just so funny. It's hard to imagine. That's so funny," she repeated.

"Anyway," said Ben, "they took me to Vantage."

"I thought you said you're in Quincy."

"I am in Quincy."

"So how did you get there?"

"Believe it or not," Ben said, "I ended up walking from Vantage to George. Cross country. Hunting chukars."

"Hunting what?"

"Little birds. Chukars."

"You walked all that way to hunt little birds?"

"Not exactly. I had some problems. There was a fellow out there chasing coyotes, and my dogs got tangled up with his dogs. And Tristan got himself killed."

"No," said Renee.

"I'm afraid so."

"Wait a minute. What happened?"

"A dog fight, a bad fight. His dogs attacked mine, and I found Tristan killed."

"Dad," said Renee. "That's terrible."

"What can you do?" Ben asked.

"You can sue the guy. He killed your dog."

"I don't even know who he is, though. Besides, it wouldn't bring Tris back."

"That's terrible," Renee said again.

"I hate to think about it," said Ben.

There was another pause, a long one. Ben shifted the receiver to his right ear because his arm was falling asleep.

"This is a really weird story," said Renee. "I can't believe I'm hearing this."

"I know," said Ben. "It's weird."

"So you walked from Vantage all the way to George? That's fifteen miles, uphill."

"Not quite. Not really."

"Dad, this is so crazy."

"There's more," said Ben. "Rex was injured. I brought him up here to the vet."

"What?"

"Those coyote dogs went after Rex. But he made it through. He's all right. I got him up here to the vet."

"Rex—that's your other dog, the one you got last year?"

"You know Rex," Ben said.

"Now wait," said Renee. "Wait a minute. How did you get up to Quincy?"

"A trucker," said Ben. "At Martha's Inn. I met him at Martha's Inn."

"A trucker took you from George to Quincy?"

"That's how it went, yes."

"You rode with a trucker."

"Rex, too. We got him up here to an excellent vet. His wounds were mostly skin wounds."

"This is bizarre," said Renee.

"It is," said Ben. "It's crazy."

"So where are you?"

"I'm at a motel."

"That's good," she said.

Ben sat rubbing his side as he spoke. He had eaten too much, and his stomach was in turmoil. He was curled on the bed with the jar of prune juice open on the nightstand.

"What are you going to do?" asked Renee. "Dad, this is just so crazy."

"I don't know," he said. "I'm so far into this thing now, there's no reason not to continue. So my plan is to wander a little and see if I can find some blue grouse."

"You're nuts, Dad. You're completely nuts. You ought to go home and rest."

"I don't want to go home and rest. I came over here to hunt."

"You can hunt anytime."

"No, I can't."

"You shouldn't hunt anyway. Go hiking with Chris."

"I like hunting."

"It's awful. It's blood sport."

"Let's change the subject," said Ben.

At the end, and in an easy way, he told Renee that he loved her. He sent his best to his son-in-law and grandson. He told her not to worry about things. He wished her the best of luck with her screenplay. He convinced her he was all right.

Afterward, he curled up but, seized by nausea, hurried to the bathroom. He sat on the toilet passing fluid from his bowels, waves of peristaltic cramping seizing his abdomen. The mango, he thought, had been too acidic. Or perhaps it was the Winesap he'd eaten. The obstruction in his colon was growing, swelling, narrowing the path of ordinary digestion—he was in need of palliative surgery; either that or stop eating altogether. But especially, he should stay away from fruit. He could not afford to eat fruit anymore. His apple days were over.

Ben left his room key by the bathroom sink and set out with his rucksack on his back, his carabiner around his neck, a traveler once more. His respite at the motel lay behind him. It was time to push toward his destination. He trudged down the road with his face to the asphalt, the wind slinging grit and sand. He passed the Custom Apple Packers warehouse, where bins were stacked six high outside and forklifts scurried about. It was the height of harvest season in the river country. The wind would shake loose apples from the trees. In a week the limbs would be bare of fruit. The orchards would look desolate, unsettling.

In five minutes he came to the veterinary clinic: inside a woman held a cat in her lap, while another clutched a small white terrier. A man sat rubbing his beard stubble, yawned, licked his lips, and stretched dramatically, twining his arms above his head.

The receptionist seated behind the counter wore a sleeveless denim shirt with pearl buttons and a necklace made of rhinestones—a woman of thirty or thirty-five who was not afraid to show her shoulders and arms and whose river-country beauty had started to fade, which made her all the more beguiling. "My God," she said. "How nasty."

"Don't ask," said Ben. "I'm here to see Rex. The Brittany, in back there."

He paid for Rex's surgery. She stood, and he took her immediately for a horsewoman, a dusty horsewoman who actually rode, who curried, combed, and lived among horses. It was in the way she moved, the economical fit of her jeans as she transferred a file from one place to another and paper-clipped ledger sheets. He followed her to the recovery room, where they stood looking into Rex's kennel. The dog twitched and shivered in his dreams, and there was something depleted in his sleeping face, something vulnerable. Reaching through the wire mesh of the kennel, Ben lay two fingers on Rex's head. "It's all right," he whispered.

Calmly examining her fingernails, the lengths of her arms sleek and honey brown, the receptionist said that Rex had been awake when she opened the clinic at eight-thirty, had taken water and food readily with every sign of returning health, but now he slept as might be expected, given all he'd been through. Dr. Peterson had examined his stitches, and things were as they might expect. Meat, she added, was good for a black eye. A thawing slab of red meat would draw the bruise right out.

"Listen," said Ben. "I can't take him right now. I have to go up to Wenatchee."

The receptionist slid her fingertips into the rear pockets of her jeans. It caused her shoulders to rotate back and exposed the blue veins branching in them. "Not a problem," she said to Ben. "He can stay with us today."

"I appreciate that."

"It's not a problem."

"I'm heading up there now," said Ben. "I'll be back before you close."

"We're open 'til five, but I'm here 'til five-thirty, so swing by when you get back." She stood with her fists against her hips and again appraised his swollen eye. "Did you see a doctor?" she asked.

"I am a doctor."

"I'm surprised you didn't take a stitch or two. Looks like you could have used it."

He followed her out of the recovery room. She was long-legged and well curved, the small of her back a deep, dark secret, and the shadow of her bra beneath her denim shirt inspired in him not desire but sadness. One of the bra's straps with its little adjuster had slipped into the open and ran over her brown shoulder in a delicate, taut white line.

Ben left and pressed on, past the United Church of Christ, past Verdah's Department Store and the Quincy water tower. The town lay sleepy and leaden, and except for the shade trees raging in the wind there was no other sound. On C Street he passed El Molino Bakery—TORTILLERIA Y PANADERIA it read in the dusty plate-glass window. There were no customers there, and none at Royer's Home Furnishing or any of the other stores. The town seemed uninhabited, yet as he crossed Central, a yard dog came out, a blunt, tough-looking stump of a dog who barked at him threateningly. Ben walked by with one hand on his hat to keep it from flying off.

The bus stop was at the edge of town, out near the Great Northern railroad tracks, beyond which lay a liquid fertilizer plant and a big diatomite processor. Tumbleweed skittered down B Street toward him, and three children huddled underneath a blanket in the backseat of a rusting, dilapidated Buick parked at the Quincy Food Bank. Across the street stood a fence hand-crafted out of stray bits of corrugated roofing metal salvaged or plundered from a refuse yard. Its gate chattered raspingly when the wind rippled through it.

At the bus stop all the planter boxes were empty. There was the red, white, and blue image of a greyhound overhead, a sign advertising WESTERN UNION, another PACKAGE EXPRESS. All were attached to a slatternly storefront, and through its grimy window Ben saw rows of unpainted ceramic figurines—dinosaurs, Indians, Pilgrims, ghosts, tigers, dwarfs, elephants—some of a size to stand in gardens, others more appropriate as mantel knickknacks or to adorn tabletops and shelves. He pushed his way through the heavy door, pulled off his hat, set his rucksack on the floor, and bought a bus ticket from the clerk at the counter, a woman dressed in purple warm-ups and a patriotic-print nylon windbreaker, who was hard at work with a razor blade, shaving clay from a figurine of Snow White. Broad liver spots mottled her hands. She was neither friendly nor discourteous to him. She expressed no curiosity about his eye, and he guessed she knew, from long experience, that there might be trouble inquiring. She made out his ticket for the Wenatchee run with a slow, troubled inefficiency, as if writing was a trial. Her letters were tall, with shaky, large loops. She paused, adjusted the set of her glasses, then finished writing his ticket. A pottery kiln gave heat beside her. The rest of the room was cold.

"Bus ought to be here in about three minutes," she told Ben, handing him the ticket. "You can wait in the doorway, if you want."

Ben half-turned to take in the displays of angels, baying wolves, Indians on horseback, impressively antlered elk and deer, fringed frontiersmen, and wood fairies. "Did you make all these?" he asked.

"I did," said the woman. "All of them."

"Can you sell them here? Do you get customers?"

"Not really," said the woman. "No."

She took up her razor blade again and went back to cutting small shavings of clay from the crown of Snow White's head. "There's no money in this," she said. "That's the way it goes."

"They're really good," Ben said.

"I've been doing it a long time."

"That's the way to get good at something."

"Well, I don't know what else I'd do. Too much time on my hands."

"It's a good hobby," Ben told her.

The woman looked up. "Hobby," she said. "I hate that word."

"Sorry," said Ben. "Me, too."

They looked at each other warily. The bus pulled up to the curb outside, raising dust in the street. The brakes gave a hydraulic gasp, and the door hinged open noisily. The driver bounded down the steps with theatrical resolve and energy, a crisp, neat man of thirty-five, his hairline prominently receding. He wore wraparound sunglasses and carried a pair of leather driving gloves. Pushing through the door of the little shop, he swung off his cap, high-stepped and saluted, snapping it low off one eyebrow. He said to Ben, "Hi-dee ho!"

"Hi-dee ho," Ben answered.

"Stow your bag?"

"I'll keep it with me."

"Where to?"

"Just to Wenatchee."

"Trip to the doctor?"

"Maybe, maybe not."

"Boxing practice?"

"Sure. You and me."

The driver whipped off his sunglasses. "Whenever you're ready," he said, grinning. "I'll tag that other eye."

The shop clerk laughed—the twitter of a bird—and her exasperation was evident. "Men," she said, shaking her head, her wrists turned back against her hips. "My God. What is it with men? Whatever will we do with you?"

To Ben's surprise, the bus was crowded. Most of the passengers looked wan, road-weary. Small televisions sat mounted on high, but no one had them on. A wastebasket, clinched by a bungee cord to the back of the driver's seat, was full of hamburger and candy wrappers, cola cans, paper cups—all the refuse of travelers passing tedious, interminable miles in a ruinous highway torpor. A teenager in the front row slept against the window, his mouth gaping wide. A bag of Cheetos lay open beside him, as well as a plastic bottle of Coca-Cola and a gaudy paperback with a submarine on its cover. Behind him sat a black man with his hair in shiny ringlets, eating an Almond Joy. On his knees was a briefcase with a combination lock. He spoke softly with another black man, who wore a Nike Air billed cap and sat with his legs crossed effeminately. In the next row a fat man with headphones clutched a tiny cassette player, drummed his prominent belly, and occasionally stopped beating rhythm to the music to caress his long gray locks. There was a cheerless couple of approximately Ben's age, looking washed-out and diminished by their journey, and even vaguely humiliated, as if riding the Greyhound was beneath them. Farther along was a very young woman traveling with three small children. A baby slept on the seat beside her, and the other two children wriggled, slouched, and slithered about as if underwater—first with their feet running up the backrests, then coiled like fraternizing sea snakes, then curled like small human seals. A coloring book lay on the floor beneath them, crayons scattered about. In the back of the bus rode three young men Ben guessed were apple pickers coming in late for the harvest, migrants following the crop even now, this far into the fall. They were all nut-brown and dusty. One sat tightly wrapped in a blanket, shivering and sweating from a fever, wracked by a sputum-filled cough.

Ben sat down amid these strangers and looked up at the bus driver, who stood before them pulling on his leather gloves, securing them against his fingertips as if he were a gunslinger or a surgeon. YOUR OPERATOR, read a sign above his head. SAFE, RELIABLE, COURTEOUS. The driver made a final adjustment at the thumbs, flicked a lever that shut the door—it gave a soft, hydraulic sigh—then took his palm-sized microphone in hand, working its handset cord. His eyes were still concealed from view behind his sunglasses. "Hey, all right," he said in the voice of a man who considers himself a stand-up comic. "We have a new passenger riding to Wenatchee, and that's good, that's excellent, so why don't we all just sit back now and enjoy the ride, let me do the driving, relax and we'll all go Greyhound together—let's get this show on the road!"

The driver adjusted himself on his throne. He pulled out, rumbled through town, and turned onto the highway. The bus shook as it picked up speed. Its ventilators hummed with a steady insistence. The passengers were jostled and stirred a little, readjusting their legs or heads or turning to look out the windows. Opposite Ben a girl slept with her face beneath her upper arm, a hardbound book propped open beside her, pages down, spine showing. *The Philosophy of Freedom*, by Rudolf Steiner. Subtitled *The Basis for a Modern World Conception*. She wore blue jeans many sizes too large, and when she moved her arm and half-sat up, he saw the ring impaling her nose. A compact girl, her hair tinted green, freckles on her cheeks and nose, fundamentally pleasing to look at. When she noticed that he was staring her way, he pretended to look past her at the orchards along the road, but she straightened up, stared back at him, and asked what happened to his eye.

"I took a baseball bat to it," Ben said, "so I'd have a conversation starter."

"It's gross," said the girl. "I mean, really."

"True, but it's been worth it," Ben said. "I've had interesting conversations."

The girl smiled, and he saw crooked teeth, but their asymmetry was a quiet thing and carried with it a certain charm. Her smile was unguarded and suggested to Ben that she was not afraid to speak to a stranger, an old and battered vagabond. "You look totally wasted," she said to him.

"I am wasted," he agreed. "That's a good way of putting it."

The bus slowed for a crew of linemen unspooling cable at roadside. There were low sloughs of water, aluminum silos, and rows of trellised apples. The sunlight pooled over everything, and the wind blew briskly in the trees. He could hear it whistling through the windows.

In the back of the bus, the sick fruit picker began to cough. A phlegm-filled cough, coarse and rough, so that Ben turned to look at him. The picker wore his blanket like a hood.

"Your book," Ben said, "looks a little profound. Not really typical bus reading, is it? *The Philosophy of Freedom?*"

"I'm just reading it," the girl replied, handing it across the aisle. "It looked kind of interesting."

"*The Philosophy of Freedom,*" Ben repeated. "Are you a college student?"

The girl touched a pimple festering on her chin. "I'm working on my master's," she said. "At WSU, on Goethe, his poetry. The author of this book—Rudolf Steiner—edited Goethe's scientific writings. I've gotten kind of sidetracked into him. Have you heard of anthroposophy?"

"I have," said Ben. "I know the term. But I don't know what it means."

"It's from Steiner here," the girl said. "It's a spiritual thing, a philosophy. And I really relate to what he's saying. To the point where I'm thinking of changing my thesis, focusing more on Steiner."

"Why not? It's your thesis, after all."

"It's just kind of late. I'm so far into Goethe."

"You've got your whole life, though."

"I don't know."

"Believe me," said Ben. "You do."

The girl turned fully toward him now. "Where are you from?" she asked.

"Here. Hereabouts. A little north of here."

"You mean you live here?"

"No, I was born here."

"You live somewhere else."

"Over in Seattle."

"Me, too. I grew up over there."

"Two west-siders," Ben said.

There was the chatter of the children in the row behind them and the hacking of the apple picker. The bus dropped toward the Columbia. A steep draw gaped beside the road, throttled by sage and sumac. In the distance ran the railroad tracks and a stark web of power lines against the dry, auburn hills.

"Anthroposophy," Ben said. "Now you've got me curious. You have to tell me about it."

"That guy," the girl said, lowering her voice. "He's been coughing like that for hours now."

"It doesn't sound good," Ben agreed.

"Well, anyway," the girl went on, "it's this spiritual thing, I guess is how to put it. It's like there's this spiritual dimension people just don't see. Because they're so occupied with the material world. And in anthroposophy you try to reach it. You train your consciousness to rise above the physical. It's mostly an intellectual thing. You use your mind, you train yourself."

"That—to me—doesn't sound so unusual. I'm no expert on these matters, but I'd guess most religions would say the same—that it takes mental discipline to find spiritual truth. This anthroposophy, as you describe it, doesn't sound so unique."

"I guess," said the girl. "Yeah, okay. But this was back around the turn of the century. People weren't thinking the same way then. Materialism had no counterbalance, except a few intellectuals like Steiner."

"Tell me," Ben said. "This spiritual realm. This dimension you use your mind to discover. Is it life after death? What most people would call heaven?"

"I can't say," the girl replied. "But no, Steiner doesn't put it like that. Angels playing harps in the clouds, if that's what you mean, no."

"But does he describe it, this spiritual place? In some other way? Not angels?"

"I haven't finished the book yet. It might be in a later chapter."

"I wonder if he will," Ben said. "And I wonder how he'll claim to know."

"You get there with your mind. You don't have to die first."

"So it isn't life after death, then. It's something else, not heaven."

"It's something else," the girl agreed. "Steiner doesn't talk about angels."

"Well, angels wouldn't be bad," said Ben, handing back the book.

She took it and set it on the seat beside her, rested her forearms on her knees, and dangled her loose hands in front of her. "You're a skeptic," she said accusingly. "You're way too analytical."

"Skeptic, yes," Ben said. "I don't accept things easily, I have questions, I'm a skeptic. Analytical—maybe, but no more than Rudolf Steiner. Didn't you say gaining the spiritual realm was a matter of using your mind?"

"Yeah, but it's also spiritual. You have to accept that it isn't just intellectual. You have to believe it's out there."

"What's out there?"

"The other world."

"I'll believe it when I see it."

"That's circular logic."

"Circular is good. It keeps me here."

"If you like going in circles," said the girl. "Okay, fine, you're here."

"Where else would I want to be? Out there with the stars?"

"If you feel that way, death is too scary. But if you believe there's this spiritual realm, you're not afraid to die."

"You're not afraid?"

"No. I'm not."

"That's good. I'm terrified."

"That's because you don't believe in something."

"No," said Ben. "It's because I'm older. Death isn't real at your age."

The girl leaned toward him, animated now. "Yes, it is. I've thought about it. Death is totally real for me. Don't say that. Death is real."

"It's easy to say," Ben said. "But try to imagine it."

"I have," said the girl. "I'm not afraid."

Ben smiled and rubbed the back of his neck. "This is why I smashed my eye," he said. "You see what I mean? It works."

The girl laughed and took her foot in her hands; she was limber in an easy, unathletic way and looked comfortable sitting tailor-fashion. "It's weird," she said, "but you remind me a lot of this doctor I had when I was growing up."

"Did he have a black eye?"

"He had glasses like yours."

"I was a doctor, too," said Ben. "I retired a year and a half ago."

"Well, maybe you should look at that guy back there, then. He's really sick, I think."

"Maybe you're right," Ben agreed. "But what if he speaks only Spanish? I won't know what to say."

"That's all right," the girl said. "I took Spanish as an undergrad."

"Are you pretty good?"

"I read *Don Quixote*."

"What did you think?"

"I loved it," said the girl.

"Quixote's mad."

"Much madness is divinest sense." She admonished him with a forefinger. "That's Emily Dickinson."

"Much madness can just be madness, too. What is it Sancho Panza calls him? Knight of the Mournful Countenance?"

"I wouldn't talk," the girl warned, "with your eye swollen that way."

Ben looked at the picker again. One of his companions looked back at Ben, calmly, showing nothing. He wore a cap emblazoned with the name of a fruit company, DOLE.

"Come on," said the girl. "The guy's messed up. Take a look at him."

Ben felt a surge of affection for her. He wanted her to believe in decency. "If you'll translate," he said.

She stood up with no hesitation. She smiled at him, her hands in her pockets. "Come on," she said.

"You keep yourself back a little. You don't want him breathing on you."

"You look out, too. Wear a mask or something."

"I don't have one."

"Use a handkerchief."

"I'll be fine. I know what to do."

"What's your name, by the way?" said the girl. "Just in case they ask."

Ben told her. Then she gave him hers. "Catherine," she said. "Catherine Donnelly."

She led the way. She stood in the aisle next to the pickers who, up close, looked to Ben like boys younger than seventeen. "*Es doctor*," said Catherine, pointing at Ben. "*Es médico. Quiere ayudar.*"

All three looked at her, then at Ben, then away again. The one by the window stared out with no expression—a dark boy with a thick pug nose, his black hair swept up and pomaded, a faint mustache above his lip. The sick one shut his eyes with a listless resignation, the blanket draped closely over his head so that only his mouth, nose, and brow showed. The one in the Dole cap removed it from his head and set it gently in his lap. His hair was shorn close to his skull, except for a long black ponytail sprouting from the base of his neck. "*No se preocupe*," he replied. "*Un resfriado. Nada más.*"

"He thinks it's just a cold," said Catherine. "What do you want me to tell them?"

"Tell him it isn't just a cold," said Ben. "Tell him the coughing is serious. And tell him he doesn't have to pay me."

"*Es muy serio*," said Catherine. "*Pulmonia. Tuberculoso. Es muy serio. El médico, no va a cobrarle. Es gratis, entiende?*"

There was no answer. The one by the window appraised her with suspicion. "*El médico generoso*," she said. "*Gratuito. Un hombre de Dios. Un ángel de Dios. Muy bien.*" She touched the sick one's shoulder, lightly. "*Hace cuánto tiempo que usted está así?*" she asked. "I asked him how long he's been sick," she told Ben. "Just to get things started."

"That's good," said Ben. "Keep it going."

The sick boy didn't answer. Ben looked up the aisle of the bus. A number of the passengers had turned around and were watching him and Catherine. The driver watched through his rearview mirror. They were passing along the river now, not far from the place where Ben had been born. Orchards stretched away north and south. The poplars stood tall in the wind.

Catherine sat down across the aisle. Ben could see the boy better now. His eyes were bloodshot, his eyelids crusted, his cheeks gleamed with sweat.

"Catherine," the girl said, pointing at herself. Then she put a hand on Ben's arm. *"Este es el Doctor Ben Givens. No habla mucho español. Comprende?"*

There was no answer. They didn't look at her. The one with the Dole cap in his lap began to finger its bill a little and pulled on his ponytail. The one with the pomaded hair looked studiously out his window. The sick boy began to cough again. He leaned forward and gagged.

"Qué le occure?" said Catherine. *"Hace cuánto tiempo que está usted así?"*

"No me siento bien," said the boy. *"Estoy enfermo. Tengo escalofríos. Tengo fiebre. Me duele la cabeza y la espalda y todo el cuerpo. Me cuesta respirar. Pero no quiero un doctor. Muchas gracias."*

"He's really sick," said Catherine. "He says he's got a chill and a fever and his head and back hurt a lot. Plus, it's hard for him to breathe. But he doesn't want a doctor."

"Tell him he doesn't have to pay," said Ben. "Tell him we won't ask to see papers. We won't even ask his name."

Catherine translated these things. They all three looked at Ben again. *"Un ángel de Dios,"* she assured them again. *"Un buen hombre. No es nada como para preocuparse. Un médico de Dios."*

The boy with the Dole cap studied her face, then began to speak in a whisper. Catherine leaned toward him.

Ben recognized place-names: Boardman and Milton-Freewater, Pasco and Walla Walla. The boy spoke evenly, rapidly, until

Catherine stopped him with the palm of her hand. "It's his brother," she said. "The sick one's his brother. He hasn't worked in three weeks. It started out he had a cold. Anyway, they thought it was a cold. They bought him some aspirin in Walla Walla. Still, he's always coughing and sweating. He can't work, he's always tired, he gets hot, his body aches. They've been all over looking for work. Pasco, Milton-Freewater."

"The coughing," asked Ben. "Does it hurt?"

She translated. "*Sí*," said the boy. "*Me duele mucho el pecho.*" He patted his chest. "*Aquí.*"

"Ask him if he's coughed up blood. Even just a little. Ask him."

She did. The travelers conferred among themselves. The answer was no, no blood, none anyone could recall.

Ben massaged his forehead. The night sweats in particular interested him. He guessed it was a case of tuberculosis, though he could not rule out pneumonia, or coccidioidomycosis, or a host of other possibilities.

He stared out the window. They were passing a dirt yard, carved from bench land, where a thousand cows thronged a feed trough, yellow tags stapled to their ears. Beyond was the old Fisk orchard, which was now Bartlett pears. Then came his family's old orchard. The house had been torn down and replaced. The Lombardy poplars were stately sentinels. In the south orchard, the ladders were up. The bins stood between the rows. He could see someone picking in the wind.

"That's where I was raised," he told Catherine. "That was our orchard, there."

"Really great," she answered. "But this guy's kind of suffering. You can't just look out the window."

Ben sighed. "I was a heart surgeon," he said. "I'm sort of shooting in the dark here."

"Well, keep shooting," Catherine said. "What should we ask them next?"

"Ask them what kind of work they've been doing."

"What's that got to do with anything?"

"Maybe he ingested a pesticide, or maybe they've been working around barnyard animals. I don't know, just ask."

She asked them about the nature of their work. The one with the ponytail answered at length. Asparagus at first, for almost four weeks. Then, in June, no work for a while. They lived at the bottom of an onion field, waiting. In July, three weeks of sweet onions. They went into Oregon for raspberries. Afterward, no work again. Then, finally, hoeing potatoes. They waited more. They picked apples near Yakima. Now they were heading north.

"*De dónde es usted?*" asked Catherine. "*Sonora? Chihuahua? Jalisco?*"

The one by the window answered. "*Tejas,*" he said. "*Somos de Tejas.*"

"*De qué parte de Tejas es usted?*"

There was no answer. The boy shrugged and looked out his window. "He says they're from Texas," said Catherine. "But he can't say what part of Texas, or maybe he didn't understand me."

"They're here without green cards," Ben said. "They're afraid they're going to be deported. Tell them again we're not the police. We're not going to turn them in—stress that. Promise them or something."

Catherine turned again to the travellers. "*No somos policía,*" she said. "*Les prometo. No se preocupen.*"

There was no answer from the one by the window, but the one with the Dole hat in his lap faced her earnestly.

"Ask them," said Ben. "Before they came here. Was anyone sick at home?"

No, none had been sick at home, not especially.

"What about in their travels?" asked Ben. "Have they met others sick like him? Anywhere? Picking raspberries in Oregon? Somewhere? Hoeing potatoes?"

Yes, there had been others ill. But there were always a few ill workers in the fields. Colds, fevers, it was to be expected. Nothing that stood out.

"Sprays," said Ben. "Pesticides. Chemical fertilizers."

"*Líquido para rociar,*" Catherine tried. "*Cebolla. Papas. Espárragos. En la hacienda . . . abono para la tierra.* I don't know. *Químicos. Respiraba químicos, acaso?*"

The one by the window seemed to understand. In animated fashion, he explained it to the others. They nodded in their understanding. But no, they said, there had been no chemicals, none that they could recollect.

"All right," said Ben. "What about skin rashes? Ask him about his skin."

There had been no rashes, no stiff, sore neck, no swollen throat. He had no lumps in his neck or armpits. He didn't smoke cigarettes and never had. He did not eat much, but in the last few days he'd had refried beans, a ham sandwich with salsa and onion, a stew of chicken backs, tortillas. He'd had coffee with sugar and milk that morning, some Kool-Aid and a Pepsi Cola. As much water as he could drink. Yes, they drank irrigation water at first. No, they didn't often wash their hands. Yes, they had all felt ill at times, mildly ill, from traveling. But the sick one had really begun to suffer about three weeks ago. He began to ache in his muscles and joints and was light-headed in the fields. He felt sleepy most of the time. Now he couldn't keep from coughing, especially in the night hours. They didn't know what to do with him.

"This is a mystery," Ben said. "If I had to guess, I'd say TB, possible TB versus pneumonia. But there are all kinds of viruses around out here, fungal infections, bacterial diseases, any number of things."

"Still," said Catherine. "We have to do something."

"He needs care," Ben told her. "He needs a clinic or a hospital. Myself, I can't make a diagnosis, much less offer treatment.

I'm out here on this bus without anything—I don't even have a stethoscope. Tell him this is serious. Tell him he should go to the hospital as soon as we reach Wenatchee."

"Now wait a second," said Catherine. "If he goes to a hospital, they'll ask for papers, won't they? Identification. A visa or something. And then he'll maybe get kicked out of the country. We can't do that to him."

"Look," said Ben. "He's seriously ill. If he doesn't get some help soon, he's going to get even worse than he is. He could even die from it."

"We promised him," said Catherine. "We promised he wouldn't get deported."

"He won't get deported," said Ben. "The main thing is, he needs treatment right away. That's all there is to it. A hospital. As soon as we get off the bus."

"You have to help him from outside the system."

"There isn't any help outside the system."

"Then what'll we do?" asked Catherine.

The boy threw another coughing fit, which brought her exhortations to a halt. He lurched forward spasmodically, whipping his head against the seat back before him, and brought up a bolus of blood-tinged sputum that spattered his blanket, red.

It was as though a demon had seized his chest. He wheezed and labored to move air through his lungs. His brother put a hand around his shoulder. "*Ángelito,*" he said. "*Quédate tranquilo. Ya va a pasar. Dios nos va a ayudar.*"

"What did he say?" Ben asked.

"He said God will help them."

TEN

The bus went past the Rock Island Dam, a silicon plant, and an aluminum smelter, and on the east side of the road a cherry orchard barren in this season. The apple orchards, though, were laden heavily, the pickers filling their canvas bags, the tractors busy pulling bins, the apples waiting at pull-outs and sidings, the branch props stacked in the crooks of trees, and everywhere on the road to Wenatchee the haul trucks ran fully loaded. Along the river course the wind blew downstream: the flag on the basalt island just south of Hurst Landing stood stiffly battered by it. The river here was a frothing lake with a few fall whitecaps blown up like tufts of scudding ocean foam.

The bus passed the Rock Island Hydro Park with its ball fields silent this time of year and its stark NO SWIMMING signs. It passed a trailer park laid out formally above the river. Across the water lay South Wenatchee with its dingy railroad freight yard, poplar trees, and more mobile homes. The rail yard had once been thronged by apples, but now it was desolate and little used, its buildings skeletal. Fruit pickers squatted in makeshift camps. One had a warming fire sparking in the wind. Children sat by the river's edge.

The bus crossed the bridge to Mission Street and came into Wenatchee. Some of the passengers began to stir and gather their belongings. It was a prosperous town—more than twenty thousand people—the preeminent city of the apple country. It sat in a bowl between bleached hills that rose a thousand feet above the river. To the east they were colored in auburns and tans, their summits and ridges forming the rim of the vast wheat plateau. To the north the hills fell steeply to the river in rippling, undulant, shadowed draws, and the river ran with the sun on it, its sinuous surface broken by bridges and by the dams at Rock Island and Rocky Reach. Everywhere on the edges of town were orchards ascending into arid heights, including the Wenatchee Pinnacles, summits Ben had scaled as a boy—Castle Rock, Squaw Saddle, and Old Butte, sun-beaten peaks of eroding basalt, tall spires against the skyline. The outlying neighborhoods were tidy and quiet, the homes with deep porches and sheltering willows, but downtown were stoplights in inordinate number, hamburger and taco joints, crowded parking lots and strip malls. The streets ran wide, two lanes in each direction. There were more trucks than passenger cars. Wenatchee hummed with fast-moving vehicles, with tractor-trailers, four-wheel-drive cars, and late-model crew-cab pickup trucks riding high above the asphalt. On the sidewalks some men wore cowboy hats, shambling along with their hands in their pockets or cupping cigarettes against the wind; they were ranchers of the sort Ben remembered from childhood, basin men with leathery faces, pearl-button shirts, cowboy boots, and emaciated backsides.

At First Street the bus careened into a covered loading bay with a broken skylight in its high roof. The driver announced a fifteen-minute pause and suggested that passengers use the station bathroom, buy coffee at Cecil's Cafe, or simply stretch their legs outside before taking to the westward road again at 2:55 P.M. He swung open the cargo compartment as the passengers filed off. The apple pickers put their heads together and spoke in a soft, rapid Spanish. From under their seats they pulled grocery bags overstuffed with their belongings. The sick one, Angel, waited wrapped in his blanket, his mouth open, sweating. His brother slipped his Dole cap on, adjusting its bill to throw a shadow across his eyes. *"Donde estamos?"* he asked.

"Wenatchee," answered Catherine Donnelly. "Wenatchee, Washington."

"Guanache," he repeated. *"Cuándo vamos a llegar a Orondo?"*

"Este bus no va a Orondo. Usted tiene que tomar otro bus para ir a Orondo. Es necesario bajarse aquí y cambiar de bus."

"Ho-kay, muchas gracias," the picker said, rose and took up his bags. The one by the window stood up, too. They helped Angel to his feet.

"They say they're going to Orondo," said Catherine. "What do you think we should tell them?"

"Ask them why they're going up there. Ask them about Orondo."

"Tienen ustedes trabajo alli?"

"Si. Acaso."

"Cosechando manzanas?"

"Si."

"Y su hermano? No puede trabajar. Necesita ir al hospital."

"No. El está bien. Por favor, no se preocupe."

"He says," said Catherine, "that in Orondo they have a job. They're going up to Orondo to pick apples. He insists Angel is doing fine. We shouldn't worry about him."

Ben looked at Angel now, directly into his eyes. "*No hos-pi-tole,*" he said to him. "*Muerte, sí? Comprende, Angel? No hos-pi-tole, muerte.*"

Angel, in answer, drew his blanket closer and turned his bloodshot eyes to the floor.

They filed off the bus with the other passengers, the fruit pickers with their plastic bags, Catherine with her sunglasses on, Angel shrouded in his stained blanket, Ben with his rucksack on his shoulder. The wind blew loud, a sudden whirlwind hurling dust down the loading bay. The driver stood with his back to it, clutching his cap to the top of his head, his pant legs billowing and his coat flailing, so that he looked as if he might blow away. A garbage pail fell over and rolled toward Chelan Street, refuse spilling onto the ground—cans, bottles, candy wrappers—and they, too, were wind-whipped north and up against the brick facade of the Labor Union Temple.

"*El remolino,*" said one of the pickers. "*El viento del Diablo.*"

"I'm calling 911," said Ben. "They'll take Angel to the hospital here, and that'll be the end of that."

"I don't know," said Catherine. "I'm back on the bus in fifteen minutes and heading over the mountains."

"You are?" said Ben. "I didn't know that."

"I just hope you're doing the right thing and all. I hope you don't get him deported."

"Better deported than dead, you know."

"That's true," said Catherine.

In the station, a girl in a pink, oversized shirt worked the joystick of a video game. A map of the country displayed Greyhound's routes as an arterial system of blue lines. Beside the map was a lost-children poster; beneath it, at the corner of the counter, sat a box of baggage tags and a stack of Gospel tracts. There was a ceiling fan, inert and dusty, a soft-drink machine, and three telephone booths, two with the phones ripped out. A hand-scrawled sign was taped to the bathroom door, NO BEER: THIS IS NOT A TAV-

ERN, and at the fountain counter—Cecil's Cafe—the stools were bolted to the floor. From behind the ticket and baggage desk, feeble radio strains could be heard, a melody Ben faintly recognized, a homely ballad, a love-gone-wrong song, a country lament from the fifties.

Angel collapsed on a wooden bench, coughing incessantly. His brother put a hand around his shoulders and spoke softly in his ear.

Ben called the emergency operator. He said he was a doctor traveling on the Greyhound, had come across a young man seriously ill, and was now in the bus station at First and Chelan. In his opinion as a thoracic surgeon, the situation was an emergency, the young man in question had coughed up blood and needed immediate assistance. The operator dispatched an ambulance and kept Ben standing by on the line to answer plodding questions: Ben's name, the sick person's name, Ben's address, more about the sick person's symptoms, more about Ben's credentials as a doctor, more about the Quincy bus ride. In three minutes, an ambulance pulled in, lurching to a halt in the loading bay. "They're here," said Ben, and hung up.

Everyone in the station gave their attention to the ambulance, a spectacle to break up the boredom. Ben raised a hand at the emergency technicians as they came through the door with their medical bags. "Over here," he called. "Right here."

They were stalwart-looking, both of them, in blue uniforms and polished shoes. Their name tags read COLEMAN and ODLE. Coleman stood as tall as Ben, at least six-foot-four. Odle was short, with tight curls at his brow and thick, veiny forearms. Ben pointed to Angel and said he suspected tuberculosis. The boy had expelled a bloody bolus and needed a workup immediately, and good hospital care. Coleman, listening, set his medical bag down. "What happened to your eye?" he asked.

"Car accident," Ben said.

"Looks like you should have had it stitched," said Coleman. "It's going to leave a scar."

"The boy," said Ben. "Come on now."

The apple pickers whispered among themselves, their bags against their legs. Catherine squatted on the floor with them, as if she were a picker herself. "*No se preocupe,*" she said. "*No es la policía. Les prometo.*"

Angel's brother replied, at length, eyeing the EMTs.

"They don't have money for a hospital," said Catherine, coming across the room. "He says he won't let Angel go. He's Angel's brother, he can't let him go. He feels responsible for him."

"Tell him they don't have to pay," said Ben. "Tell them it'll all be taken care of. It won't cost them a dime."

"But they do have to pay," said Coleman. "We'd better be clear about it."

"No, they don't," Ben said. "There's federal assistance for this. But anyway, that's irrelevant. The important point is to get him treatment." He put a hand on Catherine's arm. "Just tell them they don't have to pay anything, that's all they need to know."

Coleman shook his head emphatically. "There's no federal assistance for wetbacks," he said. "I've been through this before."

"Now wait," Odle countered. "That isn't really right, is it? The hospital can apply for welfare assistance with the Emergency Medical Office."

"Not for these guys," Coleman said. "These guys are wet, it's obvious. They don't have permission to be in the country. Like I said, I've been through this."

"They still get assistance," said Odle.

"All right, forget it," Coleman said, snatching up his medical bag. "Fine with me. Let's go."

The technicians slipped on filter masks and pulled on rubber gloves. Odle eased Angel down against the bench, put a thermometer in his mouth, and took a blood-pressure reading and a pulse while Coleman wheeled in a chrome gurney. The passengers in the station watched in silence. "The bus for Seattle waits for no man," the driver announced from the doorway. "Let's wish this fellow the best of luck and hit the westbound highway."

Catherine anchored her hair behind her ear and began to hop in place. "Hey," she said. "This looks good. You think he's going to get better?"

"He should," said Ben. "With antibiotics. If he has what I think he has."

"Just so they don't get deported or something."

"You really ought to stop worrying about that."

"All right," Catherine sighed. "I guess I better go. It was nice meeting you and everything. Later on, I guess."

She turned to the boy with the long black ponytail, the brother of Angel. "*Hasta luego,*" she said. She nodded at the other boy, the one with the pug nose and pomaded hair, and he nodded back at her. "*Angel,*" she called. "*Buena suerte. Ahora vas a mejorarte.*" Angel smiled weakly.

"What did you say?" Ben asked.

"I told him he's going to get better."

"You'd better catch your bus now."

"Okay," said Catherine. "Later on."

She left then, without looking back, her jeans hems scraping the ground. The driver hopped onboard behind her. The door closed, the air brakes gasped, and the bus pulled out of its covered bay, described a wide and steady arc, and disappeared into the west.

Angel's brother got in the ambulance, but despite Ben's polite entreaties, Coleman refused to take the other boy. There was no legal place for him to ride, they couldn't stow him in the back with Angel, and besides the hospital was on Fuller Street, he

could walk it in less than an hour. The ambulance pulled out
with Angel and his brother, and the third boy watched it go. He
stood in the loading bay with his plastic bags, his collar turned
against the cold. To Ben, the cold seemed to rise from within.
He felt sick to his stomach, feeble, and listless. The wind had
subsided, the sun was out, the bay stood empty of passengers;
there was only the boy with the pomaded hair standing there,
scratching his chin. Ben watched him and then, sighing, limped
back into the bus station. He slumped on a bench, rubbed his
side, and watched the boy beyond the window, who seemed content to stare down the bay where the ambulance had disappeared. After some time, the boy trudged through the door and
stood by the window with his bags beside him. He didn't look
at Ben.

"*No hablo español,*" said Ben. "*Habla* you *inglés?*"

"*No,*" said the boy. "*No inglés.*"

"*No inglés,*" Ben said. "That makes things difficult."

They watched each other. The boy shrugged. He was short
and sturdy, with a smoky complexion. "*Hos-pi-tole,*" Ben said.
"Your *amigos* went to the *hos-pi-tole.* Do you think you might want
to go there?"

"*No hospital.* Apples. *Trabajo.*" The boy's fingers plucked invisible
apples, placing each in an invisible picking bag belted at his waist.
"*Manzanas,*" he said. "*Trabajo.*"

He swiped his brow in stylized fashion, then flicked his wrist
toward the bus-station floor, as though flinging sweat away. "*Trabajo, trabajo.*" He tapped at his chest. "*Quiero trabajar.* Apples."

"Okay," said Ben.

They went out into the loading bay and walked down First Street
with the wind at their backs, the boy trailing slightly behind as if

in deference to the gringo doctor, Ben limping and laboring beneath his rucksack, stopping twice to lean against streetlamps while the boy waited patiently. In the bookstore on Wenatchee Avenue, Ben bought a copy of *Spanish for Travelers* and an English-Spanish dictionary. Then he and the boy sat down on the sidewalk, their traveling gear against their legs, while Ben leafed through the books. Through his one good eye, the print wavered, but he found the word *to harvest.* "*Cosechar manzanas?*" he asked the boy. "Is that what you want to do?"

"*Si,*" said the boy. "*Manzanas.*"

"*Cosechar manzanas,*" Ben repeated. "*Muy bien.* Okay."

He pawed through the gear in his rucksack carefully until he found the map of Chelan County rolled up in its cardboard tube. Then he unfurled it against the sidewalk, where the boy held two of its corners down, and pointed out the town of Wenatchee— "*aquí*" he said, "Wenatchee, *aquí*"—and with a finger Ben followed Highway 2 until it reached Orondo. "Orondo," he said. "*Amigos?*"

"*No le comprendo a usted,*" the boy answered. "*Orondo? Sí? Orondo?*"

"Do you want to go there? *Cosechar manzanas in Orondo? Amigos* in Orondo?"

"*No,*" said the boy. "*No amigos aquí.*" He tapped his chest, his breastbone. "*Solo,*" he said. "*No amigos aquí. Solo, comprende usted?*"

"*Comprende,*" said Ben. "Me too."

He sat for a moment looking at the boy's shoes—battered black chukkas coming apart at the welts, probably salvaged from a Dumpster. The boy's odyssey, clearly, had been much longer than Ben's brief trip across the apple country. He was dusty, sun-beaten, and smelled of earth; his plastic bags were tattered. He had probably traveled a thousand miles, sleeping under trees and bridges, out in the open country. Ben paged through his dictionary again, looking for the right words. "*Hambre,*" he said, after some time.

"*Hambriento. Restaurante. Alimento.* Something like that. Let's go eat, okay?"

They went to a restaurant on Wenatchee Avenue, mostly empty at that hour of the day, a close place smelling of cigarettes. Ben ordered tea for himself and a T-bone steak with fried potatoes for the boy, and while the boy ate a roll and butter, Ben struggled with his Spanish books and tossed garbled questions across the table. The boy's name was Emilio—he offered only that, no surname. He was not a brother to the other two, whom he'd met picking pears near Yakima. The others knew of apple-picking work, so Emilio had accompanied them northward. Now they were gone, but he still wanted to work. In Orondo, somewhere else, anywhere.

His plate of steak and potatoes arrived, and Emilio pondered it. "*Muchas gracias, señor,*" he said, then rained salt and pepper over the potatoes, steak, and boiled green beans. He ate neatly, unhurried, using his knife deftly. Scratches—white streaks—crossed the backs of his hands. His fingers were thick and callused, blunt and cracked at the nails.

Ben sipped his tea and asked no more questions. The hardship of communicating allowed for silence, as did the boy's reserve. Ben didn't ask Emilio, though he wondered, how he'd come to be alone, how he happened to be separated from his family, if he had any family to speak of. What sort of world he'd left behind, what sort of life he'd lived until now, how it felt to be rootless and adrift, always in pursuit of work, unable to speak the language. These things were beyond telling, certainly beyond Ben's *Spanish for Travelers,* since the life of the boy—of anyone—was a life, in the end, and no mere story to be told across the table. The essentials could not be culled from the rest without divesting both of certain meanings.

As he watched Emilio at work on his food, cutting and eating with instinctive dignity, Ben accepted that the boy wouldn't trade his story for a meal. It was really a desirable thing in a companion, this reticence, this taut reserve, because if it meant no answers, it also meant no questions. The boy had not used his talents as a mime—as a wielder of gesture, expression, and signs—to interrogate Ben about his black eye, as if to suggest that Ben, too, was entitled to his secrets. So if Emilio preferred to have no story, Ben was happy to oblige. Just a boy eating a lucky meal, a thousand miles from home.

Ben bought him a piece of apple pie a la mode and a second glass of milk. Then he went to the phone booth by the rest rooms and called the Job Services Office. "Apple-picking work," he told the receptionist, and she transferred his call to a job specialist, who introduced himself as Hector Martinez. Yes, there were jobs in agricultural labor, but these were all of short duration, the apple harvest was nearly over, the work would be done in days. "Where?" said Ben. "Where do I go?" "That depends," answered Martinez. "Where are you right now?"

"I'm at a phone booth here in Wenatchee. Wenatchee Avenue."

"Okay," Hector Martinez said, in the tone of a public servant trained to be empathetic, within limits. "Have you been into our office before, or have you registered with us recently, or did we refer you in the last twelve months or anything like that?"

"No," said Ben. "None of the above."

"Okay," said Martinez. "Just let me get to the right screen on my computer and . . . okay, your name."

"Larry Miller," Ben told him. "L, A, double R, Y. Miller as in the beer."

"As in Miller beer, okay. Your social security number?"

Ben made one up. He invented a date of birth, too, and an address and telephone number. The act of formulating a false identity with such ease and authority made him feel pleased with himself. "A few years back I was out here," he said. "Up by

Malaga, the Wolfhound Orchard. Something like that. Wolf-hound."

"Wolfhound Orchard," said Martinez. "Let me check my job list."

"I'd like to get there again, if I could. It was out of Malaga, I think."

"Wolfhound Orchard. It's not a problem. They have some positions. We can do you a referral."

"I appreciate that," said Ben.

When he was done on the phone, he limped back to the table and nodded at Emilio. *"Trabajo,"* he said. *"Manzanas. Trabajo.* There's work for you *en* Malaga." He dug out his map of Chelan County, unfurled it across the table, and traced for the boy the route to Malaga, down the west side of the Columbia on the Malaga-Alcoa Highway. *"Cosechar manzanas,"* he said. *"Manzanas* to pick, *aquí."*

They walked up Wenatchee Avenue, passed Kim's Tae Kwan Do School, the Central Washington Water office, assorted furniture and auto parts stores, a tavern called Brews And Cues. Outside the Valley Pawn Shop, Ben slung his rucksack onto the sidewalk and leaned over a newspaper vending machine with his head propped against his forearm. The urge to vomit swelled and subsided while he rubbed his side in that stooped posture and gradually came to feel up to the task of pushing forward once more. But the boy reached for the rucksack when Ben did, and looked at him inquiringly. *"Muchas gracias,"* Ben said, putting a hand on his shoulder. *"De nada,"* the boy answered.

They continued up the avenue, Emilio hauling both their bags, Ben shivering in his tin-cloth coat, until they came to the U-Save Auto Rental. The clerk eyed them suspiciously—an old man with a battered eye, at his side a dust-bitten apple picker, shoes split open at the toes, loaded down like a hobo. She could not conceal her disdain, but she rented them a half-ton Ford for thirty-seven dollars a day with a reminder to return it full, lest there be a surcharge for gasoline they wouldn't feel happy about. When she dropped the keys into Ben's hands, she made certain not to touch him. "We expect the truck back clean," she said. "I don't know what you're planning with it, but we expect to get it back clean."

"Medical waste," Ben said. "Plus landfill runs for a rendering plant, and some organic fertilizer."

The woman blanched and touched her hair with the tips of her painted fingers. "Well, I don't know," she said.

It was a new truck with cloth seats and big padded armrests, its cab done up in royal maroon, and as they drove down Wenatchee Avenue, luxuriating in the motor's smooth silence, Emilio tried the power window. He worked it down a few inches at a time, then up until it sealed out the road noise. Next he worked the power locks and felt the nap of the seat. "Try the radio," Ben suggested. "*Música,* or something like that." He turned it on and searched the channels until he found a station broadcasting in Spanish. "*Aquí,*" he said. "Okay?"

"Okay," the boy said. "*Gracias.*"

"*De nada,*" said Ben. "*Está bien.*"

They came to the river bridge but didn't cross, and passed into South Wenatchee. There was laundry hung to dry in the wind, a car without wheels on jacks in a yard, a tractor-trailer parked in front of a dilapidated two-story warehouse. The road ran high above the old rail yard and looked down onto the decrepit roundhouse, icehouse, and sand house, the turntable with weeds growing through it, abandoned boxcars of the old Great Northern and Burlington lines, and a web of iron tracks. The Appleyard Terminal Ben remembered from long ago was empty of apples now. Glass insulators still decorated the power stanchion cross beams. In a corner of the yard sat dry, weathered bins stacked six and seven high. The paint had peeled in scabrous blisters, and the plywood beneath had been bleached by the sun to a washed and pale gray.

They passed the Shaw Orchard and the Atwood Orchard—
full bins waited at the sidings there—and came to the Stemilt
Creek–West Malaga cutoff, where Ben paused at roadside, idling,
to consider the way to Joe Miller Road. The country before him
lay dense with fruit trees, all the way to Jump-Off Ridge, the roads
winding among canyons and draws and up through the manicured
Stemilt Hill orchards, which looked as graceful as the plain of the
Po, as undulant as the vineyards of the Apennines. A listless pond
sat in the shade of Russian olives where Stemilt Creek ran out of
the mountains. A brace of widgeon milled on the far shore, feeding in the interstices of marsh weed.

"*Madre y padre hacienda,*" Ben said, pointing east and south across
the river. "I grew up right over there."

"*Bien,*" said Emilio, and smiled.

They drove up into the Stemilt Hills, the orchards large and
well kept, the hills above Malaga that had once been in grapes,
English walnuts, and pears. They gained a thousand feet until
they were high above the river and traversing switchbacks and
tight-loop turns through orchards cut into the sides of hills; past
a tarp encampment of fruit pickers and a few worn trailers along
a creek; past a row of pickers' cabins; past a silent cherry-packing
shed tucked under a turn in the road; up to the crest of Stemilt
Hill, where the wind blew hard across cemetery stones and beat
against the windows of the Grange Hall. Here the view gave out
to the east, a long vista over the tops of trees and beyond the
river to the wheat plateau, and all down the hill were pickers on
their ladders, working in the apples. "*Manzanas,*" Ben said to
Emilio. "*Aquí, manzanas. Cosechar manzanas aquí.*"

Emilio nodded and scratched his head. "*Está muy bien,*" he said.

Ben pulled over at the community church and sat with the engine idling. He didn't feel he could continue. His side felt as if it
might burst, and it was painful merely to sit upright.

"I have to get out for a few minutes," he said. "*Un momento,
Emilio*. Okay?"

He stumbled out into the cherry trees behind the Stemilt Hill
Community Church and lay in the grass battling the urge to
vomit and slowly rubbing his side. In this position, curiously, his
nausea felt endurable. He curled up around his tumor and suspended it there at the heart of his viscera as gently as he could.
He understood that the cancer in his gut had a mass and density,
a friction and gravity. A dark stone weighing in among his organs, a rotten pit nestled in his flesh. The cause of his illness was
something tangible: a festering object in the mucosa of his colon,
penetrating through the muscle wall but also narrowing the
bowel lumen, causing serious constipation. He was headed for
perforation, with its accompanying infection and septic death;
his colon would be split open like a banana skin, its contents
would spill into his abdomen—his watery excrement, his meager
diarrhea, curdling and sloshing between his organs.

There was a quiet, humble fluttering—small birds on distant
limbs. There was the pale heat of the sun against his cheek, the
smell of orchard grass. Ben became aware of his breathing, and
of the steady rhythm of his heart. He became aware that he
wanted to live, to have and hold such things as a cherry orchard
in midautumn in river country. It was this world he wanted and
no other. There was no sweeter world he knew of.

Despite himself, he vomited, slouched on his hands and knees.
Stomach acid burned hot in his throat. His nostrils stung, and he
panted heavily, at the mercy of his body. The pits of cherries
were everywhere. Fallen leaves stirred in the wind.

On Joe Miller Road, Ben slowed to a crawl to pass by sidings
bristling with apples, the trees flowing down and out across the

hills, the rungs of ladders disappearing among leaves, the bins laid out between the shaded rows, the tractors hauling bins to the sidings. In some places, at the edge of the trees, pickers rested in groups of three or four, but mostly they worked with dogged persistence, with the patient madness of harvest. It was the time of year when the silence of the orchards was subsumed by the voices of pickers. Hung from limbs were coats and hats; propped between branches were canteens and bottles. In the orchard grass the dogs lay about; children sprawled in sunlight, dreaming; men and women stood high in their ladders, reaching into the tops of trees, leaving limbs bereft of fruit. They pulled the branch props one by one and descended rungs with their bags bursting-full, easing the apples into the bins for fear of bruising them.

Ben asked a woman at her mailbox if this was the way to the Wolfhound Orchard, then drove another mile south. On the west side of the road was the Hardens' mailbox, just before a siding thronged with bins, two men laying hands on the fruit. A tractor emerged from between the trees to set another bin in place, and a forklift loaded a truck. Ben pulled over and, though the hour was late, slid his sunglasses on. He felt ridiculous, doing it. He felt he must look like a blind man, wearing sunglasses at dusk, in October, with the sun behind the hills. But one of these workers—the tractor driver, say, or the man on the forklift—might be the night rider who had stolen his shotgun, the thief Ben had come looking for, yet whose face he had never seen. This William Harden who ran his wolfhounds after coyotes in the moonlight. Harden would remember the battered eye, Ben's signature feature of late, Ben's calling card in the world.

He recognized his entire day as a kind of protracted stall. Things had gone awry, aslant, but now he was back on course. There was no turning back now, nothing to lose that wasn't lost. What could Harden do to him? In the morning, when he had rested enough to gain the strength, he would find Harden and take his gun back.

Ben parked the rented truck around a bend and stepped into Joe Miller Road, one arm wrapped across his gut. Emilio emerged from the truck, too, and hauled out their traveling gear. Ben paused to button his jacket and to take in the color of the sky in the west, which had gone purple now. The shadows were deepening across the hills. The timbre of the light was quieting. The orchards that had looked so inviting in the sun were sullen now in the desert gloaming. The world lay altered by the imminence of night, as though a curtain was dropping over it. Yet out on the low rim of the western horizon the sun streamed into the high eastern sky, which held its unearthly light.

ELEVEN

The contractor at the Wolfhound Orchard, a man named Lyle
Parmenter, squatted with his clipboard and a carpenter's pencil,
filling in the blanks on a Department of Justice Employment El-
igibility form. He pondered Emilio's employment card, tattered
and worn along its edges and bearing the name Raul Ramirez; he
examined Ben's Washington State driver's license and social security card. Parmenter eyed Ben's photograph, scratched his forehead, scrutinized Ben—who wore dark glasses at the hour of
dusk—then considered the license once more. "There were
Givens," he said, "other side of the river. You related to them?"

"No," said Ben. "I'm not."

"You ever picked apples?"

"I have, yes."

"Where at?"

"All over. You name it."

"But you're from t'other side of the mountains."

"I can still pick," said Ben.

Parmenter tapped his nose with the pencil. He was a red-skinned man with pointed sideburns and a chapped, cross-hatched neck. "This is a young man's work," he said. "It's harder than it looks."

"I'm old for picking, that's true," said Ben. "But you can figure at my age I know better than most how to do it right."

Parmenter seemed to take this as a challenge. "We'll see about that," he replied. He turned to size up Emilio. "You speak English, señor?"

"No," answered Ben. "He doesn't."

"Raul Ramirez," Parmenter read. "Does he know what he's doing with apples?"

"Yes," said Ben. "He's good at it."

"How do you know?"

"I've seen Raul pick."

"Where was that?"

"In Yakima."

"Well, I don't know how they do it down there, but here I don't want any broken branches or crashing around with the ladders. And I want people handling the fruit gentle. You start bird-dogging or bottoming trees, I'll pull you off your ladder fast and send you down the road."

"Understood," Ben answered.

"We've got to be this way," said Parmenter. "Better to make it clear beforehand than have trouble because we didn't."

"I'd do the same," Ben assured him.

Parmenter handed Ben the clipboard and showed him where to sign. "It's late for them sunglasses, isn't it?" he asked. "There's not much light anymore."

"I've got cataracts," Ben answered. "In both eyes."

Ben and Emilio were passed into the hands of a field boss introduced as Sanchez, who was told to show them to the pickers' camp. A small, crisp man in cowboy boots, Sanchez wore a rawhide belt with a silver buckle embossed to depict a bucking bronc. He wore a lightweight cowboy hat high on his bronzed smooth forehead. The hair at his neck was closely cropped. His breath smelled of menthol cough drops.

Ben, walking, took off his sunglasses, but when he went to tuck them in his pocket, they tumbled to the ground. Emilio picked them up for him, and they hiked on toward the pickers' camp. "Wolfhound Orchard," Ben said to Sanchez. "That's a peculiar name."

Sanchez nodded, inaccessible. He was quiet in a perturbing way and would not look at Ben's face.

"Are there wolfhounds out here or something?" prodded Ben. "Or did they just make it up?"

"There are wolfhounds," Sanchez answered.

"A lot of them? A pack or something?"

"Yes," said Sanchez. "Twelve."

"Twelve hounds," Ben said. "You'd think a guy with an orchard this size wouldn't have time for that."

"His brother is the keeper of the dogs," said Sanchez. "His brother is always the dog man. We have to turn left on the path right there and go down that hill."

They followed Sanchez along a dirt track, past dark orchards and stacks of pear branches ravaged by fire blight. The camp lay in a hollow of hoary pines, cottonwoods, and tall poplars. There was a row of cabins sheathed in graying plywood, a cinder-block washhouse beside a creek, and a vast, dilapidated equipment shed thronged with the rusting detritus, the trim and tackle, of an orchard. In a flat, dusty field beyond the pines sat a ragged arc of pickers' trailers, moonlight playing off their sides through the vertical lines of the trees. Sanchez led them past a shed half full of neat apple cordwood. It was cold now, with the sun's descent. A girl labored at a chopping block, splitting stove wood with a short-handled ax; she didn't look at them, resolutely, as though it was dangerous to look.

Sanchez showed them the features of the washhouse: hot-water tank, two shower stalls, a wall heater, a washing machine, a Manila line for drying clothes. He and Emilio spoke in Spanish, then stopped when Ben collapsed on a bench. "You look pretty sick," said Sanchez.

"It's nothing," said Ben. "Indigestion."

"I hope it isn't contagious or nothing."

"It isn't," said Ben. "Indigestion."

Emilio helped Ben to his feet again by pulling on his left arm. They left the washhouse and walked the row of cabins, which Sanchez explained were the dwelling places of the unmarried pickers. Lights glowed in most of these; smoke blew from cinder-block chimneys. Ladders and bins lay scattered about. Two cars sat parked in front, one with a crucifix, one with foam dice hung from their rearview mirrors. On each small porch sat a hatchet and cutting block, pine kindling and scrap wood. A man emerged onto his porch as they passed—a shirtless man, in jeans and slippers—hung a mesh bag of onions from a hook, and spoke to Sanchez in Spanish. Sanchez answered, and they talked for a while. From the man's open door came the hiss of meat frying, the smell of onions simmering. A cat slipped noiselessly between the man's slippers, rubbed its flank against his leg, and stalked out into the pines. A car pulled in beside another cabin, and two young men piled out of it, laden with groceries. Ben heard the blaring of the car radio while the doors stood open. There was the smell of wood smoke and pine needles; the heat and light from the man's cabin spilled into the night.

Sanchez unlocked the next cabin and handed the key to Ben. He pulled a beaded chain inside to switch on the overhead light.

Emilio surveyed things at Ben's shoulder, his face impassive, neutral. They stood together, taking everything in, the lightbulb swinging on its cord. The cabin was the size of a garden shed, with a buckling, warped linoleum floor and slap-painted walls of plywood. A scanty, red-checked gingham curtain was drawn across a small window. A cast-iron cookstove sat on a fire pad; oilcloth covered the little table. From hooks just over the sink hung a fly swatter, a potato masher, and a ladle. Sanchez waited with one hand on the doorknob. "You have to be careful with that hot plate," he advised. "We don't want to have any fires."

"I don't plan on cooking," Ben said.

"There's a little trail across from the washhouse. You walk up there at six A.M., and we'll put you up in a ladder."

Ben nodded. "I'll be there."

"This is a cabin for one person only. They don't want more in here."

"What about my *compadre*, though?"

"He sleeps next door," answered Sanchez.

He said something to Emilio in Spanish, and they all said *buenas noches* to one another, and *gracias*, and see you in the morning, and finally the two others left.

Ben collapsed on the cot. A paltry mattress on a loose web of springs, it put him in mind of Camp Hale. Pulling his knees up toward his chest, he wrapped his arms around his gut and moaned softly with each breath. The moaning soothed him a little. He didn't have the energy to pry off his boots, so he untied them and left them on. It was silent except for a bluebottle fly that landed on him now and then. The naked bulb had ceased its swaying and cast a bald white light.

Ben sat up and fumbled in his rucksack for the drifter's breath-mint tin. There was one marijuana cigarette left, and he lodged its tip between his lips and lit it with a kitchen match he found in a dish on the cookstove. Standing in the doorway, Ben blew smoke toward the pines. The moon's glow lay over the world. The girl splitting wood had left the ax in the chopping block. A light was on in Emilio's cabin. Ben drew smoke into his lungs again, and while he kept it there, holding his breath, an owl hooted in the hollow. A strident and mysterious call, somehow disconcerting.

He turned out the light, lay on the bed, and in his thick, slow, narcotic way, took note of disconnected details. The stovepipe had a right-angle bend above the damper key. On an open shelf stood a candle, a flashlight, and a spray can of Barbasol. The ceiling was made of square fiber tiles coming loose in two corners. A bottle of castor oil stood beside the sink, slightly less than half full. Ben weighed the merit of taking some, desiring its purgative effect, but chances were it was rancid, old, and in the end he decided against it.

His mind shifted, dancing. He thought of Catherine Donnelly, then of Christine Reilly. He thought of the horsewoman at the veterinary clinic, the blue veins in her shoulders. He was half in dreams, mired in marijuana, when someone knocked on the cabin door and opened it tentatively. In the darkness Ben made out only a shape, a figure hovering silently, and his heart raced, panicked. "Who is it?" he called. "Who's there?"

The answer came, indecipherably, in Spanish, but Ben was familiar with its pleasant lilt, and the figure resolved into someone he recognized—Emilio, or Raul Ramirez, whatever his name was, it didn't matter. Stove wood heaped in the crook of his arm. He waited patiently by the door. *"Qué pasa?"* Ben asked. "What is it?"

"Hace mucho frío," the boy answered.

He set the wood on the floor by the stove and brushed his shirtfront clean. In the darkness he moved about silently. He put Ben's rucksack on the room's only chair, lay a blanket over Ben's legs. Next he built a warming fire, slowly feeding the flames. The light reflected against his face, the cleft in his chin, his bold forehead. He sat on his ankles comfortably, a stick in his hand, poking. Ben lay listening to the spit of the kindling. The boy looked contemplative with the fire's glow in his pores. "*Gracias*," Ben said. "*Muchas gracias.* I appreciate the fire."

"*De nada,*" Emilio answered.

He adjusted the damper, closed the firebox, and fine-tuned the draft. He sat for a moment looking about, then took the candle from the shelf, set it in the sink, and lit it. Candlelight fluttered across the room. Trembling shadows, the borders of things muted. Emilio came to Ben's cot and knelt. "Okay, *señor,*" he said.

Ben lifted an age-mottled hand and settled it on the boy's forearm. "Thank you," he said. "*Muchas gracias.*"

Emilio nodded and made the sign of the cross in the air in front of Ben. Then he rose and went to the door. In silhouette he was featureless, dark. The shape of a boy, slender and easy. "*Buenas noches,*" he whispered.

But a good night wasn't possible. In this world of shifting, quivering shadows, Ben fought with his disease. The chill of death was upon him, he felt, though it might have been something less than that, mere exhaustion, nausea—marijuana obscured the truth. Marijuana stood between him and knowledge of his condition. Yet to the best of Ben's ability to perceive, he felt the blowing of the Last Wind, heard the scraping of the scythe, smelled the grave. And for how long had he anticipated this, expecting it with dread? How long afraid of its coming? Outwardly he'd been stalwart and stoic, but privately he'd quaked like a child, trembled in apprehension, lived with a constant, quiet fear below the surface of everything.

Ben lay on his cot in the fruit pickers' hut, listening to the ticking of the fire in the cookstove, and felt the carabiner against his chest and the length of the ring-angle piton. In their classic application, they held a climber in the throes of ascent fixed to a wall of rock. Bits of human ingenuity standing between the climber and death. As if death was a game, as if challenging it was recreation. Ben thought of the young people in the Volkswagen van, eagerly headed for the Sawtooth Range, the mean, sheer faces there. The two of them thought of death romantically. They hadn't reached their apex yet. In their blood they had no inkling of decline, could hardly imagine it.

Dazed, Ben sought some view of death that made leaving the world endurable. No matter how often he'd turned it over, no matter the years he'd passed with it, there was still no answer to the final riddle, or an answer lay beyond his reach. Always his search had led him nowhere, and the next day he was one day older, with no greater wisdom as a shield against death, no revelation to pit against its strength. And this was how a person aged. Suffering in astonishment the progress of the days. One moment puffed up by a blustery denial, the next drowsing in blessed forgetfulness. Ben's life was an ocean of fear punctuated by islands of calm acquiescence, by well-lit places in which he forgot because his work or love or the mere light distracted him from the truth.

He had not found any way to proceed beyond such distractions. It was not the life of the spirit at all, in which mortality inspires a course of right action and humility. It had been instead a willful turning from the true conditions of existence. And, for the most part, this had been fine. He'd partaken of life with appetite. But now he found—he'd known it since Rachel's death—that this forgetting couldn't sustain him to the grave. The interludes of ignorance had grown shorter. And now there were none, there was only knowledge, and he wasn't ready for it.

Ben recalled how, on ten thousand nights, he'd watched Rachel undress at her armoire—turned from him, her long torso in the lamplight, her hands reversed at the small of her back swiftly and deftly to unclasp her bra—and the memory deepened his sadness. It was something that had never ceased to move him or to prompt in him a momentary reflection on the nature of love's good fortune. He did not take such a thing for granted, even after fifty years: always he celebrated what he'd been granted and admired what he saw. When they'd argued or carried some silent grievance or were divided temporarily by ill-chosen words—still Ben clung to her. She'd carried a tranquil grace at her center. A poise he could not limn, in the end, which had kept him turned toward her.

Now her poise had left the world. In the seasons since, he hadn't learned to live—he hadn't let go of mourning. The arc of his grief had been willfully long. He had indulged and extended its trajectory.

His death would solve that problem. It was nice to think of it that way. But death presented a thousand other faces. His thoughts on it were madly circuitous. Inevitably, there was no other subject, and he forced himself to muse on death as though it were simply a form of sleep, warm and full of dreams.

His musings finally gave way to sleep, and Ben dreamed he was traveling in the desert. On a journey whose purpose he couldn't guess. Underfoot, a fine sand shifted and confounded his progress. A strange apprehension haunted his limbs. He changed his direction twice, three times. Low, barren mountains appeared on the horizon. A lunar barrenness, the topography of dreams, stones strewn artfully down an arroyo as if laid by a Japanese gardener, a sinuous bend in the dry bed of stones, one stone, two, a stone carved in runes, the inordinate size of his walking shoes, an anxiety over the lack of water, he carried nothing, went empty-handed, looked out over the land from a ridge where the desert shuddered and disappeared, trembled and folded into itself: waves of heat, burning sheaves of air, a pall obscuring his view. He followed a trail of cobbles then, and knelt beside a rivulet. Christine Reilly knelt there, too, and placed the lucky carabiner once more around his neck. Which made no sense, since he wore it already. The illogic of that jarred him loose. He was in the fruit pickers' cabin, he was at the Wolfhound Orchard. The fire in the cookstove ticked and popped. The candle in the sink cast a wavering light. He thought of the girl with the nose ring, Catherine Donnelly with her book by Steiner, a pimple on her chin, the hems of her jeans dragging. What he wanted was gently to hold her, nothing more than that.

The boy, Emilio, knelt at his side, uttering repeatedly the word *señor*, until Ben opened his eyes. "*Necesito un medico—rapidamente,*" said the boy. "*Rapidamente, señor, rapidamente, por favor.*"

The field boss, Sanchez, was in the cabin, too. He pulled the cord on the overhead light, and its white glare blinded Ben. "He says you are a doctor," explained Sanchez. "There is a woman in the camp having a baby tonight. Maybe there is something you can do."

"Okay," said Ben. "I'm with you."

"Please hurry," answered Sanchez. "That baby is stuck tight in her. It's trapped there. It doesn't move."

"Okay," said Ben. "Let's go."

Beneath stars, as in a dream—Emilio before him, Sanchez at his back—he stumbled through pines and into an orchard where the dark apples had not yet been picked, on between rows of silent trees, until he emerged in a dusty field. The lights of a dozen trailer homes burned; pickers stood about. The place seemed blurred, but flat and still, as in a photograph.

They hurried past the first three trailers, where pickers gawked like spectators at a race, men and women standing in the cold, their hands stuffed in their coat pockets, their hats pulled low on their foreheads. It was clear that few were abed in the camp, dogs wandered in agitation, children ran footloose and dumbfounded in the night, their faces tired, quizzical. Emilio ran through without stopping to speak, without apology or explanation, and the pickers moved to make room for him and for the strange-looking doctor with one eye swollen shut, wearing steel-rimmed spectacles, his boots untied, limping. Emilio pressed on toward a silver trailer hulking in the dark like a dry-docked submarine or airplane fuselage. Its low door was thrown open, and a woman waited there, in vigil.

As they approached, she clasped her hands beneath her chin. She was fat and wore a parka patched with duct tape. "You are the doctor?" she asked.

"Let us through," said Sanchez.

"Thanks to our God," the woman said. "I have been praying for you."

"Let us through," repeated Sanchez.

Ben put his head in the trailer door. The room had the feel of a cave or chamber; distorted shadows shimmered against walls of riveted, contoured aluminum. The spectral light of a kerosene lantern illuminated a macabre scene. At one end of the trailer, on a bare mattress thrown there as if by a tornado, a woman—a girl—was in the throes of labor, naked and twisting on a nest of blankets, bucking and swaying on her hands and knees, her eyes shut, her belly heaving. Her hair had matted to her shining face, obscuring half of it. She tucked her head between her breasts and groaned until the cords in her neck bulged; then she fell onto the lengths of her forearms and paused to catch her breath. Her feet kicked spasmodically, she cradled her head in the palms of her hands, her face lay against the rough mattress. She rolled on her side, flailing, and a wail escaped from her lips.

A young man in stocking feet knelt beside her, brushing the hair from her cheek with his fingernails. A woman knelt on the mattress, too, speaking urgently in Spanish. A second woman, short and large—a dwarf, Ben realized: she was four feet tall— stood with rolled sleeves at a propane stove, dipping a towel into a kettle of steaming water, then wringing it with muscular vigor. "It's good you're here," she said to Ben.

"How long has she been in labor?"

"A long time. Too long," said the dwarf.

Ben ducked inside, carefully. The ceiling loomed claustrophobically low, and he couldn't stand without stooping deeply, which hurt his neck and back. He moved closer, knelt beside the mattress. The girl, he saw, was very young, a child giving birth to a child. "What's your name?" he asked.

"Her name is Doris," the boy answered, and draped a blanket over her.

"How old?"

"Fifteen."

"Are you the father?"

The boy nodded.

"What's your name?"

"Jimmy Perez."

"This is her first?"

"Her first, yes."

"Okay," said Ben.

The woman on the mattress caressed the girl's damp forehead. She seemed to Ben to have an eye of glass, or a wandering, unfocused, dead pupil—he couldn't tell which. He couldn't tell if she was looking at him. She seemed to look sideways, or through him, or beyond. "Are you her mother?" he asked.

"No," said the woman, her eye roaming.

"How long have you been here?"

"I came last night."

"Twenty-four hours?"

"More than that."

"She's been in labor twenty-four hours?"

"Longer," said the woman.

Ben shook his head. "Are you a midwife?"

"I don't know anything," the woman answered.

Ben put a hand to his forehead, pausing. He had not attended a woman in labor since his internship in obstetrics forty-four years earlier. For six weeks in 1954 he'd assisted in delivering babies. "We need to call for an ambulance," he said. "She needs to go to a hospital."

As if in response, Doris heaved painfully onto her back, seized the hands of the glass-eyed woman, and bore down with so much force, her lips whitened, her eyes squeezed shut, tears leaked from their corners. She flung her legs wide unabashedly— a seething mass of dark tissue, her purple rectum swollen. The vulva had stretched to the limit; her perineum might rupture. An episiotomy would have helped, but that was impossible now.

"Can you do anything?" asked the glass-eyed woman. "What are you supposed to do?"

Ben didn't answer. He kept his hand on his forehead. The girl panted, gasped, and grunted, then bore down again. Ben saw the swelling of the baby's head, the wet, dark oval of its hair. "The head is showing," he said.

"What does that mean?" asked Jimmy.

"It means it's too late for the hospital." Ben turned to the propane stove. "How hot is that water?" he asked.

"It's too hot," the dwarf said. "I'll put some cold in it."

Ben took off his hunting coat and rolled up his shirtsleeves. The dwarf poured dish soap into his hands, and he washed, adjusted his glasses on his face, and knelt again by the girl. "You're all right," he said.

"Are you a doctor?"

"Do I look like one?"

"No," said Doris.

"Well, I am."

As if in answer, she pulled at her thighs to spread them as wide as possible. Then she buried her chin against her chest and bore down with the concentrated force of a woman trying to move the earth. Her skin went from gray to blue, her brow furrowed, her eyes narrowed, it appeared as though she was being crushed by something enormous and invisible. Ben watched while the baby's head crowned, and then Doris's perineum ruptured. There was blood now, but not very much. The tear looked relatively superficial, involved the fourchette and mucus membrane but not the underlying fascia. "Your baby's coming," said Ben.

The dark wet head emerged gradually. It came face down, then turned sideways—a natural restitution. The features were scrunched, constricted, crabbed, the eyes clenched, the mouth closed, the skin tinted a shade of blue far darker than the blood of veins. The head stopped, came no farther, and seemed to retract or shrink again, like the head of a turtle or snail. An odd, swollen, parasitical growth attached to the girl's groin. Her gaping legs with a head between them—a neckless, embryonic head. It hung suspended, a third appendage, Doris impaled on it. Ben lay on the floor beside the mattress to wipe its strictured face with a towel and swab its mouth with his forefinger. He wished he had an aspirating syringe, and even more, a fetoscope. The baby wasn't breathing, it was stuck at the shoulders. He wasn't sure what to do about it, but he knew there was no time to lose. The cord might be fatally compressed.

Ben pulled up Doris's left knee until it pressed against her swollen belly, and then he brought up the right. Doris held them there. Awkwardly, low against the mattress, he pried hard at the baby's head, stretching the neck unnaturally, then gave up and slid two fingers in, next to the baby's ear. Doris shrieked and swore at him in Spanish, and Jimmy Perez put a hand on her back and leaned close to her. Ben was relieved to find that the umbilicus wasn't tangled, but he still felt time was running out. He slid in a third finger and tried to twist the baby, turn it in some subtle fashion, unlock it as though the passage to birth were a Chinese puzzle of sorts. He tried clockwise and counterclockwise. He couldn't think what else to do. He withdrew his fingers and pressed on the girl's pubis, as though the baby might be popped free, as in a Heimlich maneuver. It didn't work, and he pried again, gripping it behind the ears. The baby remained intractable.

"Is it dead?" asked Jimmy Perez.

"No," said Ben. "We'll get it out."

"Its face is blue."

"It isn't breathing yet."

"It's dead," said Jimmy.

"No, it isn't," said Ben. "It's still getting blood from the umbilical cord. That blue will go away."

"It's dead," said Jimmy. "I know it."

"No," Ben repeated.

He slid his fingers past the baby's neck—slid them into Doris's vagina. He knew he was hurting her—she was trying to pull away and shrieked at him in Spanish—but he had no choice anymore. His hand was in, now, to the third set of knuckles. Doris winced, holding her breath; her face blanched, her eyes closed. Ben crouched with his fingers inside her, seeking with his fingertips. He followed the length of the baby's upper arm, which was folded across its collarbones, until he came to the little elbow. It took awhile. He searched. Finally he found what he was looking for. When he drew out his hand, he had the baby's small blue fist trapped between two of his fingers, as in a magic trick.

The baby's arm hung quivering near its head while Ben popped the shoulder free in a gradual release of traction. The other shoulder came much more easily, and the baby—a girl—slid out like a fish, awash in blood and amniotic fluid, the umbilicus wrapped around her. "You have a new baby," announced Ben.

Catching her, he trembled. He held her, a jewel, in his palms. "It's a girl," he said. "She's beautiful."

"A girl," said Jimmy Perez.

"Thank God you were here," exclaimed the glass-eyed woman, her pupil crackling with light.

"Let me," said Doris. "Let me see her."

Ben ran a finger inside the baby's mouth, then blew in her face to startle her. Next he turned her upside down, his hand locked around her ankles, flicked the bottoms of her feet gently, then slapped her on the back. The girl began to wriggle in his grasp and made small squawking noises. She turned pink gradually. When she started to cry, her father crossed himself. "A miracle," he said.

Ben was still trembling. With a towel he swabbed the baby clean, then set her, covered, on Doris's belly. Jimmy lay down to look at his daughter. He covered his mouth in disbelief.

"What do you need?" the dwarf asked.

"A sharp knife," said Ben. "And some twine."

Sanchez, from the doorway, produced a lock-back blade. Ben sterilized it in rubbing alcohol brought from a neighboring trailer. Then he tied the umbilicus in two places, using bits of Manila twine, and made his cut between them. The placenta delivered of its own accord. Ben made sure it was all there, then dropped it into a plastic bag the dwarf held open for him. He washed and looked again at the child, who was nursing vigorously. Her color was substantially better now. She had a lot of dark hair, and a cowlick.

Ben pressed gently on Doris's lower belly, assessing the condition of her uterus. It was hard to the touch and had contracted swiftly to the size of a small grapefruit. She was not bleeding, and he felt satisfied that there was no immediate danger. "You should take them both to see a doctor," he said, addressing Jimmy Perez. "After she's rested, but as soon as possible. Just to make sure everything's all right. That there aren't any problems."

"Okay," said Jimmy. "Thank you."

"There should be a clinic in Wenatchee," said Ben. "They'll have a doctor who knows about this, who knows about newborn babies. And someone for Doris. She needs stitches."

"Okay," said Jimmy. "We'll go."

"It's dangerous not to," Ben warned.

When he went outside, it was first light. The orchards nearby were hung with ripe apples. The broad sky was pale, cloudless. Things looked different now.

TWELVE

He slept all morning in the picker's cabin. At ten Sanchez came, bringing a woman. They stood in the doorway looking at Ben. "This is the doctor," said Sanchez.

"This man here?"

"Yes."

Ben put on his glasses. He had folded his hunting coat into a pillow and lay with the side of his face against it, in the smell of blood and bird feathers. "Excuse me," he said. "I'm not very well. Excuse me for not getting up."

"Please," said the woman. "Don't."

She was almost his age, Ben guessed, a gray-haired woman with deep wrinkles and liver spots who wore a housedress, a cardigan sweater, and calf-high rubber boots. Her hair was amiss, her dress front stained, and there was hay stuck to her. She looked as if

she'd been milking cows or working in a stable. The handles of a
pair of pruning shears stuck out of her sweater pocket.

Sanchez took off his cowboy hat and held it by its crown.
"This is the woman of the house," he said. "This is Mrs.
Harden."

"I'm Ben Givens," said Ben.

"I'm Bea," said the woman.

Sanchez put on his hat again. "I'm going to head back to my
pickers," he said. "Unless you need me for something."

"You go ahead," said Bea.

Sanchez walked to the door and turned. His face was as quiet,
as inaccessible, as it had been the evening before. "We just went
to look at the baby," he told Ben. "She was sleeping, and so was
her mother."

"What did they name her?"

"Ellen Dolores."

"Remind them to go to a doctor, okay? Mother and baby
both."

Sanchez nodded and went out. Bea Harden took her pruning
shears and put them in the opposite pocket. "I heard all about
it," she said.

"Heard about what?"

"You and the baby. Gustavo told me." Bea rubbed her nostrils
with a handkerchief. "I heard it was stuck at the shoulders for a
while. That can be dangerous."

"You're right. It's very dangerous."

"Then it's lucky you were there."

"It was lucky," said Ben.

Bea stuffed her handkerchief away. Her nostrils looked in-
flamed and tender. She had an equine, pop-eyed face. The space
between her lips and nose was deeply etched with wrinkles.

"Your name," she said. "I know it."

"Plenty of Givenses used to live around here."

"But you used to live across the river when I was growing up in Wenatchee. My name then was Beatrice Cade."

"Cade," said Ben. "I don't remember."

Bea kneaded the fingers of her left hand, which were bent, knobby, arthritic. "My dad worked with your dad on the Icicle Ditch. And we had the milliner's shop in town. Your mother used to come there sometimes."

"My memory's bad," said Ben.

"Her name was Lenora. One of the Chandlers. I knew your aunts, too."

Ben didn't answer. He tried to remember. Where had the milliner's shop been in Wenatchee? He thought back sixty years.

"Lily," said Bea. "That was my sister. She was your age—one year younger. And my brother was Andy. He worked for the utility. You remember him. Andy Cade."

"Andy," said Ben. "No."

"They're gone," said Bea. "But you had a brother. Aidan— wasn't it Aidan?"

"He's gone, too," said Ben.

Bea picked the hay from her sweater. Her large, worn fingers worked slowly at the task, absently, as she spoke. "I knew there was something going on last night. There were so many lights on down in the hollow. They said there was a picker delivered the baby. A picker who was a doctor, maybe. Why would a doctor be picking apples? It didn't make any sense."

"It doesn't make sense," answered Ben.

"So why are you picking?"

"It's a long story."

Bea poured a cup of water at the sink. Ben sat up and drank all of it. "Is your husband named William?" he asked.

"William is my brother-in-law."

"Does he have wolfhounds?"

"He raises them."

"He stole my gun," said Ben.

Bea took the cup again. "He's always been the terror of the country," she said. "Nothing he does surprises me."

"A varmint hunter."

"Worse than that."

"He sends his hounds out after coyotes."

"He sends them after anything that moves."

Ben nodded. "Like my Brittanies," he said. "His hounds killed one and maimed the other."

Bea shook her head regretfully. "I wish he had another hobby."

"I killed the one that got after mine."

"You killed one of Bill's hounds?"

"That's why he stole my gun."

Bea put the cup in the sink. She grimaced, angry, and shook her head. "I'm going to talk to him," she said.

Ben rubbed his side. It hurt relentlessly. "Don't bring it up. He can have the gun. I don't want it back. Forget it."

"It's yours, though."

"I don't want it anymore."

"It's the principle."

"Just let him have it."

"We'll get it back."

"I don't want it, though. The only thing I want is to go home."

Bea, again, kneaded her fingers, the swollen, misshapen knuckles. "Where is home?" she asked.

"I live on the other side of the mountains."

"You're a transplant, then."

"I guess I am."

"Can I bring you an aspirin?"

"Aspirin doesn't help."

"What does?"

"Nothing, really."

"What do you have?"

"Cancer. Of the colon."

"Oh, no," said Bea.

She took him in her car, an El Dorado, up past an orchard of trellised Fujis and another laden with Granny Smiths. A day of full sun, warm and well lit, the pickers working in their shirtsleeves. There were orchards rolling across the hills, a vast plot of spindled Galas, Braeburns on vertical trellises, seasoned Red Delicious. Off in the distance, across the river, a delicate web of power wires ran over the hills. In the hard light they looked as fragile as gossamer, their pylons and stanchions complicated, and at the crest of the breaks they disappeared across the wheat plateau.

Bea, driving, offered comfort—people she knew in remission. A cousin who'd outlasted lymphoma, the daughter of a friend who'd licked Hodgkin's Disease, an orchardist in Mattawa who'd overcome lung cancer on a diet of raw calf's liver juice and organic Winesaps from Manson. "I hadn't heard about the Winesaps," said Ben. "But the calf's liver juice sounds familiar."

"Well, what about it?"

"It's not for me."

"Why shouldn't it be?"

"Because it doesn't work."

Bea gave him a crestfallen look. "You sound like a doctor," she said.

They passed a weathered maintenance shed, then mesh-wire kennels housing Bill Harden's wolfhounds, who lolled about in their cramped dark cages like circus animals. Around the corner was a barn, a shop—ladders stacked up under its eaves—and a clapboard house with dormer windows and a broad, wraparound porch. There were stacked bins in front of it, a forklift and Farmall tractor. A box of tools sat on the ground, and a case of motor oil.

Bea urged Ben to come in for breakfast, to rest on the couch, use the bathroom. He told her about the rented truck, parked overnight on Joe Miller Road. If she could drop him there, he asked.

"You can't drive, the way you are."

"I can, too. Once I'm settled at the wheel."

"No, you can't. I'm not going to let you."

Ben frowned stubbornly, but Bea only put her open hand out. "Give me your keys," she told him. "I'll make sure we get your truck back to the U-Save in town."

"I don't have any other way home."

"I'll drive you across. Don't you worry about that."

"It's a long way."

"I'm a good samaritan."

"You don't even know me."

"It doesn't matter."

She got out and spoke through the window frame. "Give me about five minutes," she said. "My husband is up in the orchard somewhere. I'm going to tell him about driving you."

"But you really shouldn't," said Ben.

She walked away, to the house. Ben watched her go. She had a vegetable garden laid out in tidy rows, free of weeds, bountiful, the plants poking up out of black tarp. The potatoes grew inside of old tires. The tomatoes were staked with twine to tall poles. Purple grapes hung from a willow arbor. A rototiller sat in the yard, beside a pile of bark mulch.

Ben sat with his window open, smelling apples on the air. The five minutes became fifteen. He shut his eyes and dozed a little. He was worried that Doris could hemorrhage still. He decided to tell Bea about that possibility. The girl should see a doctor right away, go to the clinic in town.

He heard the racing of an engine behind him, and then a crew-cab pickup pulled in, a little fast, raising dust. A man got out, big, in his fifties, gray and weather-furrowed. He wore his hair cropped close to his head, suspenders over a sweatshirt, stagged logging jeans, and worn boots: the steel toes showing through the leather. In one hand he carried a power drill, in the other a leather carpenter's belt and a plastic bag of nails. Walking, he spat into the grass.

He had taken ten steps toward the maintenance shed when Ben struggled out of the car awkwardly, stood in its door with his arms around his gut, and called to him, weakly, by name. "William Harden," Ben said.

Harden turned and looked at him. His eyes were small, his shoulders sloped, his face tense, pale. "What the hell?" he said.

"It's me," said Ben. "Remember me? The hunter you stole the Winchester from a couple of nights ago."

William Harden spat again, then wiped his lips with the back of his hand. "'Stole' ain't the right word," he said.

"I came to get my gun back," said Ben. "But I've changed my mind."

Harden snorted. "Good," he said. "Then get the hell out of here."

Ben walked toward him, limping. It was hard for him to walk. He came close enough to see Harden clearly through the old, steel-rimmed glasses. Harden's eyes were uncertain, but he held the power drill firmly, like a weapon, something to club Ben with. He set down the nails and the carpenter's belt. "It's your call, old man," he said.

"My call is this," said Ben. "That gun was in my family sixty years. My father used it before I did, hunting birds. He killed a lot of birds with it. After him, I killed my share, too. But you know something about that gun? It was never anything but bad, really. A bad thing, that gun."

Harden didn't answer. He wiped his mouth instead.

"That gun is cursed," Ben said. "All guns are cursed."

He moved closer, pulled off his glasses. Harden raised the drill. "You go ahead and take it," said Ben. "I pass that gun on to you, Harden, and wash my hands of it."

Bea drove the El Dorado upriver, and they crossed the Columbia at East Wenatchee. There were apple trucks going both ways on the road. There were pickers working the last of the fruit. Bea drove past Rock Island and came down into the country Ben had lived in as a boy, orchards spread out on both sides of the wide water, sagebrush and groves of Russian olive. "Where was your place?" she asked.

He pointed it out when they came to it. The apple trees fell in a sweep toward the riverbank, the tan hills rose in the west. The new house sat behind willows grown to splendor with the passing of the years. Bea slowed and sat on the road shoulder. "It's pretty," she said. "All those poplars."

"Things have changed. A lot of things."

"It's good to get to see it anyway."

"It's still beautiful."

"That it is."

They lingered there a little too long. Bea made no move to drive on. "Let's go," Ben said finally.

In Quincy they picked up Rex at the clinic. Ilse Peterson was occupied, but the horsewoman at the reception desk promised to relay Ben's gratitude and brought the dog for him. Ben checked the staples, stroked Rex's coat, and carried him outside. He arranged the dog across the backseat, on a blanket. "We're going home," he whispered.

The road to George, at noon, was sunlit, and the big irrigators sat in the fields. The vacancy and magnitude of the land struck Ben, and its fertility—false—struck him, too. The edges where the fields met the desert were sudden: clean lines of demarcation. Whatever was not cultivated was steppe, haunted and beautiful. The arid plateau lay under the fields. The sage had been pulled out whole, by the roots. When the water no longer arrived here, the fecund crops would die of thirst. The land desired dryness.

Long before George, Bea asked about his eye, and Ben began at the beginning. Rachel's death, first of all. His daughter and his grandson. He didn't go into the details, but he did tell, in linear fashion, the story of how he had come to this pass, his shotgun lost, his dog wounded, his eye blackened, his transience. It felt good to speak of it all. She seemed the right person, a stranger.

"Suicide," Bea said when he was done. "I couldn't imagine it."

They passed a feed lot, peppermint fields, a walnut grove, a new orchard. Ben, experimentally, pressed on his eyelid. "I didn't want to burden my family," he said. "Put them through nine months of it. I didn't want to make them miserable."

"It isn't a burden," Bea said firmly. "Think what they'll learn from it."

"That sounds good, in principle."

"It is good," Bea insisted. "Seeing you die, it'll make them compassionate. It'll help them be more compassionate."

They came to the interstate and turned toward the Columbia. Bea kept to the right-hand lane, both hands high on the steering wheel. "What did your wife do?" she asked.

"My wife was a nurse. She started in the war. For thirty-four years, a hospital nurse. In a burn unit, for a long time. The worst cases. Burns."

"A doctor and a nurse," said Bea.

"She took off eight years when our daughter was born, but then she went back to work."

"She must have liked it."

"She did like it."

"I admire that," said Bea.

Ben fell silent. "I admired her, too," he said after awhile. "She was a better person than I am."

Bea nodded. She made a small adjustment to her rearview mirror and changed lanes to pass a truck. "Well, I don't really know," she said.

"She was," said Ben. "She gave everything."

"I guess you'd have to, being a nurse."

"A burn-unit nurse."

"It's so."

They came to the bend where the plateau broke, high above the Columbia. Ben looked toward the Frenchman Hills. A flight of ducks passed over them. To the south lay endless sagelands.

"So why did you change your mind?" asked Bea. "What made you change your mind?"

"Cowardice, mainly. Try shooting yourself. It isn't easy."

"There's sleeping pills."

"I couldn't do it."

"You didn't really want to."

Ben shrugged.

"Think of this," Bea said. "You saved a baby last night."

There were geese on the river, three dozen of them, down toward the Wanapum Dam. The wind blew north, up the canyon. The light lay bronze on the hills. Beyond rose the Saddle Mountains.

When they had crossed the river, Ben spoke again. "When we married, we made a pact," he said, "to bury our ashes together."

"That's very romantic."

"Well, we felt so."

"I like the idea."

"I like it, too. And if I'd gone through with shooting myself, it probably wouldn't ever happen."

"Coyotes and worms instead, you're right."

"So I'm going home because of that, too."

"I understand," said Bea.

They came up over Ryegrass Summit, into the Quilomene, then the Kittitas Valley. The trees along Manastash Ridge had gone russet red and yellow. "October," said Bea, "is a beautiful month on this side of the mountains."

"The fall is more vivid over here," said Ben.

"On the coast you just don't get the same colors."

"It's a trade-off," said Ben. "Our weather's more temperate. We don't have quite the extremes."

"There's a price for everything," said Bea.

They came into a country of evergreen trees and left the sage and canyons behind. The mountains rose in front of them, snow-swathed, in the west. Forests covered Easton Ridge; already the light had softened. They came up toward the Stampede Pass cutoff, between slopes of Cascade blueberries. There were fields of burnished, dying red where the berries grew among mountain heathers. The old clear-cuts were full of them. They made a kind of heath.

In Snoqualmie Pass—the crest of the mountains—they stopped at the Traveler's Rest. Bea had to use the rest room, she said. She was going to get a cup of coffee and a donut. She could bring him something, if he wanted it. He answered that he had no appetite. He thanked her for her attentions to him, and thanked her again for her generosity in taking him back home. "It's nothing," said Bea. "It's useful to you, and interesting for me. I don't ask more from any day."

She went into the Traveler's Rest, and Ben turned to check on Rex. "You look okay back there," he said. "Better than me, really."

He rolled down his window with effort. He wanted to smell the mountains. It was getting on toward midafternoon, and an alpine chill was in the air. He remembered walking the crest of the Cascades from Windy Gap to here. Silver Peak was a few miles off. He thought of his promise to climb it with Chris. He would have to explain that now.

It was a long way down to the west side, home—almost three thousand feet. Bea drove with her coffee in one hand, a maple bar on a napkin in her lap. The sky here was a muted gray. There was nothing to see but mountains, forest. By North Bend, it was raining gently. Mount Si lay veiled by clouds.

Everything at home was as Ben had left it; nothing had gone awry. His neighbor had taken out the garbage that morning and had seen to the newspapers and mail. The VCR had made its recording of *Great Railway Journeys*. The bird plucker sat on the kitchen table; the recipe for quail on toast poked from the recipe box. There were four messages on the answering machine: Bill Ward's nurse confirming an appointment, another doctor Ben sometimes hiked with, the auto shop that had towed his Scout, his car insurance company. He would have all these calls to return, but not now.

He fed Rex, and while the dog ate, he slumped at the kitchen table, his head against his arm. Through the window he could see the dog kennel and the Summer Damasks his wife had planted between the pad for the garbage can and the wall of the neighbor's house. A few leaves were left on them, and the unpicked blossoms had turned to hips. The plants were tall now, profuse.

Ben turned up the heat in the house and made his way to the bedroom, where he had left the copy of *Scientific American* open on the side table. He pried off his boots, settled back on the bed. He curled up as comfortably as he could. His dusty hunting clothes smelled of sage. There were bloodstains on the front of his coat and feathers in his pockets.

Rex limped in, looked at him, and lay down on the throw rug beside the bed. Ben rested a hand on his flank. "I guess you can stay," he whispered.

After awhile he took the telephone receiver and punched in his daughter's number. "Hello," she said. "Renee Givens-Kane."

"It's me," said Ben. "I'm home."

ACKNOWLEDGMENTS

For generosity in Washington's apple country, Doug and Sue Clarke, Ed and Virginia Clarke, Thyra and Doyle Fleming, Mike Robinson, Brian Vincent, Grady Auvil, and Mary Pat and Jerry Scofield. For assistance in historical research, Barbara Walton and Karen Ashley of the Denver Public Library, Moya Hansen of the Colorado Historical Society, Franco Polegato, Frank Chuk, Ken Hanson, Bob Ellis, Ken MacDonald, and Matteo Bavestrelli. For help with medical and veterinary questions, Will Toth, David Cowan, Bob and Bea Bourdeau, Mike Hobbs, Carol Riley, Laura Hoyt, and Mark Swaney. For expertise regarding medicine and war, Dr. Albert H. Meinke. For days afield east of the Cascades, Ralph Cheadle, Trip Goodall; Taylor, Travis and Henry Guterson; Ellensburg writer Joe Powell; Tess, Jack, Thorn, Gus, and Sam.

For kindness and help in Italy, Norbert and Pepe Cristofolini. For information on migrant workers, Victor Rodriguez and Dr. Patricia Ortiz. For assistance with Spanish translation, Sue and Luis Koch and Karla Sullivan. For help regarding birth and shoulder dystocia, Susan Anemone. For expertise on the flora of Central Washington, Bill Barker. For office help, Angelica Guterson.

I am grateful to Drenka Willen for her help in shaping this book and to Anne and Georges Borchardt.

Sources include Dr. Albert Meinke's *Mountain Troops and Medics: Wartime Stories of a Surgeon in the U.S. Ski Troops*; Robert Ellis's *See Naples and Die*; H. Robert Krear's *Journal of a U.S. Army Mountain Trooper in World War II*; Ken MacDonald's unpublished memoirs; Diane Burke Fessler's *No Time for Fear: Voices of American Military*

Nurses in World War II; Barbara Brooks Tomblin's *G.I. Nightingales: The Army Nurse Corps in World War II*; Lt. Col. Marjorie Peto's *Women Were Not Expected*; Al C. Bright's *Apples Galore*; Isabel Valle's *Fields of Toil*; Ronald J. Taylor's *Sagebrush Country: A Wildflower Sanctuary*; Toby F. Sonneman and Rick Steigmeyer's *Fruit Fields in My Blood: Okie Migrants in the West*; and Daniel Mathews's *Cascade-Olympic Natural History: A Trailside Reference*.

To those I have neglected to mention from sheer failure of memory or character, please accept my apologies. I owe all a great debt.